CW01500181

Naming the Dead

By Karen Haden

Also by Karen Haden

Paying in Blood

Visit https://karenhaden.blogspot.com for character lists and maps.

For Ethel Webb

You are of your father the devil … there is no truth in him

When he speaks a lie, he speaks of his own, for he is a liar, and the father thereof

Geneva Bible, John Chapter 8 Verse 44

NAMING THE DEAD

Prologue

January 1613

Dear Reverend Sculthorpe,

Since we last spoke, Geoffrey has used an informer to extract intelligence from your prisoner Alexander Baxby. I could not deter him without drawing attention to the sensitive nature of this case.

As a result of this informer's testimony, Geoffrey is sending me north to search for an official called Julian Felde, who supposedly committed crimes in the Diocese of Lincolnshire whilst you worked as the bishop's secretary there. Given I shall be away from London for a few days, I thought it wise to share my concerns before I left.

The timing of this manhunt is suspicious. I may miss the royal wedding festivities. Why is Geoffrey pursuing historical feuds at this time of heightened security risk? Does he not realise the seriousness of the ongoing threat from Catholics, and the increasing number of subjects who deplore King James' Scottish favourites? We should be devoting our energy and resources to delivering a spectacular and safe event, of which the King and the whole of England can be proud.

In my opinion, Baxby still has questions to answer from his time working in the Nottinghamshire village of Scrooby. Geoffrey is placing too much trust in his word. Also, there is a risk that the informer could supply further information about more recent events, which we would prefer to remain secret.

I am sending this letter with Pusey, who will destroy it once read.

Your faithful servant,

Leonard Redfern

Friday

1

Amsterdam 1608

Although Matthew Mobley's hearing was poorer than mine, we both heard the flour store door slam open below us. His lantern flickered on the long table, as a cold draught of air rose up the stairs. Mice darted across the bare boards when the door banged shut again.

We were the only two remaining in the first-floor meeting room, my old master having delayed his departure so we could talk. It had been a delight to discuss symptoms and treatments again, after a year apart.

I had not seen Matthew since the previous spring, when he fled into exile with the first group of Separatist believers led by Pastor Smyth. They left Gainsborough without warning such was the danger they faced. Those of us living in nearby Scrooby survived another year, until we too sailed from England illegally.

Amsterdam offered an exciting opportunity for me to start my life anew, free from my former spymaster Geoffrey and his devious schemes. Geoffrey had tricked me in my youth. Now I was an experienced physician, almost twenty-six years old.

My respect for Cambridge-educated Mobley had not waned, nor the gratitude I felt. The physician taught me well during my apprenticeship, about medical matters and much more besides. He had amassed an impressive set of patients since arriving with Pastor Smyth. I felt like a novice again, having only disembarked that morning with my Scrooby friends.

Assuming Pastor Smyth had not fastened the door properly when he left the flour store, I offered to go downstairs to secure it. Over fifty years old, Smyth still suffered from consumption, which he contracted whilst imprisoned for preaching without a licence.

"Shh, Baxby," Matthew moved a finger to his lips, then pointed to the wall behind my back. What had he seen there?

NAMING THE DEAD

Nervously, I turned to observe the glow spreading upwards from the ground floor. We heard the first thud on the bottom tread. Someone was climbing the stairs with a brighter lantern than Matthew's.

Instinctively, I drew my rapier, fearing Archbishop Bancroft's henchmen had tracked our Scrooby group across the Narrow Sea. How else could anyone find this hiding place in a narrow alley outside the city walls? Had I endured a winter in a safe house and survived a storm at sea, only to be captured on the day of my arrival?

Whilst working for Geoffrey, I had seen how tenacious Bancroft could be. Until the outside door slammed open, I assumed we would be safe in Amsterdam. Now I feared the archbishop's network of informers, spies and pursuivants had spread its tentacles beyond England's shores.

My sword arm trembled, watching the light spread up the wall.

Before emerging, the nocturnal visitor coughed, no doubt afflicted by the flour which had caused me to sneeze earlier and aggravated Pastor Smyth's condition. Only then did I relax my guard.

A woman was ascending the stairs below. English clerics and their accomplices were always men. Matthew and I were not about to be arrested by a member of Archbishop Bancroft's spy team.

As the woman's head appeared above the banister I rubbed my eyes in disbelief, momentarily convinced the building was haunted by a bodyless ghost. The woman's millstone ruff reflected the light upwards to her face and embroidered cap, whilst her dark clothes were indistinguishable from the shadows below.

If Matthew had not whispered her name I would have assumed Temperance Knowsley was Dutch. Although narrower than some ruffs I had seen on the trek from the harbour, hers was formidably starched. Typically, our women wore smaller, neater collars and plainer headwear. None of us were that well fed. She addressed Matthew in English, "Praise God, you're here, Doctor Mobley."

In all my subsequent years in Amsterdam, I never saw Temperance so flustered again. Trembling and out of breath, she gripped the baluster for support. I presumed this was due to climbing the long flight of stairs from the flour store, until Temperance explained she had run all the way from the Blue Bridge.

Matthew sympathised, "Dear Mistress Knowsley, you look tired. Please sit with us and rest. My friend and colleague, Doctor Baxby, arrived this morning with the congregation from Scrooby. They didn't drown as we feared."

"Praise God for this answer to prayer, but I need you to come with me immediately."

"Yes, of course. Is someone ill?"

"My son Michael spotted a suspicious object in the river, on our way home from *Vloonburg* Island. Being taller, he had a better view. I saw the body once I leant over the parapet."

Matthew asked the most obvious question, in a suitably respectful tone, "A living person or a deceased one, Mistress Knowsley?"

"Most probably dead, but neither of us are doctors and it was dark. That's why we need your help."

Already Matthew was fastening his cloak, preparing to leave. Physicians are used to responding quickly after such a request is made. I remained seated, shocked to receive such news on my first night in Amsterdam. There was a man in the Amstel, just upstream of the Blue Bridge.

However, I was delighted when Matthew suggested I join them.

"Doctor Baxby is a proficient physician with extensive skills and experience, including three valuable years in London."

What a gratifying endorsement, one I hoped he would repeat in the coming days. No longer reliant on Geoffrey, I needed to find patients in the city. This would be quicker and easier with Matthew's help.

Temperance moved towards me, bringing her lantern near to scrutinise my hair and beard. Fixing her eyes on mine, she posed an unexpected question, "Are you Spanish, Doctor Baxby? You're tall, and your features are very dark for an Englishman. Was your father born elsewhere?"

"I can assure you I am English, completely English, Mistress Knowsley."

No one had been so impertinent as to question my allegiance before. I was angered by the suggestion.

My face had tanned on the deck of the ship, so might look darker than Matthew's in the lantern light, but how could she mistake me for the enemy? All the Spaniards I had met, whilst working overseas for Geoffrey, sported rounder bellies and smarter clothes.

"Your hair is dark too, and what a monstrous beard! My Michael's would not grow that bushy if he failed to shave for a year. What about your mother? Was she foreign?"

"My mother was born near Boston in Lincolnshire, where I grew up. It's kind townsfolk helped facilitate our escape from England."

As Temperance looked unconvinced, I added, "I served at the Battle of Nieuwpoort, where I killed the last Spaniard I met."

This admission had always been well received in England. No one sympathised with the enemy there. Temperance stepped back in horror, clutching her hands to her breast.

How bizarre! Did she not know Dutch and English regiments had been fighting King Philip's army for decades, since the northern Low Country states won their independence from Spain? Catholic Dunkirker pirates still sank our ships in the Narrow Sea.

"The war with Spain has lasted long enough," Temperance pronounced, "We should be leaving now. Michael won't be able to stand guard for long. The Blue Bridge is a popular route."

Matthew replied, "Of course, Mistress Knowsley. Please lead us back the way you came."

With parts of the city flooded by recent downpours, she would know the best route.

Assuming we might need a stretcher, I took two brushes from the ground floor flour store. If the bakehouse owner was kind enough to let penniless Separatist immigrants stay in his building, he was unlikely to object to me borrowing them.

2

Venturing out into the damp night, I did not know if Temperance Knowsley's discovery was commonplace in Amsterdam. Did unsuspecting citizens regularly drown in its rivers and canals? Her demeanour suggested this was not the case, yet I knew the pavements were treacherous when wet. Anyone could miss their footing if distracted momentarily.

My old comrade John Crackleton had slipped twice on our journey from the harbour. Having grown close since removing his injured foot at the Battle of Nieuwpoort, I sympathised with the difficulties he faced. Even the most prominent waterways were not protected by fences or walls, particularly difficult for a man with one leg.

I had clung on to Crackleton's two children, terrified of losing one, whilst young Margaret Deryngton assisted him. A former maid at Scrooby Manor, Margaret was a sensible girl. If she had not caught Crackleton's arm, he would have fallen in.

Back home, drunken Londoners regularly tumbled into the Thames and its tributaries. Southwark's south bank was notorious, as were the rapids beneath London Bridge. Otherwise, people kept away from the water and fretted whenever it rained.

Here, locals carried on regardless. Crossing the city, we had seen all manner of people stacking crates, carrying sacks, and rolling barrels back and forth, whilst others swept floodwater away.

When the captain brought our ship past the palisades, which protected Amsterdam's long harbour from the north, I had been excited and eager to disembark. The River Ij was brimming with vessels converging on the port. All the berths on the quay were full.

Beyond the waterfront, the New Church spire rose to a great height. The exotic onion dome of the Old Church was unlike any I had seen before. I was ready to start my new life in this intriguing city, no longer beholden to Geoffrey. How shocked he would be if he saw me arrive.

My friends had their own reasons to rejoice as we waited to dock.

Crackleton, Margaret, my former servant Nicholas and other Scrooby-believers had reached the goal of their pilgrimage, a place where they could gather and worship as they chose, free from English Church control. Although I did not share their faith, I admired their courage and sympathised with their cause.

Our guide Thomas Helwys would be reunited with the oldest five of his seven children. The youngest two were still in York gaol with his wife, Joan. Thomas had been a respected lawyer prior to joining Smyth's Gainsborough congregation. He had escaped from England with them, and lived in Amsterdam for a year before returning to rescue us.

My former adversary Sir Julian Felde stood alongside me on the deck. During a private conversation on the voyage, Felde had confessed to heinous crimes whilst spying for Robert Cecil. The others did not know he was fleeing prosecution.

Despite our differences, we were all delighted to arrive at last. None of us were safe in our homeland while Archbishop Bancroft retained his power.

Yet, as our ship pulled alongside the quay, I felt nervous. The neighbouring Dutch fluyt, flying the colours of the East India Company, had crossed oceans to deliver the spices being winched from her holds. Our little hoy seemed insignificant next to its towering hull.

The sailors shouted across to each other in Dutch. I was familiar with some phrases from the voyage, but our group relied on Thomas Helwys, our only fluent speaker, to translate, "Dam Square is knee-deep in water. The council has suspended trading at the Exchange and ceased work on the new bastion walls. We will need to take care crossing the city."

Surveying the busy quay from the deck, Julian Felde sought to reassure me. He had visited the city previously, when helping Thomas arrange our escape, "Don't worry, Baxby. Amsterdam often floods. Its capable burghers and guildsmen know how to handle this."

Our leader thought highly of Felde, unaware of his heartless disregard for those less fortunate than himself. Although the former deputy no longer wore a fancy cape or drenched himself in foul lemon scent, he still annoyed me intensely. I did not trust Felde.

Thomas chose the quietest route across the city, not wishing to draw attention to our group. He would not let us stop to admire the grand canal houses as we walked. Regardless, they looked magnificent even in rain. Hundreds of merchants and businessmen lived in the imposing dwellings, five or six stories high.

Some canal houses backed onto wharfs, with convenient warehouses for storing goods. Others faced each other across smaller waterways. With varying brickwork patterns and gable designs, each complemented its neighbours in a satisfying way. The Dutch had created an elegant, ordered city, affirming their superior wealth and skills.

As we neared the outer walls, I imagined visiting patients behind the imposing front doors, then later living in such a home myself. When I asked Felde if he had been inside one, he shook his head, less impressed. Unlike me, the former deputy had known considerable financial security in England after inheriting land.

It was hard to keep up with Thomas' pace. He did not stop until we had passed through the *Munt* gate and crossed the *Singel* canal. Pausing at last, the rest of us stood in silence, surveying the cheerless scene beyond the walls. Densely packed yards and mills jostled for space between the river and the marshes, like human ant colonies.

Crackleton's daughter Anna started to sob.

"What is this place?" he spluttered.

The noise and stench of the industrial suburb threatened to overwhelm our senses.

Thomas led us up the dark alley called *Bakkersstraat,* where the bakehouse was squeezed between a busy brickworks and dairy. Little Anna did not stop crying until she saw Matthew Mobley's eldest son Luke sitting on the flour store step in the yard, a face we recognised from England.

Thomas opened the gate, "Welcome to your new home. It's safer for us outside the ramparts. Immigrants are tolerated in Amsterdam, not loved."

What I witnessed beneath the Blue Bridge would cause me to question his claim.

Striding out across the bakehouse yard, Temperance's appearance and manner led me to believe she must live in a grand canal house in the city. She managed to avoid the puddles. My shoes were soaked for a second time.

Before she reached the gate, we heard Julian Felde's deep voice behind, "Perhaps I could be of assistance, Mistress Knowsley. You may need someone to keep order or clear a safe route. I worked for the Lord Lieutenant of Lincolnshire for many years, so have experience in such matters."

Felde must have overheard our conversation from the attic above the meeting room. Most new arrivals slept up there until they could afford more suitable accommodation. I was not surprised that Felde had been listening, having previously worked undercover for Robert Cecil. However, we did not need his assistance now. Felde was pushing his bent nose into other people's business.

Conversely, Temperance seemed impressed with the former deputy's credentials. She thanked him before asking his name, "Please join us at the bridge, Sir Julian. Anything out of the ordinary can draw a crowd."

Felde lifted the latch and held the gate for the others to exit, then let it swing for me.

Accompanying Temperance down *Bakkersstraat* towards the River Amstel, I felt the same trepidation as when we arrived. Although we could not see the windmills, we heard the disconcerting *swosh, swosh* of their sails slicing the air behind us.

Emerging onto the river pavement, we saw a light ahead. Temperance's son Michael was leaning on the parapet, with another lantern. The bridge's narrow walkway disappeared into darkness beyond, barely wide enough for two people to pass.

After waiting for a couple to cross, Michael lowered the light for Matthew and me to look beneath. Nervously, we peered over the side. The water level had receded. The man's head was clear above the swirling waters, a few feet below. When the current turned him, we could see his eyes were closed.

Matthew exchanged a glance. We both knew the man was dead, but were unsure how to proceed.

On first sight, there was nothing to arouse my suspicions. It was easy to slip and fall, especially in such weather and poor light. Nevertheless, this was an inauspicious start to my life in Amsterdam.

3

Felde drew his rapier, a sleek weapon I had long envied, before returning to stand guard at the entrance to the bridge. Temperance brought her lantern closer, giving us a better view. When we tried to lever the body up with the brushes I had brought from the flour store, it quickly became clear it was attached in some way.

As the younger physician, Matthew suggested I descend to investigate. Michael and Temperance swiftly agreed. She seemed a little less cold towards me after I passed my weapons into her care. I left my cloak and shoes there too.

Michael showed me the steep steps reaching down into the water, with a gap in the top rail where I was expected to climb over the lower two. No bridge in England was designed in this strange way.

Slowly, I tested my weight before trusting myself to the broken treads. The Amstel waters swirled beneath me. It would be easy to fall. I could not swim.

Matthew and Temperance called words of encouragement, and warned, "Be careful, Baxby. One of the boards is missing."

They had the advantage of having seen the structure in daylight before.

Nearing the bottom of the steps, I discovered planks beneath the surface on which I could walk. They formed a platform running parallel to the pier, with another rail I could grip. The water came above my knees, but I reached the body without incident, after inching my way along.

Once Matthew directed the light in the right direction, I could see that the man looked relatively young. He was clean-shaven, with a neat crop of hair. One of his ankles was secured to the wooden slats by a tangled rope. That was the reason we could not lever him up with the brushes. I would need to sever the rope before we could lift the body to the bridge.

Wading back, I called for Temperance to pass my dagger down. "Be careful, Doctor Baxby. We don't want to watch you drown."

On the third attempt, I managed to cut the man's ankle free by wedging one of my legs against the pier and the other against the rail, whilst clasping his belt with my free hand. However, the water was too strong. I had to let go to save myself from being swept away.

I watched in horror as the torrent crashed his head into the brick pier, then rotated him to point towards the nearest arch. I feared the poor man would be washed away by the swollen Amstel, out into the River Ij and *Zuider Zee* beyond, to never be seen again.

Urged on by Temperance and Matthew, I lurched to catch the nearest severed end of rope with my cold, numb hands. With enormous effort, I reeled the body in until it was close enough for Michael to lean down and clasp a foot. Only then did I realise how tired I was.

As the others hauled the body up, I waded back even more slowly than before. They did not see my exhaustion or the relief I felt.

Wringing my clothes on the top step, I heard Matthew exclaim above, "Good Lord, it's Peter Weekes, one of my patients."

I did not recognise the name, but looking down at the body lying on the bridge, there was something familiar about his face despite its wrinkled texture.

Felde joined us, clearly shocked himself, before disappearing back to his guard duty.

Understandably, Matthew was upset by the loss of a patient in such horrendous circumstances. Temperance knew Weekes too, a fellow member of her English Reformed Church. She clasped her hands to her bosom again, clearly distressed, but remained pragmatic, insisting we take Weekes to her home.

I asked, "Shouldn't we call a constable? Won't the city authorities want to investigate?"

"The Night Watch would come if Peter were a burgher or reputable guild member. They won't venture beyond the ramparts for an immigrant death."

Our lives mattered less than the Dutch citizens who lived within the walls.

NAMING THE DEAD

Concerned that moving the body might attract attention, Temperance instructed us to move quickly, before setting off to help Felde.

As Matthew and Michael constructed the stretcher with the brushes, I looked at Weekes again. His shoes were missing, but the fitted jacket and breeches suggested a man who could afford to dress well. Also, he had visited a competent barber recently.

Michael led the way to the Knowsley's home. My previous assumption was wrong. They lived just outside the walls, in one of the narrow three storey houses on the Amstel pavement, between the *Munt* gate and *Bakkersstraat*. I had passed the row earlier in the day with Thomas and my Scrooby-friends. The exterior was plainer than the city canal houses, but well-maintained.

"I don't think Temperance likes me," I confided in Matthew, while we waited for Michael to rearrange furniture inside.

"Don't be silly. Temperance Knowsley is a remarkable woman who merits our respect."

She had been a founding member of the Ancient Brethren Separatists, who escaped from Norfolk during Queen Elizabeth's reign, before moving to Amsterdam's English Reformed Church.

"Although Reverend Paget is the vicar, sometimes it seems as if Temperance is actually in charge, a tremendous asset to them all."

"She thought I was Spanish."

"She just needs to get to know you better."

Michael used the ground floor of the Knowsley's home to make and sell pots, which were arranged in neat lines on shelves. He had moved his wheel out of the way by the time we entered. There were several stools by the large window at the front of the long room, and a table at the back on which we could lie Weekes.

While Michael found a sheet to replace the cloak we had used to cover his body, Matthew and I were able to inspect it more thoroughly on the table. There was a purple wound on his skull, which could have been caused when his head hit the pier, or from an earlier blow, perhaps causing him to fall. Whatever the reason, the water had subsequently washed the blood away.

Temperance reappeared as I was removing the last section of rope from Weekes' shin, then went upstairs to fetch beer, and dry clothes which belonged to her husband. We did not see him while we were there.

Sitting on the stools by the window, our hostess divided the most urgent tasks between us. Temperance would take responsibility for contacting Reverend Paget and the leaders of other local immigrant communities who would be concerned about this tragic death. She would take care of the funeral and burial arrangements too.

Matthew agreed to call on Peter's wife on his way home. He had his own reason for wanting to speak to Alice Weekes, which he did not reveal at the time. We agreed to return in the morning to decide what to do next.

As the two of us walked back along the Amstel, to a similar house in the same row, I asked Matthew if Peter Weekes had been ill recently.

"The poor lad suffered from painful symptoms, primarily with his bowels."

Constipation can be debilitating. This might explain a fall. Weekes could have staggered when feeling unwell, then become entangled in the rope.

"When did he arrive in Amsterdam?"

"Peter was very young at the time, but managed to get a good job at the Weighing House in Dam Square."

This meant it was unlikely I recognised him from England

"Peter was my wealthiest patient. That wasn't the reason I liked visiting him, though. He was a lovely young man. This is a sad day indeed."

The Weekes rented the ground floor of a house identical in appearance to Temperance's. No one answered the door. Disappointed, Matthew escorted me back to the bakehouse and left me at the gate. He was keen to return to his wife Agnes and the children.

Like many in Smyth's group who arrived the year before, the Mobleys rented a small house on *Vloonburg* Island, on the far side of the Blue Bridge. New arrivals, like me, had to sleep in the attic above the flour store meeting room. Sympathetic to our cause, the bakehouse owner, Jan Munter, allowed us to use it free of charge until we could afford to move out.

Although we were more fortunate than other exiles arriving in Amsterdam, it was a basic arrangement. The attic was divided by partitions. There were insufficient mattresses for everyone. I had to sleep on straw, with a worn blanket my only protection from the cold.

Wearily, I climbed the ladder to join my friends. Peter Weekes' death had unsettled me, but eventually I fell asleep. I dreamed I entered a smart canal house with my physician's bag and left with a purse of gold.

4

London 1613

Neither of the cell-mates listening to Baxby' story has ever boarded a ship. The printer on his left is keen to learn more about the faraway land of windmills and canals, then remarks, "How strange that you're sleeping on straw again here."

Baxby replies, "I did not understand the challenges I would face in Amsterdam, nor those of my friends, but we were free to speak and meet as we pleased, unlike here."

The Dutch Reformed Church and States General in the Hague do not enforce religious conformity as rigorously as King James and the English Church, attracting persecuted groups from all over Europe.

"It's hard to imagine such freedom. What about the presses? Does the Church control them there?"

"Dutch citizens are able to print and read more of what they choose. Burghers and guildsmen read copious quantities of pamphlets and books on all kinds of subjects, along with immigrants who can afford to do so."

The vicar to Baxby's right does not join in the conversation. Although previously talkative, he has not spoken since returning from interrogation in a nearby crypt. During this ordeal, Leonard Redfern ordered a guard to kick him. His shin still hurts. The bruises are darkening.

Geoffrey promised he would renew the vicar's licence in return for information, then quickly reneged. Now, the vicar's future well-being is contingent on providing further information about Baxby's contacts in Amsterdam.

Baxby does not expect to be freed. Telling his story provides welcome respite during his captivity. Rightly, he assumes Sculthorpe arranged his arrest. In addition to his other duties on behalf of the Archbishop of Canterbury, Sculthorpe is now secretary to the High Commission, the highest Church court in the land.

5

Amsterdam 1608

My former servant Nicholas Barton woke me in the morning, bright and cheery as usual, "Baxby, please can you help me get Crackleton to breakfast? Margaret's already taken his children down."

Young Nicholas had been besotted with Margaret throughout my time as Scrooby's physician. Having spent the winter in a safe house together before escaping from England, they understood the challenges Crackleton faced with his wooden leg. The attic ladder was too steep for him to descend alone.

The four of us sat at one end of the long table for breakfast. The mice from the night before had disappeared. Flour still seeped from the store below, triggering another sneezing fit.

We ate bread and pliable Dutch cheese, along with broken ships' biscuits from the bakehouse owner Jan Munter's ovens. Crackleton and Nicholas, who were always hungry, consumed all they could at speed. The beer was paler than English brews but palatable nevertheless.

Despite his wiry frame, Nicholas was strong and resourceful. In Scrooby he had even helped the thatcher mend my roof. That morning Nicholas had a particular reason for encouraging haste. While we were eating, he announced his intention to visit Dam Square to find work.

Dam Square sounded a good place to look, having been the centre of Amsterdam's trade since fishermen first dammed the Amstel to form a settlement in the marshes. The Town Hall, Exchange and Weighing House were all located there.

However, John Murton, an ex-tanner who had lived in the flour store attic since arriving with Pastor Smyth, warned Nicholas this might take time. Murton was earning his keep as a hod bearer whilst training to work with bombazine cloth.

Nicholas was not deterred by Murton's story. He said he would return to Dam Square tomorrow if he was unsuccessful today.

Similarly, I was determined to start working as soon as possible. There must be plenty of patients for me to treat in a city of this size. I hoped to find an opportunity to discuss an initial list of names with Matthew soon.

Of course, my friends were horrified to hear about Peter Weekes. None of them recognised his name, but were worried to learn of a fellow countryman's death, especially so soon after arriving.

When I mentioned wading along the jetty to retrieve Weekes' body, John Murton laughed, "It's not a jetty. Didn't you see the wooden stalls?"

Murton had been prone to swearing in Gainsborough, but seemed more amiable now. Seeing our bemused expressions, he continued, "They're called *stilletjes*. Men use them to piss in the water under the bridge, or at least that's the intention of the council members who are trying to keep the city clean."

Weekes might have got into difficulty when relieving himself, rather than falling from the bank. Although awful to imagine, Nicholas and I thought this an interesting theory.

Crackleton remained convinced someone had pushed Weekes in the river, possibly due to his own experience of being jostled on Amsterdam's pavements.

Ex-lawyer Thomas Helwys cautioned against hasty conclusions, reminding us there were few clear facts. He offered to ask Jan Munter if the Crackletons could sleep on the first floor, an excellent idea.

Margaret wanted to say a prayer for Weekes' widow. Murton recommended another for Nicholas, concerned for his safety after the recent floods, "The city gets busier each month, and the weather seems worse this spring."

Pastor Smyth arrived during the discussion and led the prayers instead, once he had recovered his breath. Despite his dishevelled appearance and age, Smyth's powerful voice still commanded the attention of everyone in the room.

During the day, Pastor Smyth taught the group's children in the flour store meeting room.

As others cleared the table ready for them to use, Crackleton drew me aside to talk. Looking out a small window overlooking the bakehouse yard, he said, "I haven't seen Isobel yet. Do you think she's alright?"

Having previously confided in him, Crackleton knew about my feelings for the attractive widow of an alderman. I had not seen Isobel Greenacre since a memorable walk by the River Trent, just before she fled Gainsborough with Pastor Smyth. Bound to silence, she could not say a proper goodbye.

Back then, I believed Isobel loved me as I loved her. The longer we were parted, the less certain I became. Thomas had told me she was hoping to set up a bread charity on the islands, similar to the one she managed in Lincoln, but nothing more.

"I hope Isobel hasn't met with an accident too," Crackleton said.

Although he was convinced Peter had slipped, it was imprudent to suggest this. I was anxious myself. Why had Isobel not been there to greet me?

I replied more confidently than I felt, "Agnes Mobley is bound to know more. I will talk with her when she arrives."

Hopefully, whatever the news, Matthew's wife would be more tactful than Crackleton.

Matthew had arranged for her to take me to the Knowsleys' home to meet with Temperance again.

Despite being unable to have children herself, Agnes resembled a mother duck with ducklings as she led Matthew's three and her nephew Toby up the stairs. Matthew had married Agnes after his first wife Eunice died in childbirth. Toby was the son of Agnes' late half-sister Susannah.

Whereas the children had grown, Agnes seemed to have shrunk. Her chestnut hair still spilt from her cap, but she needed a belt to keep the familiar dress in place. It was hard to believe this was the buxom landlady who once enticed me during the early months of my apprenticeship.

Once she had settled the children, Agnes came across to greet us, "Baxby! Crackleton! Welcome to the flour store. Praise God, you're alive. Isn't this a wonderful place? Jan Munter is a kind man."

"It's good to see you looking well, and the children too. You're a great mother, Agnes. Matthew's fortunate to have you for his wife."

"I'm relieved you've come to assist him, Baxby. There are lots of sick people on the islands, and Peter's accident has troubled him greatly."

Crackleton expressed sympathy for all who knew Weekes. Having lost his wife Catherine in dire circumstances, he understood the pain of such a loss.

Walking down *Bakkersstraat*, it was hard to break into Agnes' torrent of praise for her new home. She loved the city and islands, where no one gossiped about her past.

On reaching the Amstel, I saw the Blue Bridge for the first time in daylight. It was painted the same colour as the stripe on the Dutch flag. Two long lines of wooden stilts supported a curved walkway, reaching its highest point in the centre of the river. Boats and barges passed beneath at speed, aiming for different archways appropriate for their height.

People were filing across the bridge from *Vloonburg* on their way to work. Some had blond hair, others darker colouring than mine. Residents were opening their doors, offering glimpses of their ground floor shops and businesses. The pavement was drier now. Despite the numbers, no one walked perilously close to the edge. Murton's *stilletjes* accident seemed more likely than Crackleton's theory.

When we paused to let a laden donkey through, I managed to interrupt Agnes. My heart filled with dread as I asked, "Where is Isobel? I haven't seen her since arriving in Amsterdam."

Agnes smiled, "Don't worry, Baxby. Isobel hasn't forgotten you. She's raising funds for her bread charity project in the Hague, then plans to visit Leiden. No doubt she will charm its university professors into giving generously. I will let you know once I hear from her."

What a relief! Isobel was alive and well, pursuing the cause she held dear.

"Thank …"

I stopped, distracted by the sound of shouting emanating from the Knowsleys' home. Temperance was arguing with a loud man inside, both alternating between Dutch and English languages, speaking each with equal force.

Having already encountered one dead body since arriving, I ran the length of the row, fearing the worst. Agnes lifted her skirts to follow behind. A barge was moored outside.

6

Two tall Dutchmen blocked the entrance to the house, wearing bright sashes across their chests. Both carried pistols, and sturdier blades than my own. They were waving other onlookers past. We had to get inside.

Agnes managed to wave to Matthew. I attempted a greeting in Dutch. Eventually, one of the sentries understood our demands sufficiently to let us through, whereupon we witnessed the altercation within.

Despite being unarmed and considerably shorter, Temperance was not deterred by the enormous Dutchman gesticulating in her home. His thick cloak could not hide his wide girth, nor the distinctive smell of strong wine. I found his presence intimidating. If Temperance did, she hid it well.

The two switched between languages, so I could not understand everything they said, but clearly this was a heated exchange. Temperance spread her arms to block the giant's path to the table at the back of the room, "No, you can't take Peter away. However important you are, you must respect his wishes."

The feather fell off the man's wide-brimmed hat. His extravagant moustache quaked when he spoke, "Madam, I merely wish to honour the memory of a valued employee."

Michael looked nervous, clearing precious pots to safety upstairs.

Seeing Agnes and me, Matthew hurried across to explain. This was Cornelis van Giessen, Peter's employer at the Weighing House or *Waag*. He had come as soon as he heard the news.

A wealthy burgher, with friends on the council, Cornelis was used to getting his own way.

Temperance was similarly determined, insisting, "Peter was a member of our English Reformed Church. He must be buried in accordance with its traditions."

"I came here to help," Cornelis boomed, before returning to impenetrable vocabulary.

NAMING THE DEAD

Brandishing a letter, Matthew tried to attract his attention without success.

With considerable skill and patience, Agnes succeeded in distracting Cornelis. She motioned for him to sit with her on the stools, a difficult manoeuvre for a man of his size. After lowering himself carefully, he spread his knees wide to balance, taking more than his fair share of the space.

Temperance sat too, positioning her stool between Cornelis and Weekes' body for the duration of the conversation.

As Matthew read the letter in a slow, deliberate voice, both antagonists quietened. Peter Weekes had written and signed it in the presence of two witnesses. Like the others, I was astonished by his request.

Weekes wanted his body to be dissected in the event of his death in order to identify the cause of the severe pain he had suffered for several months. I had seen illustrations in Matthew's medical books, but never known anyone volunteer for such butchery. The others seemed less squeamish.

Temperance nodded, "An autopsy could confirm the true reason Peter died."

Cornelis was intrigued by the idea. Professing an interest in scientific discovery, he offered, "You can use my loft. It's a more suitable place to cut him up. I will pay for the coffin too."

"As long as you return Peter in time for the funeral," Temperance was determined to keep control of that event.

"Just let me know when you've made all the arrangements, so I can transport him to the *Begijnhof* chapel."

Amsterdam's Dutch Reformed Church had shown preference to their English fellow Calvinists by providing a former Catholic building for them to use.

Thus, Matthew secured an excellent compromise with the help of reassuring murmurs and nods from his wife.

Van Giessen's men brought a large wooden chest from the barge outside. Each surface was marked with the letters VOC, indicating it was the property of the renowned Dutch East India

Company. The chest would have been too short for me. Weekes' body fitted inside easily.

As we watched them carry it away, Cornelis reminded us we would need to perform the autopsy quickly. He and his wife often entertained guests in their home. Although the cold, damp weather would delay decay, she would not tolerate unpleasant smells. We should come that afternoon.

"Why not print your findings?" he added, "Many guildsmen and burghers are interested in anatomy."

"Do you think they would buy such a book?"

"You need pictures. People like pictures. Do you know anyone who could draw?"

Matthew shook his head. I could see he was tempted by the idea, though. This would be a way of using his experience to benefit others and honour his patient's memory.

After Agnes left us, already late for her cleaning job, Matthew and I watched Cornelis' barge disappear into the city, through the *Munt* gate.

"Peter was convinced he suffered from an undiagnosed condition," Matthew said, "I found no evidence, but now wonder if I missed something. The autopsy will settle this, once and for all. Will you help me, Baxby? We can follow the procedure in my book."

Matthew knew I performed emergency surgery at the Battle of Nieuwpoort before starting my apprenticeship with him. The day I removed Crackleton's foot was one of the most distressing of my life. Although I had not been troubled by recurrent nightmares since surviving the storm on the voyage, they could return at any time.

Would opening up a dead body be easier than a living one? Traitors' entrails looked vile after they were hanged.

"Together, we will be able to solve the mystery of Peter's pain. You could co-author the book," Matthew tried to tempt me.

I did not want to draw attention to myself in that way, knowing I still had enemies in England who might hunt me down. However, it might prove beneficial to learn more about the innards of a corpse. Also, I was interested to see inside Cornelis's canal house. Even Julian Felde claimed not to have entered one.

When I agreed to help him, Matthew echoed Agnes' earlier sentiment, "I'm glad you've come to help. There are too many patients on the islands for one physician."

Unlike her neighbours', Alice Weekes' door was shut and her curtains closed when we walked past. Previously, Matthew gained her permission for the autopsy when he called. However, having broken bad news on many occasions, he had been surprised by her muted reaction, "I think Alice had been drinking. She took a long time to open the door, then seemed distracted."

"Were you suspicious? Do you think Alice might be complicit in Peter's death?"

"Oh no, Alice is a quiet little thing, who couldn't push anyone in the Amstel. She said Peter left in good spirits that morning. He often worked late, and they slept in different rooms, so she didn't notice he hadn't returned home."

By the time we reached the Blue Bridge, my thoughts had returned to Isobel and my precarious financial state. In England, I had been a respected physician, with a cottage and a servant. Now I slept on straw in the attic of a flour store.

Isobel was the widow of a wealthy alderman, who had bought her jewels and fur. She would meet eminent professors at Leiden University, who might own land and several houses like him. Although I longed to see her again, I feared she might politely reject my advances on account of my poverty, an unbearable thought after waiting so long.

Perhaps Isobel's delay would be beneficial after all, giving me time to improve my position. Matthew had suggested patients on the islands. Hopefully, before long, I would find richer ones in the city too.

7

As was his custom in England, Matthew had written a list of patients to visit. The number looked optimistic, given how tired he looked. His hearing was poorer on his left side. He walked more slowly than before. I would assist the older physician until I found patients of my own.

However, I was surprised when Matthew asked me if I still spoke Spanish, "There's a patient I'd like you to meet on *Vloonburg* island."

Matthew knew more about my background than I realised. Geoffrey arranged Spanish lessons before I accompanied him to Cadiz. Then I worked as a translator for a sweet wine importer for a few boring years.

"I haven't had cause to speak the language since starting my apprenticeship with you."

"Do you speak Portuguese too? Some Jews have fled persecution there."

Jewish patients! Matthew had never expected me to enter their homes before. In England they lived separately from everyone else.

"Please try to be understanding, Baxby. They have escaped persecution like us."

Matthew had a reason for asking me to visit a particular one. Raphael Barr's artist son might be willing to sketch illustrations of the autopsy, not an easy conversation in a language I had not used for several years.

The wind was strongest at the apex of the bridge, which provided an expansive view across *Vloonburg* to the other islands and the shipyard beyond. How could Matthew and Agnes live in such a place? Descending, I smelled it too. Rubbish and sewage spilt into the Amstel from numerous narrow channels, to the delight of enormous rats.

Vloonburg's once orderly pattern of dwellings and wharfs had been blighted by hundreds of interposing sheds and shacks, which poor yet innovative immigrants had constructed from misshapen off-cuts of wood. Some were topped by reeds, offering poor protection in recent weather.

Matthew recommended we use one of the main thoroughfares to reach Raphael Barr's home. Forming the shape of a cross, they were lined with rows of single-storey houses, following an identical pattern to his own.

I had grown accustomed to hearing Dutch and Turkish sailors on the ship. Now, a bewildering mix of strange sounds and cooking odours piqued my senses.

According to Matthew, this reclaimed rectangle had a reputation for disease and destitution, but not crime. We were not accosted by grimy whores or tiresome pickpockets, who were commonplace in Southwark on the south bank of the Thames.

"Don't worry, Baxby. You'll soon find your way around here, as you did in Lincoln at the beginning of your apprenticeship."

Vloonburg was very different. Despite the overhanging storeys and central drains, Lincoln streets were named and wide enough for two donkeys to pass.

When I told Temperance I killed a Spaniard, I did not expect to meet another so soon, albeit a Jewish one. Raphael Barr was slow to open the door of his one-room home. After introducing us, Matthew left, grateful for the opportunity to attend to another urgent case.

Barr offered me delicious pastry sweets laced with ginger, of which I ate several. He insisted I sit on his sole comfortable chair, whilst I bled him with Matthew's leech.

Although Barr spoke with an unfamiliar accent, I understood most of what he said and felt more at ease than I expected as he talked about his homeland. Barr missed the sunshine, the coast and olive groves. It was hard to reconcile his description of idyllic scenery with the carnage I witnessed when we captured Cadiz. I asked him why he left.

"We fled an even greater evil than you and your friends. Given the choice between adopting the Catholic faith or death, what would you do? The Inquisition tortures anyone it disagrees with."

It was a moving testimony. His wife died on the journey. Barr raised their two boys alone. She had taught him how to make the sweets. He thought of her every time he took them from the oven.

"Amsterdam has given us back our lives, our hope, and our faith about which we have lots to learn. Our rabbi wants to build a synagogue. However, we must remain vigilant. The Spanish have informers everywhere."

He was proud of his two sons. The elder worked at the Hague, whilst the younger Samuel painted portraits of Dutch families who appreciated the way he depicted their homes. Hopefully, Samuel would be willing to produce autopsy illustrations too.

As I struggled to explain Matthew's request, Raphael Barr looked horrified, "My Samuel would never touch a corpse. You should bury it today."

"Your son wouldn't need to make contact with the body, just sketch details for medical purposes."

I failed to persuade him, due to a religious rule, but Barr insisted I visit again next week and promised more pastries. He gave me a few Dutch coins, my first ones. Despite being from one of the largest Jewish families on *Vloonburg* island, he could only afford a small sum.

As a capable, Cambridge-educated physician, I had assumed Matthew would live in a grander home than Barr's. Perhaps the Mobleys' finances were depleted by looking after so many children. Thomas' eldest three offspring had stayed with them whilst he returned to organise our escape from England.

Retracing my steps to the Blue Bridge, the rows of one-roomed homes all looked the same. They shared an identical layout, with which I was to become familiar. Samuel Barr slept in the attic space, reached via ladder-stairs directly opposite the front door. His father slept in an alcove bed behind the ladder, which gave some separation from the cooking and living space.

Where once Agnes had complained about the lack of glass in her upstairs windows, in common with their neighbours the Mobleys only had one here, looking out onto the street. I hoped to afford somewhere better, preferably within the city.

I paused when crossing the Amstel, admiring the view to the north. A shaft of sunshine broke through dark clouds to illuminate the walls. Beneath, the glistening *Singel* and *Kloveniersburgwal* canals provided the city with the protection of a moat. Most boats headed in through the *Munt* gate, towards the *Rokin* and Dam Square. Others turned left to circumnavigate the city on their way to the River Ij, or right towards St. Anthony's gate. In contrast to the island I had left, it was a delightful scene.

The *stilletjes* were fully visible now the water level had dropped. Two boys were fishing with a line, oblivious to the offensive stench from the stalls. I stepped over the rails to take a closer look, descending the steps with care.

On reaching the end of the *stilletjes* platform, I made an astonishing discovery which caused me to reconsider my previous assumptions about Weekes. A length of rope was still attached to the slats where I retrieved his body, fastened by a knot. Although not one a boatman would use, the knot was secure enough.

Someone had tied Weekes there. Here was evidence his death was deliberate. Whatever Crackleton or anyone else believed, the young man had not caught his foot when falling.

Naturally, my suspicions fell on King James and Archbishop Bancroft. Intent on enforcing religious conformity, they had sworn to harry Puritans out of England or do worse. Subsequently, several had moved to Amsterdam and now worshipped at the English Reformed Church. Since being given the *Begijnhof* chapel, they would be easier to hunt down than our Separatist group or the Ancient Brethren who met on *Vloonburg*. Peter Weekes would have been particularly conspicuous given his job at the Weighing House.

Bancroft's pursuivants could have boarded a ship to Amsterdam. Would a passerby have noticed if one tied Weekes to the slats and left him there to drown, given how dark and wet it was at the time?

Who would they target next? It could be any one of us. Any immigrant tripping across the Blue Bridge could be an informer.

Were any of us truly safe?

I had come a long way to escape Bancroft, Sculthorpe and Geoffrey's grip. Surviving the storm at sea had strengthened my resolve. I had taken the tiller to steer my own course through life. I would not give up without a fight.

The lads were impressed with my dagger, which is common at that age. After cutting the rope, I kept the knot as a reminder. I would not forget Peter Weekes.

8

When I returned to the flour store meeting room, Margaret Deryngton was assisting Pastor Smyth. Watching her write neat letters for the children to copy, I remembered how she drew pictures during our time in the safe house. If Raphael Barr's son could not help us record the autopsy, perhaps Margaret could instead.

Scrooby Manor's owner, William Brewster, had found Margaret a reliable servant. I was pleased with the way she followed my instructions for dressing Crackleton's stump and her mother's swollen legs.

Margaret was intrigued to know more, concluding, "If this helps people understand more about diseases and cures, I will gladly draw for you."

I knew Margaret was not afraid of blood. The first time we met, in Scrooby Manor's buttery, she had been keen to calm the Brewsters' cook, despite suffering from a nasty head wound herself. Margaret had fallen in the hunting forest whilst running away from a man near Mattersey bridge. She used the route each Monday, when visiting her mother.

However, none of us had knowledge of what a dissection would really be like.

Matthew was pleased to learn Margaret would help us. Given Jan Munter's concern about Weekes' death, Pastor Smyth assured us the bakehouse owner would be happy for Margaret to use the paper and black chalk he provided for the children.

Matthew wanted to leave straightaway. He had not had time to read Temperance's instructions for finding the Giessens' home. It was situated on the *Achterburgwal* canal, a name which explained its position to those who understood the language, but was unfathomable to everyone else.

Unsurprisingly, we got lost. Once inside the walls, the smaller canals and bridges all looked the same. Although each house was unique, they were similar enough to confuse. The city was like no other, magnificent and disorientating in equal measure.

Matthew said we should head for the New Church spire, our destination being between it and the *Haringpakker* tower. After retracing our steps, we found the *Achterburgwal* at last. It followed the curving line of the wall, marking the city's western edge.

The van Giessens' house was six stories high, with a basement beneath, and pots of plants on either side of steps to a solid black door. I rang the bell and waited, then Margaret tried again.

Having expected a maid or Cornelis, I was surprised when an attractive woman opened the door, quite possibly half his age. She wore a ruff even wider than Temperance's, above a bright orange gown which showed off her figure to good effect. This was Sophie, Cornelis' younger wife. She explained, "Cornelis is at a meeting. He should be home in time to eat."

When Matthew explained our business, Sophie did not seem perturbed by the presence of the corpse in her home.

Entering the ground floor of the burgher's house for the first time, it was hard not to stare at the high ceiling and sumptuous furnishings. Cornelis was a wealthy man. His wife beckoned us through to a comfortable vestibule, apologising for her pretty accent by explaining she was born in France.

Catching sight of myself in a mirror, the first opportunity for several weeks, I wished I had visited a barber. My hair and beard needed urgent attention. Crackleton had cut my hair on the ship, not an experience I wished to repeat. Certainly, my face looked darker than my friends', closer to Sophie van Giessen's shade.

Sophie pointed to the stairs, "The body is in the loft. I hope you don't mind if I don't accompany you up. I need to finish arranging flowers."

Two vases were waiting on a polished table with carved legs.

"I have one request," she continued, "Please complete your work as soon as possible. We don't want unpleasant smells to ruin our evening with my husband's business associates."

"We hope to finish before dusk."

"Good. Keep walking until you reach the top."

When Sophie's skirt brushed against me, I realised it was made of silk. English noblewomen wore the fabric at court. How amazing that a burgher could afford this for his wife.

Margaret and I followed Matthew up in silence. There were no noisy children or servants in the house. The stairs narrowed and steepened the higher we went. I would have liked to peep in the rooms off the higher landings, but all the doors were closed.

Being older, Matthew tired first. As we passed him at the third storey, I remarked, "It must have been difficult to carry Peter's body up here."

"Didn't you see the rope hanging from the loft doors outside? They probably attached the chest and winched it up."

How had I missed this ingenious Dutch idea? Reaching the top landing ahead of the others, I paused before going inside alone. The winch drum was positioned in front of the loft doors. I decided to open one to let in more light, then stepped back abruptly, buffeted by cold air. A fall from that height would kill me instantly. However, it was hard to ignore the magnificent view across the flat landscape.

Beyond the walls and *Singel,* workmen were hammering pre-cut timbers into the marsh by lifting heavy weights on poles. Previously on the ship, we had seen windmills which powered saws to cut these. I could see rows of similar ones stretching into the distance.

Although not visible from the opening, I knew where the border with the Spanish-held Low Countries lay. The Dutch commander Maurice of Nassau-Orange had made further gains since Nieuwpoort, alongside our English regiments led by Sir Francis and Horace Vere, but the enemy was only a hundred miles away to the south.

Several chests were stacked beneath the eaves of the loft, all marked with the letters VOC. Cornelis' business interests extended beyond his post at the Weighing House. Weekes' chest was by a table in the centre, marked with chalk. Otherwise, it looked no different to the rest.

I stepped away as Matthew prised the lid open, my nose being more sensitive than most. It took three of us to lift the body onto the table, a serious undertaking.

Lying there, I studied Weekes' features again. I was certain I had seen him before, but where? If he had returned to London in the last few years, I might have seen him whilst working there. If an opportunity arose, I would ask his widow, Alice. She should know.

As I laid out the tools on another chest, my mind returned to Nieuwpoort where I removed Crackleton's injured foot. Back then, I did not know whether my friend would survive the operation, but felt compelled to try to save his life. I experienced a similar sense of trepidation now. Would this procedure have long-lasting consequences, too?

"Hurry up, Baxby," Matthew interrupted my thoughts, "Sophie van Giessen wants us to finish before her visitors arrive."

I was pleased to be sharing the responsibility with him this time.

9

According to Matthew's book, we needed to examine the external appearance of the body first, the gash on the head being the obvious place to start. It could have been caused before death, by Weekes hitting his head as he fell, or afterwards when it crashed into the bridge. However, we should not ignore the possibility that someone had hit him with something solid.

As we undressed him, Margaret noticed strange marks on Weekes' underside. There were three small ones on his left buttock, a darker shade of red than the flesh beneath.

After measuring them and the head wound, Matthew instructed Margaret on what to sketch, then turned back to his anatomy book, "Generally, the colouring is correct for a two-day old body. The blood has pooled in the lower extremities. However, there's no mention of anything that could cause such marks. They're unlikely to be significant, but we must document everything."

How strange. None of us knew why they were there.

"Is there anything else before we open him?"

"Weekes' face has been shaved and his hair cut recently," Margaret observed.

Matthew agreed this could be relevant, "Peter was seldom this tidy when I visited him. Perhaps he was due to meet someone important at work."

Margaret wrote everything down and completed her first drawings, accurate depictions of head wound and pattern of marks.

As I chose the most suitable knife, Margaret asked if I had done this before. Crackleton's friends posed a similar question in the surgeon's tent at Nieuwpoort. How inept I had been back then.

"I'm sure you'll cope admirably," she added, "I remember the first time we met. You bandaged my head and reassured me, after I fell over running away from a man called Gilbert Grey near Mattersey bridge. I was relieved when you said you'd investigate. He never threatened me again."

As Margaret had already heard me recount the story of how I removed Crackleton's foot, I told her about severed ears, split lips and missing fingers instead, which proved a useful distraction. I was ready to make the first incision.

After slicing the torso, we could see that the lungs had expanded and were pressing against the chest cavity wall. Margaret captured this well.

"Does this prove Weekes drowned?" she asked.

"It's more complicated," Matthew frowned, thumbing through his book, "We need to weigh both lungs."

After convincing ourselves there were no scales in the room, I offered to return to the lower floors to ask if we could borrow some. The autopsy was going to take longer than we expected.

Before I reached the bottom of the stairs, I heard Sophie conversing with a man in Spanish. She was showing him out the front door. I could not detect whether they used the formal or familiar form of address. She let him kiss her hand before turning and smiling at me, gawping on the stairs. What a beautiful woman!

"I'm sorry to disturb you, Mistress van Giessen. Could we borrow some scales and weights? We should have brought them with us. Unfortunately, we forgot."

"Please call me Sophie. Of course, you can borrow them. Our maid does not work today. You'll have to come to the kitchen with me to find them.

Her ruff prevented her from reaching a low cupboard, and caught my face as I crouched to help. How ridiculous to wear it at home. Also, it was unusual for such a wealthy couple to only employ one maid.

"Did you know Peter Weekes?" I asked as she stacked the weights.

"He worked for my husband at the Weighing House. We never spoke."

"Peter must have been an exceptional candidate to get such a prestigious job."

"I think he was recommended by a business associate of my husband, a long time ago. Can you carry all these up to the top floor?"

I said I could, despite considerable difficulty. My hair was an unruly mess. I did not want Sophie van Giessen to believe I was feeble too.

After making several cuts, I severed Weekes' windpipe and the tissues which held the lungs in place. We carried them between us to the scales. They proved heavier than typically expected, which meant Weekes most likely drowned. Although the book insisted there was always room for doubt, this was the most probable cause.

I showed the others the knot I had found. The poor lad must have been alive when the rope was tied around his foot. Had someone knotted it and left him to drown in the river? There was more to discover yet.

As I cut further into the abdomen, the autopsy took an unexpected turn. Weekes' internal organs were not the same as the wood-cut illustrations in Matthew's book. Most of the stomach was intact, but what remained of the liver was covered with hideous bulging growths. Smaller protrusions spotted his intestines and bowel.

I turned away, disgusted by the sight. Margaret was undeterred, "They look like the fungus which infected trees in Scrooby Manor's hunting forest. Do you want me to draw them all?"

Matthew did not answer. Instead, he crumpled on a chest by the open loft door, holding his head in his hands. Being fond of his patient, this was harder for him.

"Peter told me he suffered from serious abdominal pain. He pestered me for months, insisting he was afflicted by a hidden disease. To my shame, I didn't believe him."

This was not the first time the physician had admonished himself. He still felt guilty that his first wife, Eunice, died in childbirth, yet there was nothing he could have done to save her.

"Could these be cancerous tumours, caused by an excess of black bile?" I suggested.

Matthew nodded, "I saw a breast tumour once. Although smaller and pinker, it was growing in a similar pattern."

I turned the pages of his anatomy book without success. Those dissected in the wood-cut pictures had not endured such horrors.

Margaret took some time to draw the tumours, as they had not grown in a uniform way. The result was an excellent likeness. No one could doubt their virulence.

When she finished, we returned the lungs and sewed up the chest. Matthew refused my pleas to investigate further, insisting this was unnecessary because we knew why Weekes died.

"No longer able to bear the pain, Peter must have killed himself. He tied his ankle to the platform, knowing the Amstel would rise. We can't save every patient, but I should have done more."

"You shouldn't blame yourself," Margaret uttered the words before me, "You couldn't have known how serious his condition was."

"I should have listened to his pleas."

Matthew made us promise not to tell anyone that Weekes had killed himself, not even his wife. He knew of a previous case where no Church would bury the body. Catholics and Protestants believed suicide was a grievous sin, something they agreed on.

"Could we determine the time of death?" I posed, still keen to learn more.

"If Peter was wearing this shirt and breeches when you found him, he probably died in the middle of the day," Margaret said, "Otherwise, it would have been too cold."

"He could have removed his cloak before killing himself," Matthew contradicted.

"Or someone could have taken it."

Nevertheless, Margaret had spotted an interesting clue. Why was Weekes not wearing more? Alice might know what he was wearing when he left home. I needed to find an opportunity to talk with her.

10

When we descended to tell Sophie we had finished, her husband met us at the foot of the stairs. He had left work earlier than usual, with the intention of speaking with us. Cornelis invited us into the family's grand reception room before asking his wife to fetch wine.

As we waited, we admired the large portrait above the fireplace. Cornelis was smiling in the centre, with his arms around Sophie and a younger woman. They were standing in front of the same fireplace.

"What a marvellous likeness," I exclaimed.

"I'm a very lucky man," Cornelis winked, "My daughter Amalia is taking her flute lesson, otherwise I would introduce you to her too. We're very pleased with the artist and have recommended him to several friends."

Sophie must be his second wife. She was too young to be the mother of the daughter in the portrait. Cornelis went outside to shout at her, impatient for his drink.

While we waited, I crossed to the generous window with a delightful view of the *Haringpakker* tower.

"The *Achterburgwal* canal looks charming from here," I commented, not realising Sophie had returned.

"The New *Achterburgwal*," she corrected, "We live on the new side of the city, not the old."

Cornelis laughed and winked, "The Old *Achterburgwal* has notorious brothels, conveniently close to the harbour. My wife doesn't want people to think we live there. She prefers to call the old side *De Wallen*, so as not to confuse the two."

My subsequent attempt to steer the conversation to a less contentious subject proved unsuccessful. The couple disagreed about the impact of the building work, too. The piles were intended to form the foundations of new defences, the first stage of an ambitious plan to expand the city outwards.

"Once they've finished the new bastions, they will pull the old wall down. We will be able to see the *Singel* from here. I can moor my barges there."

"When they've filled the gap with new canals, we should move to a more modern home there."

"This house is big enough for three and convenient for my work."

Sophie served us on the sofas, without hiding her displeasure at her husband's remarks.

Despite switching between languages when arguing with Temperance, Cornelis conversed with us solely in English, which he spoke more fluently than his wife.

"Was the dissection worthwhile? Did you discover anything interesting?"

Matthew answered positively, without mentioning the cancer or his conclusions. Margaret declined to show him the sketches, cleverly saying she was too nervous.

Nevertheless, Cornelis made a generous offer, "Anatomy is a fascinating subject. I know some printers who might be interested in your work. Would you like me to make enquiries on your behalf?"

As Matthew thanked him, I could see Margaret was thrilled by the suggestion too. Cornelis said they should return in a couple of weeks, by which time he should be able to provide names.

His kindness surprised me. It was hard to reconcile his geniality with his earlier belligerence towards Temperance. Why had he not shown more respect to her? She was a well-respected member of a Reformed Church, the type the Dutch preferred.

Sophie perched on the edge of a soft leather chair throughout, smiling widely once to reveal a spotless line of white teeth. Her fingers were long, with jewelled rings on both hands, possibly one set with a diamond.

Cornelis was not only rich he appeared well-informed too. The shelves on either side of the fireplace were filled with books, arranged in height order, covering a greater range of subjects than William Brewster's in Scrooby Manor. Here, Cornelis and Sophie enjoyed an equally comfortable life, with more privacy.

In truth, I envied the burgher's fine canal house and married status. How long would it be before I owned such a home of my own? When Isobel and I sat on comfortable chairs by our own fireplace, we would not bicker like Cornelis and Sophie. I might even commission Samual Barr to paint our portrait. We would live in greater luxury than her first husband provided.

The walk back was quicker. The three of us followed the canal south until we reached an alleyway with a view of the New Church. Matthew pointed to another wider one which led to *Begijnhof* island, before reaching the now familiar *Munt* gate.

Shopkeepers were shutting their doors along the length of the Amstel. The Blue Bridge was dotted with immigrants filing home from work.

Alice's curtains were open this time. Matthew planned to report our findings to her, without mentioning suicide.

Although I respected his judgement and experience, I was not convinced by Matthew's conclusion about Weekes' death. There were easier ways for an enterprising young man to take his own life. Weekes could have hanged himself below the bridge. Also, why remove his outer garments beforehand? Where had they gone?

However, as Alice opened her door, I agreed with Matthew's earlier statement about her innocence. Weekes' wife was too tiny and timid to push anyone in the Amstel. She was dressed more simply than Temperance and was more hesitant.

The Weekes' ground floor was divided into separate rooms, but the stools by the front window were identical to those at the Knowsleys' home. Plain and undemonstrative, Alice sat quietly on one while Matthew told her about the cancerous growths.

"Did they cause Peter's death?"

"We think your husband drowned. The pain could have been a contributory factor. Few of us know how well we would function in such circumstances. It is easy to slip and fall."

Alice twisted strands of hair protruding from her bonnet. Having seen other widows receive bad news, I was surprised by the fortitude with which she discussed distressing details, "I still find it hard to believe Peter is dead. He left in good spirits yesterday morning."

"Was he wearing warm clothes?" I enquired.

"Peter liked to dress well. He was wearing his favourite blue cloak and wide-brimmed felt hat."

On hearing they were missing, she suggested someone might have stolen them, as Margaret had before.

I would have liked to ask Alice if her husband had visited London in the past few years, but this was not the right time. The city remained the most likely place I had seen him before. Thousands thronged through the gates each day. We could have met in a shop, an inn or at a theatre. However, I had a nagging sense the encounter had been more significant.

Remembering more might help to explain the remaining mystery surrounding his death, which had unsettled me more than others I had known. Women frequently died in childbirth. The young and elderly were vulnerable too. Peter Weekes was a seemingly healthy, successful young man who yet suffered from a hideous, hidden disease. He said goodbye to his wife, as was his practice when leaving for work, then never returned.

I suspected foul play, but knew I should not make hasty judgments. If I were to establish myself as a serious physician in this city, an equal to Matthew, I needed to approach this and all cases in a sober manner.

11

London 1613

The vicar to Baxby's right has grown increasingly agitated whilst listening. Will his leg recover? What if his own pain becomes unbearable?

Previously, the cleric hoped to be released in time for the royal wedding fireworks and sea pageant, marking the marriage of Princess Elizabeth to Elector Frederick of the Palatinate. Now he just wants to regain his licence and return home to his wife and children. Will he ever see them again?

"Can you move your leg nearer?" Baxby asks. The chain attaching his ankle to the wall prohibits him from shuffling closer to examine it.

The vicar shakes his head and looks away, "What have I become? Other clerics envied my parish. I baptised thirty babies last year. My vicarage wasn't grand like Cornelis' home, but it was a good place to raise a family."

"You mustn't lose hope."

The vicar sobs, believing he has lost God's favour along with his benefice. If his leg were less painful, he might be able to understand why. He longs to go home, yet would struggle to walk to the cell door.

Wincing, he manages to move his leg sufficiently for Baxby to get a better look, "These are nasty bruises. Your leg has swollen, too. Did you fall on the stairs, or otherwise injure yourself while out of the cell?"

The vicar does not respond.

"Perhaps the guards will take pity on you. I will ask them to remove your chain when they bring our next meal."

If the leg blackens, the vicar will lose it.

12

Amsterdam 1608

On my first Sunday in Amsterdam, my believer-friends gathered for a service, as was their custom. With the benches moved to the perimeter, the flour store meeting room reminded me of Gainsborough Old Hall and Scrooby Manor in England, although smaller and more austere.

Former neighbours and friends squashed together, plus others who had joined Smyth's congregation in the past year. Older children sat on the floor around the long central table, smaller ones on adults' knees. It was reassuring to see so many familiar faces and be surrounded by English voices again.

Matthew and Agnes had placed her young nephew Toby between them to afford some control. He still resembled his late mother Susannah, but not as strongly as before. Only she and Agnes knew who his father was. His hair was not as red than theirs.

Nicholas was sitting between Margaret and her mother, a noteworthy achievement. Crackleton looked brighter, having slept better since Thomas arranged for him and his two children to sleep in a former office on the first floor.

Pastor Smyth stopped shaking hands, and moved to the centre of the room to commence the service. Black buttoned doublets looked smart on most men, but his was a little too large. However, his powerful voice commanded attention instantly, "Most of you will have heard about the tragic death of Peter Weekes. He was a valued member of the Ancient Brethren Separatist congregation before moving to Amsterdam's English Reformed Church. Please pray for his widow, Alice, and all who miss him. The funeral will take place at the *Begijnhof* chapel this week, with refreshments afterwards at Mistress Knowsley's home."

After psalm-singing and noisy prayers, Smyth introduced William Brewster to those who had not known him in England. Brewster worked for a privy councillor, before inheriting his father's position as Scrooby Manor's postmaster. After Bancroft's High Commission issued warrants for his and Pastor Robinson's arrests, Brewster led our group's escape to the coast with remarkable strength of purpose and courage. All were keen to hear him speak.

Brewster hesitated before addressing us. Both he and Pastor Robinson had seemed less confident since being forced to leave their wives and children behind in England. As he explained their plight and that of other missing Scrooby members, silence settled in the room.

"Soldiers arrested our women and children at the final hour, after their barge lodged in the Humber mud. We were already on board our hoy. The captain refused to delay. There was nothing we men could do but watch the horror unfold from the deck."

Even the smallest children stopped fidgeting during his moving account. Our Gainsborough-friends imagined the women's heart-rending cries. We relived them again.

"Do you know where they are now?" Pastor Smyth asked.

Overcome with emotion, Brewster turned away unable to answer. It was unbearable to witness his distress. After leading our 'pilgrim' group to the coast and through dark days imprisoned in Boston Guildhall, his wife Mary, daughter Patience, and baby Fear had been taken. None of us knew where.

Matthew's daughter Constance sobbed, "Where's Patience Brewster? Patience is my friend. I want to play with her again."

Agnes apologised for the little girl's outburst, but Constance expressed the pain adults felt, separated from those they loved. How could children understand?

Pastor Robinson read a passage from the big Geneva Bible, which he had carried on his back from Scrooby. The verses explained the sorrow we all felt. Whether together or separated by the Narrow Sea, we were closely linked like parts of a human body.

By one Spirit we are all baptised into one body, whether we be Jews or Greek, bond or free, and have all drunk one Spirit
For that body also is not one member but many

KAREN HADEN

Therefore, if one member suffers, all suffer with it

It was a wise choice in the circumstances, with particular resonance for those of us who dissected Weekes' corpse. The cancer could not hide the fact that the body's skeleton, organs and muscles fitted together well.

When Pastor Smyth finished his sermon, he shook Pastor Robinson's hand, explaining to those unfamiliar with the practice, "This is how we recognise one another as fellow members of one body. There is no distinction or hierarchy in a believers' church. God calls us all by His grace. Jesus is our Lord."

Pastor Smyth shook William Brewster's hand next, then his ward William Bradford's. The clamour in the room grew as existing members of the bakehouse church shook newcomers' hands. Smyth organised a line enabling them to greet each believer-brother and sister in turn, an emotional reunion.

Agnes wiped tears from her eyes. Like others who feared our ship had been lost, she attributed our deliverance to the miraculous providence of God.

I held back, having previously made the decision not to join the church in this way, feeling it would have been fraudulent. Although I sympathised with the believers' cause, I did not fully share their faith.

My friends valued my contribution, including my medical skills, but did not know about my past. Also, I had questions and doubts. If God loved them all as they claimed, why submit them to such suffering?

However, tears formed in my own eyes when they sang my favourite psalm, one hundred and seven, in which weary, hungry, and imprisoned souls are rescued after crying out to God for help. I had been saved from my own foolishness after calling out in the storm, and prevented Felde from being washed overboard.

It might have been easier to participate if I had not retrieved Peter Weekes' body from the Amstel. Given everything that had happened before, I was hoping for a calmer introduction to life in Amsterdam.

NAMING THE DEAD

During the discussion at the subsequent business meeting, William Brewster proposed that he return to rescue those left behind. Thomas Helwys, whose own wife Joan and youngest two children had been imprisoned by the Church in York, advocated a gentler approach. He would return to England, discover their whereabouts and charter another ship.

Agnes made a plea on behalf of Thomas' older children, who would miss their father if he left again, but after a long debate, the meeting accepted Thomas' offer. The Mobleys would need to look after young Edwin Helwys and his sisters again.

The meeting agreed that William Brewster would be the group's elder in Thomas' absence. Also, they needed a replacement translator. Having been impressed by my attempts at Dutch on the ship, they recommended I take lessons with Temperance Knowsley. I willingly agreed. Learning the language could be beneficial in other ways, too.

Julian Felde was not at the service or the business meeting. Although he helped Thomas arrange our escape, Felde had not been part of a Separatist group in England, so I was not unduly concerned at the time. I had not seen him since carrying Weekes' stretcher from the Blue Bridge.

As the others filed down the flour store stairs, Thomas came across to talk, "Temperance gave me my first lessons. She's a good teacher. You'll learn quickly."

"I sense she will organise Peter Weekes' funeral well."

"Indeed. Peter's death is a tragic loss for her church. He was very capable, but sometimes spoke when it would be more prudent to remain silent. People can be jealous of success, particularly that of immigrants."

"Are you suggesting Peter brought his death upon himself?"

"Certainly not. I'm warning you to be careful, Baxby. Remember, we're tolerated here, not loved."

As always, I was grateful for Thomas' advice. When my financial position improved, I would need to be discreet.

Thomas was not surprised by Felde's absence. He thought he might be staying with a friend or associate nearby. The former deputy had visited the Dutch Republic on several occasions before.

"I'm due to meet Jan Munter before I return to England. I will introduce you then. If Sir Julian hasn't appeared, we'll ask Jan to make enquiries amongst his contacts in the city. He might know more about Weekes' background, too."

Thomas did not admit to knowing anything about that.

13

In addition to paying my respects, Peter Weekes' funeral might provide an opportunity to learn more about his life. Nevertheless, I was nervous about entering the English Reformed chapel. In the past, Pastor Robinson had explained religious differences to me patiently. It seemed inappropriate to ask him in his current circumstances.

Crossing the little drawbridge onto *Begijnhof* island with Matthew felt like stepping back to an earlier age. Its little courtyard provided a welcome respite from the busy city, with a patch of grass and trees which were rare elsewhere. The surrounding stone and wooden houses had been constructed long before the Alteration, when Amsterdam became Protestant following independence from Spain. The once-Catholic chapel in the centre now affirmed the Dutch Reformed Church's generosity towards its English co-religionists.

"Surprised?" Matthew asked.

I nodded, having never expected an English congregation to worship openly in such a charming setting.

Cornelis van Giessen had delivered Weekes' coffin as promised. It sat on a table beneath the enormous pulpit at the front of the chapel, with the young man's bible on top, along with a small bowl of white flowers called tulips. They were similar to the ones I had seen Sophie arranging.

Unlike parish churches back home, the chapel walls and windows were plain and bare. People still sat on pews which gradually filled from the rear. There were more mourners than I expected. Colleagues from the Weighing House squeezed between black-clad members of the English Reformed and Ancient Brethren congregations. Matthew said the pair had over three hundred members in total.

The front rows were reserved. Alice, Temperance and Michael filed in ahead of a line of English and Dutch officials whom Matthew did not recognise. Peter's little widow kept her head bowed throughout.

If Thomas' theory was correct, Weekes' killer could be sitting amongst us now, a thought I found hard to believe. Were any of these respectable citizens really capable of murder? They looked too satisfied with their own lives to envy Weekes' success.

Sitting there with Matthew, I could scarcely believe my eyes and ears. John Paget conducted the funeral service without reference to the Book of Common Prayer, and read from a giant Geneva Bible rather than the version approved by the English bishops. He wore a black cassock, not ornate robes and headwear, blatantly flouting the Church's dress codes too.

The English cleric was breaking all the rules, leading an English service in this way. Why take such a risk? If Archbishop Bancroft learnt about this subversion, I doubted any member of Paget's congregation would be safe. Bancroft could have spies in the congregation, deciding who to target next. They were more likely culprits than Thomas' theory about a jealous local.

After lengthy prayers, Reverend Paget climbed the high pulpit staircase to deliver his address, "Peter Weekes was an esteemed member of this church, a loving husband and valued colleague at the Weighing House. He worked hard and persevered for what he knew to be true and right."

No one echoed "Amen". This service was much more restrained than our recent gathering in the flour store meeting room.

The New Church bells rang again. We had been listening to Paget for over an hour.

I learnt that after meeting on the ship from England, Peter and Alice had married young, but nothing more about his early years. The Ancient Brethren had provided initial assistance before the couple moved to the English Reformed Church. Paget's smile betrayed his assumption that this was a wise choice.

Opening the big Geneva Bible, he read a passage he obviously knew well.

For those whom he knew before, he also predestined to be made like to the image of his Son, that we might be the first born

50

NAMING THE DEAD

among many brethren
    Moreover, whom he predestined he also called, and whom he called he also justified, and whom he justified he also glorified

Paget explained the importance of these verses. He was preoccupied with Weekes' eternal destiny not his past.

"Although Peter was taken from us in this untimely way, we do not grieve his passing as the ungodly do, for we know he was Elected by God. Redeemed by irresistible grace, Peter now shares the blessings of the heavenly kingdom, our future hope too."

Studying the glum faces of my fellow mourners as they trudged out, I doubted they found comfort in the service either.

Cornelis' barge took Temperance, Michael, Alice and Reverend Paget to the burial site with the coffin. Matthew and I had to walk. We were slow to leave the island. *Begijnhof's* winchman Smeets had opened its little drawbridge to let another boat past, a clever design.

As we waited, I asked Matthew about Weekes' Election, assuming Paget had been talking about a position the deceased held.

Matthew quickly corrected me, "The Elect are those God predestines for heaven. It's a key doctrine of Calvinist theology. I'm surprised you don't know that."

"Have they got a name for everyone else?"

"Those predestined for hell are called Reprobates, or the non-Elect."

It was sobering to think the impatient dignitaries, also waiting to cross, probably saw me in this way. Stoic Smeets ignored their complaints. The winchman's weathered face and strong arms suggested he had been doing this job for many years.

None of the dignitaries attended the committal. A handful of fellow English men and women trudged with us to St. Anthony's gate, using a route which avoided *De Wallen*.

As Amsterdam's New Church cemetery was no longer large enough for its growing population, Weekes was buried with numerous other immigrants in open ground allotted for a new

Zuiderkerk church.

Temperance seemed more upset than Alice as we watched the coffin lower. I found an opportunity to talk with Weekes' widow when we moved away from the graveside.

"Thank God, that's over," she sighed, "Peter was always more religious than me."

"Reverend Paget seems to think highly of him."

After checking the vicar was not looking, she produced a flask of liquid from her bag and sipped some discreetly.

"Paget's certainty scares me. Once he called at our home after I'd been drinking. I shouldn't have argued back, but I meant what I said. He wasn't interested in Peter before he acquired his well-paid job."

"He thinks Peter is in heaven now."

"Who is Paget to judge who goes where? I'm certain he thinks I'm bound for hell."

It was hard to believe this small, plain woman could show such anger. Her pronouncement worried me. If God was omniscient, as Paget had preached, He would know about my illegitimate birth and impoverished upbringing. Although I believed God saved me in the storm, Paget was unlikely to conclude that was sufficient evidence to assume a glorious afterlife.

Concerned, I accosted Matthew afterwards, "Do all Christians believe in predestination?"

"Good Lord, no."

He described the differences as being like a weather vane, with Paget's Reformed Calvinists in the north. Catholics were diametrically opposite, believing salvation depended on receiving sacraments from the one true Roman Church. Lutherans and Anabaptists were different again, figuratively in the east and west.

"What about our pastors?" I queried.

"Smyth and Robinson are still developing their ideas, but are probably nearest northwest or north of northwest. When visiting patients, it's wise not to mention religion. People can have strong ideas."

Temperance informed us it was time to leave. The next burial was due to start. A ragged line of Norwegians was queuing at the gate. Matthew did not know what Norwegians believed.

14

Matthew waited until after the funeral to shatter my dreams. Whilst I was admiring an empty canal house near the *Munt* gate, he told me about the restrictions. Our English medical licences were not valid in the Republic. This was why he only treated patients on the islands and lived in a one-roomed house. Agnes had returned to cleaning work to supplement their income. Dutch physicians could make a comfortable living, but not us.

I should have guessed. Other professions were restricted to burghers and guildsmen. Even if an immigrant was invited to join one, he was unlikely to be able to pay the fee.

"How can Temperance afford to live here?" I asked, as we passed her home.

Reginald Knowsley works with the North Sea herring fleet. He earns good money but is away for much of the year. The rules are particularly difficult for sensitive souls like Michael. His parents bought him his wheel so he could make pots."

"Will it make a difference if I learn Dutch?"

Matthew stopped and turned towards me, "That's unlikely. Don't you want to help the poor, Baxby? Many need medical care."

"Yes, but not exclusively."

I wanted to visit patients in grand canal houses, not just sheds and shacks.

Amsterdam gave me an opportunity to start my life anew, on its own terms, not mine. My new life would prove more challenging than I expected.

Matthew took me to see patients on *Uilenburg* island. There were four islands in total, each seemingly more crowded and deprived than the previous one. Although he warned me the cess channel was blocked before we crossed from *Vloonburg*, my first visit was still a shock. We had to balance on rotten planks. Women washed clothes nearby, while children argued in a language I did not recognise.

All the *Uilenburg* patients lived in damp, cramped tents or dilapidated shelters they had erected between the businesses which served Amsterdam's neighbouring shipyard. The noise was deafening at times. Hundreds worked in the lumber yards, rope sheds and forges, building and repairing the largest fleet in the world.

Matthew was keen for me to meet Elliot and Helen Kent, who lived with their children and two other families in a former byre. Whilst Matthew gave the children sweets and examined them, Elliot sat motionless, staring ahead. Helen's face was creased and drawn.

"My husband served as a mercenary under Maurice of Nassau-Orange and Frederick of the Palatinate, a record of which he should be proud. Sadly, the Battle of Nieuwpoort broke his soul."

Elliot turned and nodded, "I will never fight in sand again."

This was the reason why Matthew wanted me to visit the Kents. He had told them I worked in the surgeon's tent at Nieuwpoort.

Taking me aside, Helen asked, "What happened there? Elliot refuses to talk about his experiences."

"Please don't think ill of your husband, or press him to speak. There were horrendous deaths and injuries. Also, war leaves mental wounds which cannot be seen."

"Elliot refuses to return to England, yet struggles to find work here. I don't know how long we can continue like this."

After the battle, I had been troubled by strange waking dreams and nightmares myself. They had not resurfaced in Amsterdam, but I had not forgotten the fear I felt.

"Don't worry, Elliot," I tried to comfort him, "Keep going. You're not alone. Your children and wife need you to stay as strong as you can be."

Helen thanked me. I did not feel I had helped, but Matthew had made his point. Patients like the Kents needed my help. He was worried that Elliot might take his own life, which may have influenced his conclusion about Weekes.

Exhausted after the busy day, I was grateful when Matthew

invited to his home to eat. The Mobleys' one-roomed house seemed spacious compared with those I had visited on *Uilenburg*.

Lying awake that night, I reflected on what I had seen. Although grateful to Jan Munter for the roof above my head, I found it hard to sleep. The bakehouse noise disturbed me. The straw made me itch.

My prospects were far worse than I had expected. Archbishop Bancroft seemed to have expanded his operation to target exiles in Amsterdam. My old nightmares could return at any time. I did not know which was worse.

Were these setbacks due to mistakes I had made in the past, or those of my parents? Were they predestined by God long before both? Would it make a difference if I knew?

Finding a way to earn more money would have been a more useful pastime.

Crackleton was not bothered by such matters. He believed Weekes had slipped and fallen. It was pointless trying to argue about knotted ropes and strange marks.

Jan Munter had found a desk for Crackleton's little room. He was happy to sit there, preparing Robinson's manuscripts for publication, as he had in Gainsborough. My old comrade had little interest in venturing out, blaming the number of stairs and wet pavements.

When I attended my first Dutch lesson, I found an unlikely ally in Temperance Knowsley. With the funeral behind her, she wanted to discuss the circumstances of Weekes' death.

After forcing me to repeat basic greetings and name different kinds of food, the previously restrained older lady gripped my arm tightly, "That poor lad was murdered, Baxby. Don't let anyone tell you otherwise. Although we're free to worship as we please in Amsterdam, some would prefer we did not."

"Do you mean Archbishop Bancroft and the English Church?"

Temperance nodded, "Please find out whatever you can. Let me know if I can help in any way."

"Peter's face seemed familiar. I don't know where I might have seen him before. Do you know where he was raised, or if he visited London recently?"

Temperance confirmed Weekes had returned to sell property when his brother died. This was after King James succeeded Queen Elizabeth. It seemed most likely I had seen him whilst working in the capital.

After putting aside her initial suspicions about my appearance, Temperance proved a skilled teacher. I had lots to learn, about the language and this extraordinary city.

15

Thomas took me to meet Jan Munter before he sailed for England. Julian Felde had not reappeared. We found the bakehouse owner by an overheated oven, assigning instructions to his team. They listened intently, despite the foul burning smell, then spread out to perform their allotted tasks.

I was impressed by Munter's calm demeanour and pragmatism from the start. It was not surprising the Dutch Navy had entrusted their lucrative biscuit contract to such a businessman.

After watching a line of children pass, carrying buckets of dough, Jan invited us into a small, hot office. He introduced himself in reasonable English before switching to Dutch. I understood a little. Thomas translated the rest.

"I was very sorry to hear about Peter Weekes' untimely death. Although I only met him briefly, I could see he was a conscientious young man."

After learning more about the circumstances, Jan echoed Thomas' earlier sentiments, "Weekes should have kept quiet about his income. Anyone could be jealous and wish him ill. Amsterdam allows all manner of immigrants to live here on the condition they are discreet."

However, when I expressed admiration for the way Cornelis van Giessen had welcomed us into his elegant home, Jan laughed, "Van Giessen indeed. That rascal isn't from there or any other village in a Dutch state. His Flemish parents brought him to Amsterdam soon after the Alteration. He changed his name from De Vos after profiting from an early voyage to the east. That's how he made his money and obtained his position at the *Waag*. I don't know how he funds his fancy lifestyle now."

"I think Cornelis works for the Dutch East India Company. He stores their chests in his loft."

The bakehouse owner expressed surprise. I could not question his scepticism, given his generosity to our group.

When I asked Jan about Felde, he was not concerned that Felde was missing, but offered to make enquiries on my behalf, "Julian can't have disappeared, even in a city of this size. Someone will know where he's staying."

I managed to thank him in Dutch.

Outside in the yard, I asked Thomas why the bakehouse owner was letting us use his property and helping us so much. He suggested we move to a more private area to talk. Between the flour store and perimeter wall, Thomas explained, "Jan is from a Mennonite group, originally from the Waterland region."

This made no sense to me, until Thomas explained that Mennonites were Anabaptists.

Naturally, I was shocked. How could a reputable Dutch burgher join a heretical sect? Its adherents were burnt at the stake in England.

"The Mennonites were persecuted here before the Alteration. Like us, they understand the horrors of imprisonment and torture. They sympathise with our cause."

Foolishly, I repeated the warning I heard many years before, "But Anabaptists don't baptise their babies. They let them go to hell."

Thomas smiled, "I wouldn't summarise their faith in that way. Anabaptists love their children as much as anyone else, and want to live at peace with everyone."

"The English Church ..."

"Although some Anabaptists took control of the German city of Munster once, these Waterland Mennonites are definitely not a threat. You shouldn't believe everything you're told."

Amsterdam was more confusing than other towns and cities I knew. I had not expected to live amongst Anabaptists, nor be reliant on them for help. They kept their outlandish beliefs hidden in England, on fear of death. However, if Jan, an Anabaptist, could run a successful biscuit business, and Cornelis, a Flemish immigrant, could accumulate great wealth, there must be a way for me to make enough money to buy a home of my own.

After making enquiries, Jan found me at the flour store. Agnes was arguing with Thomas' eldest son Edwin at the time. He was refusing to sit at the table with everyone else, claiming he was not hungry. Edwin Helwys was living with the Mobleys again.

I had previously asked Agnes if she had heard from Isobel. The answer was 'no' again.

Jan called Edwin over to translate our conversation. Generally, the younger generation had a better grasp of the language than older ones, "An elderly lady in my church would like to speak with you, Baxby. She lives on *Begijnhof* island."

Through Edwin, I asked if she knew Felde's whereabouts.

"Eva Witte wants to talk about Peter Weekes. I'm not certain about Felde. She's frail and does not speak English. I recommend taking Edwin along to help."

I was grateful for Jan's assistance and keen to visit Eva Witte soon. However, Matthew and Agnes suggested we delay, until Edwin was allowed out again. He was being kept home for a period of time, a punishment for visiting the harbour when he should have been attending Pastor Smyth's lessons.

Agnes' nephew Toby wanted to accompany us too. She told him he was too young.

Temperance did not hide her disapproval of Anabaptist beliefs, "They're called that because they *re-baptise* those who've already received the sacrament as infants, showing their contempt for beliefs the rest of us hold dear."

"Jan Munter …"

"To be honest, I don't think Anabaptists understand the principle at all. They tend to be less educated than most."

Temperance did not talk for as long as Reverend Paget, but was clearly knowledgeable. She had read some of John Calvin's books. I did not dare to show her the little bible in my pocket, a parting gift from Jane Sudwell who I once wished to marry before discovering her Anabaptist beliefs. Jane had been convinced of her own faith like Temperance was of hers.

Religion is a confusing subject. Fortunately, Temperance was better at teaching me Dutch. After finishing her discourse on Reformed theology, she produced an old map. The immigrant islands were missing, having not been reclaimed at the time it was drawn. Nevertheless, it helped me learn the language and find my way around.

The map showed the walled city of Amsterdam, near the mouth of the River Ij, shaped like the tulip flowers I had seen before. At its southern base, near the *Munt* gate, the River Amstel 'stem' split to flow round the *Singel* and *Kloveniersburgwal* canals. The long, straight harbour stretched across the top, between the western *Haringpakker* and eastern *Schreier* towers.

Ships were exquisitely detailed, along with the *Oude* and *Nieuwe Kerk* churches. These prefixes were attached to features in each half of the city in a logical way. The name of the van Giessens' canal meant New Side Front Bastion Wall, an accurate description of its location.

Dam Square was located at the centre, the heart of the city from its conception. Having seen Temperance's map, it was easier to find the route when visiting the Square for the first time with Nicholas and Margaret.

16

Nicholas was pacing the Blue Bridge when I returned from *Vloonburg* one evening. I knew he had been offered work at the Exchange, a remarkable accomplishment at his age. Cornelis might have helped him secure it. Nicholas had visited the burgher with Margaret and Matthew, who still hoped to find a printer.

However, that was not the reason Nicholas was waiting to speak with me on the bridge. The young man was eager to tell me what he had discovered earlier, when crossing Dam Square on the way to his new job, "Couples can marry at the Town Hall. They just have to register, then return two weeks later with witnesses to sign the certificate. That's all."

Marriage had been a continual source of grief to us in England, where the Church had a monopoly. The civil ceremony was another Dutch invention, a welcome feature of religious toleration which Bancroft would hate.

"Will you be my witness at the Town Hall in two weeks' time, Baxby?"

"What do you mean? Are *you* getting married, Nicholas?"

"Margaret accepted my proposal. We registered this afternoon."

"What amazing news! I'd be delighted."

It was a great honour to be asked.

Margaret had invited William Brewster to accompany her. Ideally, she would have liked his wife Mary, her former mistress, to be there. We had not received word from Thomas yet, and did not even know if any Scrooby women were still alive.

Our friends waved us off from the bakehouse, not wanting to attract unnecessary attention in Dam Square. Michael Knowsley lent Nicholas clothes. Margaret wore a blue gown from Sophie van Giessen. It was hard to believe this beautiful bride was the dowdy girl I first encountered in Scrooby Manor's buttery, nursing a head wound.

On the way to the Town Hall, we passed the so-called Holy Place. Before the Alteration, it housed supposedly miraculous bread. Amsterdam's citizens were no longer interested in such superstitious relics. Trade provided their prosperity now.

The city's richest merchants owned wharfs on the *Damrak*, which connected the harbour to Dam Square. Their ships sailed in from the *Zuider Zee*. Smaller boats travelled up the Amstel and other inland waterways on the freshwater *Rokin* side of the dam.

Goods were unloaded, weighed, taxed, sold and reloaded on the same day with amazing efficiency. Burghers spilled out of the Exchange with coins for their wives to spend in the neighbouring shops. The city was building a Bank to loan money, enabling more to invest.

Brewster said, "When the Dutch first won their freedom, they asked Elizabeth to be their Queen. I don't think Amsterdam would have grown like this if she had accepted their invitation, and enforced royal monopolies as in England."

In his excitement Nicholas obstructed some labourers carrying beaver pelts, "Watch out boy. Keep out of our way."

Swerving to avoid them, he bumped into the traders coming to buy.

All manner of people came to marry at Amsterdam's Town Hall. I listened to different languages while we queued, then counted gable designs. Workmen hoisted a harpsichord through an upstairs window. An artist arrived at a neighbour's house with an easel and brushes. I envied them, living in such a prestigious location.

When we reached the grand entrance, I plucked up courage to ask an official if an Englishman could become a burgher, and if so, what was the best way? He understood my hesitant Dutch, but his answer was disappointing. Even if I found an existing burgher to endorse my application, I was unlikely to afford the fee. Few immigrants could.

At last, we reached the front of the queue. The official waved us through. We climbed the long staircase to the first-floor landing, where another made us wait whilst the previous couple married.

The registrar was seated behind a large oak table, positioned at the end of a long wood-panelled room. The high windows were draped in velvet, the floor covered with black and white chequered tiles. There were no altars, candles or stained glass as in an English parish church. The registrar wore a gold chain of office around his neck, signifying civic authority instead.

When he called their names, Nicholas and Mary walked across the tiles to the table, with Brewster and me following behind. The registrar showed them where to sign their names in his enormous book, then dipped the quill in the ink again for us to add our own. He smiled as he passed a wedding certificate to Nicholas, and told him he could kiss Margaret once. The official on the landing congratulated them on the way out. Mister and Mistress Barton were married, an efficient ceremony.

Back in Dam Square, Nicholas leapt over a pile of beaver fur when the owner was not looking. The couple skipped back to the bakehouse, hand in hand, for the party afterwards.

Thanks to Jan Munter's generosity, I ate more than I had for months at the feast afterwards. The Dutch were right to be proud of their herrings, the best I ever tasted.

Cornelis sent a box of paints as a wedding gift, having been impressed by Margaret's art. There was a palette and set of brushes too, cleverly attached inside to the lid. Nicholas said she should paint him first, others suggested prettier faces.

Temperance and Michael Knowsley joined the celebration, but left early without dancing. Sipping Jan's wine seemed to help Pastor Smyth's cough. He told tales from his time as Lincoln's city preacher, where Secretary Sculthorpe had repeatedly tried to remove him by inventing spurious charges.

The event was difficult for Brewster, Robinson and the other Scrooby men parted from their wives and children, although they tried to enjoy themselves.

I was surprised Julian Felde did not attend. This seemed strange, if not suspicious. He and Nicholas knew each other. They had chatted several times on the ship. Felde's absence reinforced my opinion that he could not be trusted.

Crackleton drank too much, "Haven't you heard from Isobel yet? Isn't it time she returned? How old are you now?"

"Twenty-six."

"I'd already had two children by your age. Nicholas is younger still. Looking at him and Margaret, I think they'll be starting a family soon."

"Agnes will let me know when Isobel intends to return. She promised."

There was still no news from the Hague.

Annoyed with Crackleton, I went outside for fresh air. Edwin Helwys was showing some pamphlets to other lads in the yard. They looked up on seeing me.

"What have you got there?"

Edwin was happy to show me his collection, of which he was proud. Most of the tracts were in English. He had gathered them by pestering sailors on English ships. That was why he had been visiting the harbour. Missing his parents, he wanted to know what was happening back home.

Why had I not thought of doing this? It was interesting to know what people were reading. I might even see an English captain I recognised at the harbour.

"Pamphlets aren't a reliable source of information," I warned the boys, "You must not believe everything you read."

Edwin had a Dutch pamphlet too. From what I could understand, it said the Spanish would respect the Republic's trading rights in the event of a truce. However, that was not what caught my eye.

"Where did you get this one?" I asked.

"I found it near the Blue Bridge. There were several there, all the same. Someone must have dropped them."

This particular article was attributed to Peter Weekes. His name was spelt correctly below the last sentence. How could this be possible? What did it mean? Could Weekes have written it before he died?

No, such an idea was nonsense. However proficient he was, he would never have written such content. The article must have been accredited to Weekes posthumously.

"Can I borrow this one, Edwin?"

"You can keep it if you wish. It's more boring than the rest."

Not to me. Who would do such a strange thing and why? I had no idea.

17

I showed Edwin's pamphlet to Temperance at my next lesson. She translated the parts I could not. Neither of us understood why Weekes' name was at the bottom.

"I can't believe he would write favourably about the Spanish," I said.

"Peter didn't spew out this nonsense, either side of the grave."

"Then why is he cited as the author?"

"Perhaps someone did this as a cruel joke."

"It's not funny."

"No, it is very serious indeed."

Noticing her face was white, I assumed this was hard for Temperance because she was fond of Weekes.

"Should we do something? Can we report this to an official?"

Temperance scoffed, "No one regulates pamphlet content. Even in England, the Church fails to control them despite its mandate. People should remember, anyone with access to a press can print whatever falsehoods and deceptions they choose."

"Hopefully, Amsterdam's citizens are too astute to believe such a tract."

Temperance nodded, picking up her bible to find a passage for me to read. She found it harder than usual to choose a suitable one. I sensed she was more concerned about the name on the pamphlet than she was willing to admit.

My mind was not ready to settle back to the lesson. Foolishly, I added, "And once the Dutch win the war with Spain, such arguments will soon be forgotten."

My teacher put her bible back down on the table, "Alexander, why do you still see things in black and white terms? Your boast about killing a Spaniard showed your ignorance. Europe isn't playing a simple game of chess, between the Protestant Republic and Catholic Spain. It's more like a card game with multiple players and complex rules. Have you ever played Karniffel? Don't try. It's much harder than collecting sets and runs."

I hated the way she used my first name. Only my late mother and Geoffrey called me Alexander. Also, I had not expected a staunch Calvinist to use playing cards as an analogy. There was much I did not know.

Temperance told me that a group of northern German princes had formed a Protestant Union, pledging military support in the event of attack. No one yet knew how the Pope, King Philip or his Habsburg relatives would respond, or whether this would make a truce less likely.

"What about England?" I asked her.

"What about England indeed, and France, and Bohemia, and Saxony, and Upper and Lower Austria."

She continued through a list of states I had never heard of. European politics were more complex than I had realised.

The pamphlet with Weekes' name remained a mystery. Soon there were other questions too.

When Edwin was allowed out again, we visited Eva Witte on *Begijnhof* island. The winchman Smeets pointed out her home. She lived on the ground floor of one of the oldest black wooden houses in the courtyard.

"The door is open, come in," Eva called from inside. She left it on the latch, painful joints making it difficult for her to reach the door.

The elderly lady was sitting in a wheeled chair by the window, overlooking the chapel outside. The room was small but comfortable, with two doors leading through to bedrooms behind.

When Eva turned towards us, I could not hide my shock. There was a diagonal scar across one of her cheeks, ending just below her eye. Clearly used to others' discomfort, she tried to put us at ease, "Don't be alarmed. I can see perfectly well through both eyes and have good hearing for a woman of my age."

Edwin translated the story she must have told many times during her long life.

Eva was disfigured as a child, before the Alteration. After rounding up Anabaptists, the Catholic authorities executed the men in Dam Square. They held the women in the *Haringpakker*

67

tower, which was used as a prison at the time, then threw them in the River Ij tied in sacks.

"I injured myself running away. Both my parents died. A neighbour hid me. That's how I survived. Praise God, those days have passed."

She stroked her scar while we waited for her to continue. This was still a difficult topic, although many years had passed.

At last, Eva stopped and smiled, "But you're not hear to listen to my family's history. Jan Munter told me you were asking after Julian Felde."

She proceeded to talk about a meeting between him and Weekes. No one had mentioned a connection between the two men before.

"Peter fetched my shopping. He was a kind lad. Last summer, I saw Felde arguing with him outside in the courtyard."

Eva had not heard what they said, but was concerned for Weekes, "I was very fond of Peter. He was like a grandson to me. He liked to sit where you are and chat."

"What about more recently? Did he appear distressed before his death?"

"I knew Peter was in pain. Something else was troubling him too. The lad was less talkative than usual. He forgot some items of shopping, which he had never done before."

Eva seemed more observant than Alice.

Bringing her scarred face closer to look me in the eye, Eva said, "I've heard disgraceful rumours. Peter did not kill himself. His beliefs prohibited suicide. He often confided in me."

Given Reverend Paget's pronouncements about Weekes' godly Election, I was surprised that he would discuss his faith with an elderly Anabaptist.

As if reading my mind, Eva added, "Peter had lots of interesting ideas and questions. He had a habit of speaking his mind, when sometimes it would have been wiser to keep quiet. We Anabaptists have learned this through experience. Peter loved his job, but the Dutch are competitive. He felt safer in the *Begijnhof* than elsewhere."

Eva manoeuvred her chair to point to the far corner of the courtyard, "Peter was fascinated by that building which is owned by Catholic nuns."

Not believing Edwin's translation, I made her repeat her claim.

How could this be true? What madness had possessed the city council? Why take such a risk? The Republic was still battling to expel Spain from the southern low country states. Nuns could undermine it from within, casting spells whilst fingering their rosary beads.

"Please, keep your voice down, Doctor Baxby. The nuns walk in the courtyard in the evening, once Smeets has raised the bridge for the night."

England would not tolerate such heretics in its midst. Guy Fawkes and his co-conspirators were hanged, drawn and quartered in Westminster. We lit bonfires each year to remember their treacherous plot to destroy our King and Parliament, then force Prince Elizabeth to marry a Catholic.

Edwin discussed the wet weather with Eva whilst I calmed down. I thanked him once we were outside. His Dutch was even better than I had realised. He had offered to fetch Eva's shopping the following week.

It was hard to believe this tall, thoughtful lad had once chased his siblings with pincers he stole from my bag. Edwin's life had taken unexpected turns like my own. If the Church had not issued an arrest warrant for his father Thomas, the family would still be living in magnificent Broxtowe Hall in Nottinghamshire. Having divulged his mother's whereabouts to my contact near Scrooby, I still felt some responsibility.

"We must find out who killed Peter," Edwin pressed me, drawing the same conclusions as me, "He was too sensible to fall in the Amstel and too religious to commit suicide."

I nodded, believing the same, but did not share my theories about Archbishop Bancroft and the English Church with Edwin.

18

Eva recommended I talk with Alice Weekes, believing she knew Felde too. It was time to visit her home again. Edwin pestered me to come, not wanting to return to the Mobleys yet.

Through a gap in the curtains, we could see a large crate inside. When a balding Dutchman opened the door, initially we assumed he was a visitor. Our mistake became obvious after three small children appeared from behind his legs.

"We're looking for Alice Weekes," Edwin started, "Have we knocked on the wrong door?"

"Alice left yesterday. We've moved down from the top floor, something Gertrude and I have wanted to do since arriving in Amsterdam."

The new tenants insisted we came inside. Stefan Lemmens was a weaver. The crate contained his loom. Sitting upright on their stools, the couple told us Alice was living with Temperance temporarily. Her son Michael had helped carry Alice's furniture out.

"That girl needs to reflect on everything that has happened," Gertrude announced, "Self-examination is essential whilst on earth. God did not bless their union with children before her husband's death. Hopefully, she will find a godly man now, like my Stefan."

I tried to defend Peter's legacy, explaining he was a respected member of a Reformed Church, similar to their own. Gertrude was not deterred, "Yes, but he did not live a virtuous life. God cannot be mocked."

After confirming Felde had visited the household on more than one occasion, Edwin struggled to translate what she said next. Fortunately, the Dutch word for sodomy was similar to the English one. Because some men used *stilletjes* for sinful purposes, in relative privacy under the bridge, she was accusing Peter of the same.

Gertrude should not have talked the way she did, without

stronger evidence. Edwin was astonished and enraged. We were both keen to leave. However, having learnt I was a physician, Gertrude wanted to discuss her symptoms with me. Here was an opportunity, albeit a challenging one. I arranged to return the following week. Thus, Gertrude became my first Dutch patient.

Matthew kept me busy. I could not return to the Knowsleys to see Alice for several days. He divided the names between us each morning at his home. His list grew longer each day.

Initially Agnes continued to accompany me from the flour store, after leaving the children with Pastor Smyth. The couple were growing increasingly concerned about Edwin Helwys' behaviour, "When not visiting the harbour, he hides in our attic refusing to speak. My nephew Toby adores him, but Edwin is a bad influence."

Unlike his younger siblings, Edwin remembered the family's former life at Broxtowe Hall. The others could not even picture their mother's face. She had been imprisoned for years. I remembered Joan as a tall, elegant woman, a kind and capable mistress of her home. Would I recognise her now?

Agnes continued, "Let's hope Thomas secures Joan's release, so the whole family can be reunited. A ship is due soon. We're hoping for good news."

At least Matthew and Agnes had agreed that Edwin could fetch Eva's shopping. Hopefully, that would help them both. I liked the boy and sympathised with his lot. Perhaps we could visit the harbour together, if I had sufficient time.

When I arrived for Dutch tuition, Temperance told me Alice had gone away. She showed me a note in which Alice explained she needed time alone, to meditate on God's word and examine herself in the light of recent events. Gertrude Lemmens would feel gratified if she knew.

Although Alice's writing was uneven and faint, the intention was clear. Having never seen her signature before, I had no way of verifying its authenticity.

This was disconcerting news. Peter Weekes had died in

suspicious circumstances. Now Alice and Felde had disappeared.

Agnes was surprised when I told her, "Are you certain Temperance does not know where Alice has gone? It's unusual to leave without someone noticing. People know each other's business here."

The letter was clear. Alice did not want anyone to seek her.

Agnes asked, "Did you know she and Peter slept in separate beds? Isn't that strange? Perhaps having married young, they regretted their decision. Alice is still only twenty-one."

"Peter must have been in pain for some time."

"Alice never conceived. Given my history, I offered to talk with her, but she refused. Alice is very quiet. She keeps her thoughts to herself."

Raphael Barr did not know Alice personally. He thought she could have gone into hiding, "The Spanish have spies in the city. The English probably do too. If they targeted that poor woman's husband, her life could be in danger now."

As always, I enjoyed his sweets, but stories of subterfuge and betrayal did not help my mood. I was pleased to leave when the leech was full.

Where could Alice be? Who would shelter her? I hoped to discover her whereabouts from other patients on the islands. None seemed to know.

My Dutch was poor compared with Edwin's, so I took him with me to visit Eva again. This time she seemed more confused, "Peter was a good lad, whatever he believed or did not. Don't let anyone tell you otherwise. I miss his company."

"Do you know where Alice might be?"

"If the letter said she wished to be alone, you must honour her wishes."

Pointing in the direction of the English Reformed chapel, she added, "Some people think it's their job to tell others what they're doing wrong. They interfere too much."

However, the visit was a success in a different way. After showing Eva a better method of raising herself from the chair, she walked a few steps to the door and breathed fresher air. Delighted, she asked me to return to help her more. Henceforth, this

Anabaptist lady became a favourite patient, my only one within the city walls. Edwin became fond of her too.

Fortunately, there was no plague that year. Consumption affected the youngest and oldest most. *Zuiderkerk*'s grave diggers were kept busy, as the wet summer progressed.

Several members of the Ancient Brethren suffered serious burns when their building caught fire. Having only purchased it recently, the loss was a serious blow.

More Jews arrived from Spain and Portugal. There were Germans and Walloons on *Vloonburg* too, alongside Turkish sailors' families, plus rumours of black people living on the far side of *Marken*.

I met Lutherans from Norway, Huguenots from France, and a Venetian who did not accept the authority of the Pope despite a strong Catholic faith.

Slowly, my attitude began to change. Despite our differences, my patients all suffered from the same diseases. I became accustomed to treating them all, whilst still hankering for wealthier patients within the city walls.

19

On *Uilenburg* island, Helen Kent did not believe Alice had gone away to reflect, "A woman in her position has more immediate concerns, such as accommodation and food. At least she hasn't got children to worry about."

As in other cities, it was hard for women to make ends meet on their own.

"We should visit *De Wallen*. Several of my neighbours work there at busy times."

"They're whores?"

"Only when the herring fleet returns or a lucrative voyage from the Indies. Other poor girls have no choice. They live there permanently. Don't look so surprised, Baxby. You must have partaken at times."

I neither confirmed nor denied the suggestion. Following Geoffrey's maxim with regard to questions about spy work, seemed the best response in the circumstances.

None of Helen's neighbours recognised Alice by her description, which was not surprising given her plainness. Knowing the best times for business, they advised us to visit *De Wallen* at low tide, ideally when the Weighing House and Exchange were also shut.

Helen arranged to meet me near St. Anthony's gate after work. Crossing the *Kloveniersburgwal* canal to enter the city, I felt eyes looking down from its turreted tower. Was this a good idea? Peter Weekes was a revered member of Paget's church. Would his widow really prostitute herself? When it started to spit with rain, I suggested we turn back. Helen refused.

At least, Temperance's map had given me a better idea of where to go. Turning left on to the Old *Achterburgwal* canal, I saw the first of *De Wallen*'s notorious alleyways. The buildings on either side almost touched. Helen insisted we walk the full length, then return via a parallel route. I hesitated, not having expected so many people.

Helen demanded, "Do you want to find Alice or not?"

I was not as certain as I had been. Back home, Southwark's stews were spread across a wider area, stretching up from the River Thames. Here buyers and sellers, along with inquisitive onlookers, crammed into a small section of city, as busy at night as Dam Square was during the day.

Helen linked her arm in mine, saying this was safer, but let out a piercing scream before we reached the first doorway. Someone had grabbed her from behind. There was insufficient space to draw my rapier. My dagger would have to suffice.

We turned to face a sniggering Dutchman, wide and well-dressed like Cornelis. His companions joined in the joke.

"What a puny weapon, young man. I hope you've got something larger to impress the ladies."

I wanted to kill him. It had been some time since I had taken a life. The same rage burned within, when he dishonoured Helen and insulted me. His friends might retaliate, but I did not care. A single stab wound would suffice if skilfully placed.

Helen pulled me towards an open door, "Madame Magdeleine might know where Alice is. Quick, get inside."

Although no one in the brothel had helpful information, Helen saved me from myself. My breathing slowed as my anger abated. By the time we left, I had regained my senses.

The next house was busier. We entered a poorly lit room with moth-eaten sofas, whose occupants took it in turns to smoke an enormous pipe. A girl fetched an older woman called Lelie to answer our questions.

Lelie held up her hands in despair, "Don't mention Alice Weekes here. That girl is a liar and a thief."

Naturally, I assumed she was mistaken and asked, "Have you seen Alice recently?"

"Not for several months. If she comes back, I'll throttle her. Whatever story she tells you, don't believe it."

"Her husband drowned beneath the Blue Bridge."

"The poor bugger deserved better than Alice. God rest his

soul."

Could Alice have committed the crimes she alleged? It seemed unlikely. Although Alice had criticised Reverend Paget, members of his English Reformed Church were unlikely to behave in such a way. As Lelie continued her denunciation, I became convinced she must be talking about another woman with a similar name.

"Thank you for your help," Helen interjected, "We've learnt a lot."

She was more ready to believe the veracity of Lelie's account. We agreed not to tell anyone what we had heard.

As Helen and I argued about whether to try another door, I caught sight of a colourful cape. Its owner was walking away from us at pace, back towards the *Achterburgwal* canal. There was something familiar about his gait, and his twitchiness when forced to wait.

I pulled away from Helen, "Hurry up. I think we've found Julian Felde at last."

In recent encounters, Felde had always worn sober clothing, in keeping with Thomas and the rest of our Separatist group. Why was he prowling *De Wallen* in his old fancy clothes? If we got closer, would we smell his foul lemon and musk perfume?

"Felde," I called out. It was a mistake, for instead of turning he increased his pace.

"Felde, it's Baxby. I've missed seeing you these past months."

I lost sight of him momentarily. Where had Cecil's former spy gone? Helen pointed to some steps, descending into the canal. A boat was casting off in the direction of the *Munt* gate. Felde jumped on board without acknowledging us.

Helen grabbed my arm, "Be careful, Baxby. Move away from the edge. You might fall in."

We watched the boat set off in the drizzle, then disappear under an arched bridge. Felde had escaped.

Walking back to the bakehouse, I tried to make sense of the encounter. Why would Julian Felde revert to his former ways soon after arriving? Had he helped Thomas to arrange our escape, then disappeared deliberately? If so, he might still be working for Cecil.

Felde's assistance could have been a pretence, an interlude in the ongoing rivalry between his master and Archbishop Bancroft at court. Our escape would have irked Cecil's opponent and other churchmen, including Secretary Sculthorpe who knew several of us from Lincoln. Was that sufficient cause?

The Amstel was rising again after more heavy rain. Pausing by the *stilletjes*, I contemplated Weekes' fate again, imagining him tied to the slats, knowing there was nothing he could do to save his life.

Did the young man's Reformed faith bring him consolation while he waited? Did his cancer pain improve? How can some people face death with courage, whilst others wilt at the slightest setback?

Why had Alice written a letter to Temperance, rather than talk with her?

Most of my friends had moved out of the flour store attic by then. Pastor Robinson was offered accommodation by a member of the Ancient Brethren, an acquaintance from his Cambridge days. William Brewster, his son Jonathan and ward William Bradford now lived near the *Munt* gate. After moving to their one-bedroomed house on *Vloonburg* island, Nicholas and Margaret were expecting their first child.

Crackleton was happy in his first-floor office, preparing Robinson's manuscripts during the day. Murton was hoping to find somewhere else to live, having been offered bombazine work. Both continued to believe Weekes had died from a fatal accident. They showed no interest in Felde or Alice's disappearance.

Was this my fate? A bastard forced to remain, while others rose to prosperity? Reverend Paget would conclude so.

On the ship, I had felt a tremendous sense of achievement in wrenching my rudder from Geoffrey's hand. Was this the limit of my success?

Sometimes, I dreamed I lived in a fine canal house with Isobel. More often I lay awake, fretting about the future. When would she return? How could I make enough money to afford a proper home?

I wanted to help poor families, without sharing their poverty.

Each Sunday, I asked Agnes if she had heard from Isobel. Each night, I collapsed on the straw, more exhausted than before.

If Isobel's plans changed, I did not know how I would cope. She might prefer a rich professor or official, in Leiden or the Hague. Such thoughts were unbearable. I had waited so long.

20

London 1613

The cell door opens, interrupting the story. The guards have arrived with the prisoners' meal. Baxby is relieved when the vicar lifts his head, having grown increasingly concerned about his cellmate since describing Nicholas and Margaret's wedding.

Talk of love and marriage has been unbearable for the cleric, loss and separation even more so. Increasingly despondent since his interrogation, he no longer expects to see his own wife and children again. How will they fare if he dies?

Only food seems to revive the vicar now. He grabs his bowl from the guards.

Baxby implores them, "Look at this poor man's leg. The cuff is cutting into his swollen ankle. He needs his chain removed."

Neither guard has authority to call the blacksmith. They are nearing the end of their shift, and do not know where their captain is. Nevertheless, they will be blamed if the prisoner dies, so agree to pass on Baxby's request.

The decrepit cleric moans, holding his head in his hands.

By the time the guards return with the captain, it is getting dark. His royal wedding security meeting took longer than expected. He would have preferred to go straight to bed. However, years of experience in this position have taught him caution. The captain has survived, where others did not, by never being the one to be blamed.

After ordering his lieutenant to bring a torch closer, they inspect the prisoner's bloody leg together. The cleric has been clawing at his shackle like one possessed.

Baxby speaks, "I was a physician before my arrest, so have seen wounds like this before. If you don't remove this man's leg-iron, you will need to amputate his foot."

The captain remembers a case where a warden was sacked after failing to warn the governor a prisoner might die. He cannot take a similar risk. However, his political masters are currently busy elsewhere.

Secretary Sculthorpe is briefing the Archbishop of Canterbury. Geoffrey is conducting a search of St. Peter's Westminster. Redfern has travelled north to find a felon, on a mission which no one has explained to the rest of the team.

Taking a cautious approach, the captain decides to send for a physician, rather than make a decision himself.

NAMING THE DEAD

Saturday

21

Amsterdam 1608

One Sunday when the days were shortening, Pastor Smyth called us to silence for William Brewster to speak. The former postmaster leant on the table for support, whilst sharing information from a leather ship which had docked the day before, "Our women and children are being held in gaol with Joan."

The soldiers had been looking for someone else on the day they were arrested. It was a coincidence they spotted their barge. Nevertheless, the soldiers handed them over to the High Commission in York, where they had been imprisoned ever since.

No one spoke, which was unusual with so many packed in the meeting room. The bakehouse church had been supplemented by further arrivals from England, and members of the Ancient Brethren who had joined since their building burnt down.

Although relieved to learn the Scrooby women and children were alive, it was distressing to imagine them in such appalling conditions. How long could they survive?

Edwin Helwys broke the silence, "Will we ever see them again? My mother has been held in York for years."

Robinson rose to respond, "This is troubling news indeed, but we must not lose hope. Your father may be negotiating their release as we speak."

Edwin studied the floor. Neither he nor I shared the pastor's optimism. Previously, Archbishop Bancroft had joined forces with his York counterpart in order to crush the Separatist threat.

When Pastor Smyth read bible passages, he no longer used the Geneva version like Pastor Robinson and Reverend Paget. Instead, he translated the original Hebrew and Greek texts into English whilst running his finger across the page. Smyth was as learned as any of Bancroft's authorised bible translators. The rest of us watched in awe whilst listening to his compelling voice.

"In the Old Testament God made a covenant with Abraham, the forefather of all Jewish people. God reckoned Abraham righteous on account of his faith, then promised to bless all nations through his line."

Smyth explained that the covenant with Abraham foreshadowed our own New Testament one.

"God accepts us as righteous on account of our faith in Jesus. He keeps his promises. God is faithful even when we are not. We must pray, not just for those left behind, but for all of us here. The tie which binds us is stronger than any human cord."

Several believers prayed after the pastor finished speaking. Mary, Constance and baby Fear Brewster were mentioned early, along with their cook and Bridget Robinson. Richards Clyfton and Jackson remembered neighbours from Nottinghamshire villages. The Bromyards prayed for dear friends. One by one they named those they missed. Some were former patients of mine.

Foxe's Book of Martyrs was full of stories of those who had died for their faith. Please God, not Joan and the Scrooby women in York gaol.

As was often the case, psalm-singing helped to soothe me. My mind drifted as I listened to the pleasing harmonies of the twenty-third one.

The Lord is my shepherd, I shall not want
He makes me to rest in green pasture, and leads me by the still waters
He restores my soul, and leads me in the paths of righteousness for his Name's sake

Busy since my arrival, I had not yet visited the countryside surrounding Amsterdam. It would be good to do this before the autumn. I might not find green pasture for resting as in the psalm. However, there must be some paths on which I could stroll.

Yea, though I walk through the valley of the shadow of death,
I will fear no evil for you are with me

NAMING THE DEAD

Your rod and staff, they will comfort me

Although I did not share the psalmist's strong faith, nor that of my friends, I had known what it was like to enter the 'valley of the shadow of death', where evil chills the soul. There would be a longer walk yet.

You prepare a table before me in the sight of my adversaries
You anoint my head with oil, and my cup runs over
Doubtless kindness and mercy shall follow me all the days of my life
And I shall remain a long season in the house of the Lord

Could it be true? Would I have plenty one day? Pastor Robinson had said, 'we must not lose hope'.

That afternoon, I explored the marshland beyond the city for the first time. After numerous dead ends and ditches, I found the muddy path beside the *Overtoom* channel which would become a favourite. Connecting the *Singel* to the lakes further west, it followed a similar line to the old Holy Way, which pilgrims once used to visit Amsterdam's miraculous bread. Some peat workers were preparing for the colder months. Otherwise, the waterway was quiet. Ambling along, I anticipated Isobel's return. Agnes had told me she would use this route when returning from Leiden.

Nearby, I discovered a little pond with a trickle of waterfall. Ducks seemed to like it too. Rising above the surface to flap their wings, their antics reminded me of home. Sitting there, surrounded by water-loving plants, a new idea formed in my mind. I spotted some I recognised. Others looked similar to those back home. Could I use these to mix medicines? Even though they were unlikely to make me wealthy, they could supplement my income.

As I balanced on tufts of spike sedge to venture further along a brook, a more intriguing thought formed in my mind. I recognised plants which were key ingredients of Geoffrey's syphilis ointment. Allegedly, he stole the recipe from Spanish monks near Cadiz. I was more interested in its potential than its source.

Sir Francis Vere, our commander at Nieuwpoort, had recommended the ointment to the Earl of Essex for his servant Crespin to use. All had been impressed by its efficacy. Although not a cure, it soothed symptoms to bring welcome relief.

The French disease must be prevalent in Amsterdam like elsewhere. *De Wallen*'s customers were likely buyers. I might be able to sell pots more widely if I was discreet. Sufferers might tell each other, as happened before.

Could I blend the right mix and achieve the correct consistency? With fewer friends sleeping in the flour store attic, I could hang plants there to dry. Michael might even make little jars for me. I doubted Temperance would approve.

If only I had thought of this idea sooner. With the weather even colder and wetter than Lincolnshire's, some plants would finish flowering soon. I picked as many as I could carry, then returned the next Sunday with a sack.

John Murton helped me carry it up the attic ladder. Agnes had left a message with him. I was to visit the Mobleys when I returned. However, I was too busy to see her immediately. There was work to be done.

After sorting my sack, I fixed plants to the beams. Jan Munter provided cord for attaching them. Although it was unlikely I would ever be as successful as the bakehouse owner, I felt a renewed sense of pride seeing the lines form above my head.

Now, I found it hard to sleep for a different reason. I was too excited, formulating new plans. At last, I had found a way to make money to leave the attic, if not a respectable one in some people's eyes.

22

Waking early, I remembered Agnes' request. When I called on Matthew, she was cross, "Why did you disappear so quickly after the service yesterday? Did Murton pass my message to you?"

"Yes, but …"

"I have news for you."

"From Isobel?"

"Come back when you've finished seeing patients. You can eat with us this evening."

How could I wait that long? Edwin wanted to show me another pamphlet. Agnes told him to take it back inside.

Matthew had given me a long list of patients to visit. Most kept me longer than usual that day. Whereas people in Lincoln had refused to talk and answer questions, here everyone seemed to want to divulge their life stories and share their ideas.

Raphael Barr was anxious about a possible truce with Spain, "There will be conditions. There are always conditions. The Dutch might sacrifice our freedom, more readily than fellow Christians'. There have been Jewish massacres before. We can't forget."

Good Lord! I had only considered isolated incidents before, not mass slaughter. It was hard to leave Raphael when he was so upset. He insisted I ate more sweets while he talked about his late wife, delaying me further.

Eventually, I managed to escape when his son Samuel arrived.

Tired after visiting Barr, and several more patients on *Vloonburg* island, I was reluctant to knock on Gertrude Lemmens' door. I had recently diagnosed green sickness, unusual in a woman of her age, but was yet to advise treatment. Could she wait until another day?

Having decided not to call, I subsequently met Gertrude on the Amstel pavement, near the *Munt* gate. She had a pamphlet with a wood-cut map, which claimed to show the most likely border between the Dutch and Spanish territories in the event of a truce.

"Can you believe this, Baxby? The map shows Ostend on the southern side. Maurice of Nassau-Orange must demand its return as a prerequisite for any truce."

The family had managed to escape from Ostend before the siege, whereas other relatives had been less fortunate. Gertrude lamented the loss of the port where she grew up and the surrounding Flemish countryside. Would she never stop?

Contrasting current morals with those she remembered from her youth, Gerturde denigrated Felde, calling him an effeminate fop who had led Weekes astray. I refused to believe her *stilletjes* gossip, but foolishly tried to reason with her. It would have been wiser to pretend I did not understand all her Dutch.

By then, it was harder to enter the city, with so many workers filing out through the *Munt* gate. After waiting for winchman Smeets to lower the *Begijnhof* drawbridge, he reminded me that I needed to return before dusk.

When I reached her home, Eva Witte was concerned, "You look pale, Baxby? Are you ill?"

"I've been very busy."

"I'm not surprised you're in demand, given how good a physician you are. I can walk to the chapel now, thanks to your help."

She insisted on proving this, by opening the door and setting off across the courtyard. I could not leave without following her. Eva was my oldest patient, but one of the most determined, if sometimes confused.

I tried to escape when she reached the chapel steps, but Eva had more to say, "Two nuns asked me about Peter yesterday."

"I thought the nuns only came out at night."

"These wanted to offer their condolences. They'd been praying for Peter's soul."

Of course, I did not believe her. If they had seen Weekes in the courtyard, they would know he was a member of Paget's church, a committed Calvinist. However, having already listened to numerous opinions that day, I did not wish to cause further delays by discussing religion now. I wanted to hear Agnes' news about Isobel. Smeets was preparing to open the drawbridge for the night, giving me an excuse to leave.

When I arrived back at the Mobleys' home, Agnes was already serving the meal. Matthew was outside fetching peat from their stack.

"I'm sorry I'm late."

"I thought you'd decided not to join us. Sit down and have some soup."

With seven children crammed on the benches, there was scarcely room. Toby moved aside for me. Agnes would not let him sit next to Edwin. They caused trouble together. Clearly, meal times were tense in this tiny home.

Once seated, Edwin wanted to talk about his latest pamphlet from England, "It says King James is weak, not a soldier like Maurice of Nassau-Orange. You worked at court, Doctor Baxby. Do you know if this is true?"

"I never met the King while I was there."

"Does he sleep with young men rather than women, because he's a crypto-Catholic?"

Essex's servant Crespin had proved a useful source of information after becoming a gentleman of the bedchamber. This was not something I could discuss at the table.

Matthew interjected, "This isn't a suitable topic of conversation. Please eat your soup quietly, Edwin."

"It's very good, Agnes. You're an excellent cook," I commented.

Edwin was not defeated. He made the other children laugh in Dutch, which neither Matthew or Agnes understood. They confiscated his pamphlet and sent him upstairs. I was relieved when the meal was over and she suggested we talk outside, while the others cleared away.

"Tell me, Agnes. I've waited all day in agony, not knowing. Is Isobel coming back? This is too much to bear."

My former landlady smiled, "Isobel's finished pestering university professors. Her mission is complete."

"When Agnes? When will she return?"

"Next month, before the weather turns colder. Isobel is looking forward to seeing you again. I'm delighted for you both."

"Thank you," I hugged her, without regard for conventions.

Agnes' early life had been even harder than my own. Her patience and resilience were greater. She had a kind heart and a simple faith which some might envy. I had treated her unfairly in the past and was fortunate to have her as a friend.

I ran back to the Blue Bridge. There was much to do. The wind was strongest in the centre. It would be easy to slip and fall. The walkway was deserted, so no one would hear my cry. I had come so far. I must not succumb now.

Gripping the little bible in my pocket brought comfort and renewed resolve, as it had on previous occasions. I had treated its previous owner Jane Sudwell badly, afraid that her Anabaptist beliefs would taint my reputation, which seemed ridiculous now.

I never told Jane about the inauspicious circumstances of my birth. Isobel deserved to know more, before I asked her to marry me.

My father John Baxby abandoned my mother when I was a baby. Shortly before her death, she told me he had been the captain of a galleon with sixty cannons. Twelve years old at the time, I imagined him sailing to distant lands to capture Spanish gold. Edmund Sibsey, the Red Lion landlord who took me in, thought it more likely he had invented the story to avoid marrying her.

Similarly, Geoffrey rarely stayed with a woman for more than a few weeks. I remember one shouting at him in the Boar's Head, when I was working for him in London. The landlord threw the woman out when she broke a jug.

"Choose your women carefully," Geoffrey had said, "Married ones are easier. They don't expect so much."

Why did Geoffrey assume I was similar to him? Although I could find excuses to avoid the conversation with Isobel, there was little point escaping Geoffrey's grip if I did not make wise decisions and act more responsibly.

23

The route Isobel would take was always interesting. Passengers boarded small boats at the *Rokin*, with hinged masts which enabled them to pass under Amsterdam's bridges. At *Overtoom* Dam they transferred to larger ships better suited to crossing the lakes further west at.

I learnt that ships from Leiden arrived on Wednesdays and Saturdays. My eyes followed the line of the waterway longing for our reunion.

Venturing further, I searched for suitable plants. Beyond the building site to the west, I discovered muddy pools where clay was scooped for bricks. To the south there was a well-kept Jewish cemetery, some distance from the city. Regardless I pressed on. It was important to collect as many ingredients as possible before the weather deteriorated.

Murton laughed at the number hanging from the attic beams. Edwin offered to help, in preference to attending lessons. Even Matthew climbed the ladder to inspect my handiwork.

Knowing how I felt about Isobel's return, Crackleton offered to help me improve my appearance. Emerging from his first-floor room, he announced, "Baxby, no wonder you're smiling. I've heard Isobel is due back soon. Would you like me to cut your hair again?"

Given his disastrous previous attempt, I promptly refused my old friend's help. That did not solve my dilemma. My thick brown mop had always been unruly. Patients commented on my overgrown beard. Where could I find a reliable barber who could cut it in the style I liked?

Most Amsterdam burghers had plain, straight beards. Younger men were clean-shaven, a fashion I did not wish to follow. Isobel liked my pencil beard before. What would she think if she saw me like this?

Fortunately, Nicholas came to my aid while visiting the flour store to see Margaret. Unlike other believer-wives, she did not need to work. When not sketching, or visiting the van Giessens to talk about babies and books, she helped Pastor Smyth with the children's lessons.

Nicholas had acquired new doublet and hose since starting his new job. He did not favour black, which Pastor Smyth and our other leaders had taken to wearing. His hair and beard were always neat and trim. It was hard to believe this smart, soon-to-be father, was the servant who mended my cottage roof.

"Baxby!" Nicholas greeted me, "We're pleased to hear about Isobel's return. Let us know if we can help in any way."

Temperance had recommended a Turkish barber on *Marken* island before his wedding, who he had continued to use since.

After giving me complicated instructions for finding the shop, Nicholas passed on rumours he had heard at the Exchange, "The Dutch may agree a truce next year. This war is costing too much."

His colleagues were worried Maurice of Nassau-Orange would concede trade routes on which Amsterdam's wealth depended. Our Stadtholder Johan van Oldenbarnevelt had gone to the Hague to argue the case.

"If Maurice allows the Spanish exclusive access to the southern oceans, we're all doomed."

"Do you really think a truce is possible?"

"Not on those terms."

Struggling to remember Nicholas' directions, and distracted by squalor and stench, I failed the first time I tried to find his barber. There were few clear landmarks after crossing the dilapidated bridge. I got lost in *Marken*'s narrow alleyways, so had to retrace my steps.

This time I found the little shop with the red door. I was glad I persisted. The haircut and shave were worth waiting for, better than others I had experienced before.

The Turkish barber pressed a hot towel against my chin for some time, before lathering it with soap, then used a very sharp blade. Unsatisfied by his initial results, he repeated the procedure again.

Although neither of us could speak each other's languages, I understood enough. When he showed me the results in a mirror, I was duly impressed. The pencil beard was the neatest it had ever been. My skin felt smooth and soft.

Hopefully, Isobel would arrive in time to appreciate his handiwork. Her own hair was dark and thick, often escaping from beneath her hat. Would she have changed since I last saw her? We were both older now.

The visit to the barber's took an unexpected turn when I rose to leave. Why was I thinking about Julian Felde suddenly, rather than haircuts? Was it because I once saw him outside such a shop in Boston? No, it was the lingering smell of musk and lemons. Felde's scent was unmistakeable. *Marken*'s poor inhabitants would not waste precious coins on such a stink. It was stronger nearer the door where I paid.

Did this mean Felde had visited the barber before me? Perhaps he was hiding locally, occasionally venturing out to visit *De Wallen* and to shave.

Detecting my disquiet, the barber tried to ask if anything was wrong. By pointing to my nose, I managed to attract his attention to the smell. It was impossible to communicate further.

Once I stepped outside, he made his assistant open the window.

Walking back across the Blue Bridge, I remembered Peter Weekes was well-groomed when he died. Was this significant? Could he have used the same barber as Felde? Probably not. It was unlikely he would have trekked all the way to *Marken* island, given his constant pain.

I needed to concentrate on my patients and plants, ahead of Isobel's return, but Weekes' death still bothered me. The Amstel was rising again. A fisherman ascended from the *stilletjes* platform, saying the water level was too high.

Revisiting the Lemmens, I asked Gertrude if Peter's nighttime guest had ever worn a distinctive perfume. She claimed her sickness limited her sense of smell. Although not mentioned in Matthew's books, I wondered whether strange theories were a symptom of green sickness.

In a brief pause from weaving, Stefan said he sniffed something unusual once, then complained about *stilletjes* until I left.

Back at the flour store, Crackleton exclaimed, "Look at you. Any woman would fall for you with that pretty beard."

I did not want to entice other women. I wanted Isobel.

Crackleton remarked that I looked thinner, "What is the point in working so hard? Isobel won't be marrying you for your money. You're a good-looking man."

"We will need to live somewhere with more privacy."

"I wish I still had your energy Baxby, but you need to rest."

With numerous patients, and plants to prepare, there scarcely seemed time to eat and sleep.

He told me not to worry, to take one step at a time, which was interesting advice from a man with one leg.

24

I will never forget the autumn afternoon when I saw her again. A strong wind was blowing from the west, but the ship was late arriving at *Overtoom* Dam. I must have paced the bank a hundred times. A mother took pity and offered me an apple. Her children ran around me playing chase. The quay grew more crowded, with increasingly agitated family members waiting for loved ones to arrive.

A ship appeared in the distance, a tiny speck which seemed to take hours to pull alongside. As it disgorged its passengers, I could not see her. Had Isobel missed the boat? Would I have to endure this again in four days' time? I had almost given up hope, when a slight figure with thick, dark hair emerged from behind more bulbous Dutch women.

I had been attracted since the first time I saw her, in Agnes and Susannah's Lincoln home. Isobel had been helping them make discreet arrangements for Toby's birth. As I watched her stride off in the direction of the supposedly haunted Greestone Stairs, I did not imagine a wealthy alderman's widow would ever be interested in a lowly apprentice like me.

Isobel looked smaller than I remembered and more fragile. However, her coat and hat were still stylish enough to impress university professors. Her genteel manners showed too. Isobel waited courteously for others to alight, rather than pushing through.

When she saw me, she waved, her smile even more delightful than I remembered. Wiping a tear away with the back of her hand, she confessed, "First I feared you would never come, then I feared you had drowned."

"I almost perished in the Narrow Sea, but now I'm here with you."

"Praise God."

Although tired, her joy was obvious. Isobel was as pleased to see me as I was to see her. She had longed for this moment too. I offered to carry her luggage, then left it behind. It was hard to take my eyes off her.

As we walked back to the bakehouse, we recalled the last time we met, before she fled into exile with Pastor Smyth. Now, we followed the straight *Overtoom* channel, where once we followed the meandering River Trent.

"Do you remember the stag the lads chased from the wood?" she asked.

We assumed the magnificent creature was trapped by the curve of the river. Instead, it launched itself into the water to escape.

"I knew I was going away," she said, "It almost broke my heart."

"You said you'd never forget me."

"I've remembered you every day since and prayed for you."

"Perhaps your prayers worked. I never forgot you either, but only realised how much you meant to me after you'd gone."

She smiled, "We've both escaped like the deer. We've been washed downstream and found each other again, far away from Secretary Sculthorpe and others who would destroy us."

I turned to face Isobel, "Please forgive me for being bolder than I would have dared back home. I need to know the answer to a question that's burning my heart."

Like a surgeon preparing to make an incision, I steadied myself to utter the words, "But first you need to know the truth about my past. I was born ..."

Isobel put a strong, slim finger across my lips.

"I kept a secret from you in Gainsborough. I knew I was going away. You can keep your secrets too. I don't care about your birth or exploits in England. None of that matters here."

Hoping it was true, I found the courage to hold her hands in mine and ask, "Isobel, will you marry me?"

"Nothing could make me happier. I'd love to marry you, Baxby," she beamed, squeezing my hands.

Overjoyed, we walked back arm in arm until we reached the dairy. Neither of us wanted to hurry. We watched a boatman lower his mast to pass under a low bridge. Geese flew over, heading south. It was hard to believe this day had come, yet in another way it seemed it was always meant to be.

Crackleton was delighted with the news, as were other friends when we told them at the next service.

"Well done," Matthew congratulated me, "You've waited a long time to find the right woman."

"It was worth every day. Thank goodness I kept away from those women in London you once suggested I marry."

Agnes kissed me on the cheek, "Do you remember what I said the first time you met Isobel?"

"You told me she was too good for me."

"Thankfully, God does not limit his providence to what we deserve. I never imagined I could marry someone like Matthew."

The believers had been good to us both. I do not know how I would have survived without them.

Although Isobel wore jewels and gold necklaces in England, she was not like other gentlewoman who looked down on the poor. She had run Lincoln's bread charity with compassion and skill, before Secretary Sculthorpe and his obedient assistant Pusey forced her out. Now, Isobel was keen to open another to feed hungry immigrants on the islands.

She was shocked to hear of Peter Weekes' death and Alice's disappearance. Like me, she thought Archbishop Bancroft's agents might be targeting Puritans in Amsterdam. If the women in York gaol confessed to our whereabouts, they might find us next.

Weekes had agreed to contribute funds to Isobel's scheme. She remembered him warmly, "Peter was a kind young man. He could be outspoken, but was never boastful or arrogant. Temperance Knowsley was impressed with the way he learnt Dutch quickly."

"She believes God chose him for Election, as does Reverend Paget."

"I doubt she thinks so highly of the rest of us."

However, Temperance surprised us by offering practical help. She recommended Isobel stay in her loft room. I could join her after we married, then remain until we could afford a home of our own. Peter and Alice Weekes had had a similar arrangement in the past.

Isobel agreed this was an excellent idea, which would help her save funds for her bread charity too. More optimistic than me, she expected to open this soon.

Our new landlady thought it inappropriate for the two of us to linger in the attic room alone before our wedding. She did not see how close we pressed on the ladder, poking our heads up to look. Temperance stood at the bottom, explaining which items of Alice's furniture we could use.

The room was larger than we expected, extending the whole depth of the house. There was a small window looking out over the dairy at the back, and a larger one at the front with a view across the Amstel to the ramparts and *Munt* gate.

Despite its sloping ceiling, I could stand upright in the centre. There was plenty of space to hang plants down each side.

Michael helped us move Isobel's possessions. She had more dresses and shoes than I imagined, along with several books.

Spotting a crumpled pile of pamphlets, Temperance picked up the nearest and frowned, "What are these?"

Isobel explained, "I collected them whilst in the Hague. So much is happening in the Republic and beyond. I wanted to keep informed."

Temperance's snort suggested she disagreed. I spotted a confusing mix of headlines. If Temperance had known some pamphlets came from England's future ambassador at the Hague, she might have approved of them.

25

After having no success with officials in Amsterdam, Isobel had travelled to the Hague to enlist Sir Ralph Winwood's support for her bread charity project. It was a mark of her determination that England's foremost diplomat in the Republic had given her an audience at such a critical time. Isobel is a formidable woman.

When I worked in London, Winwood had been one of Robert Cecil's privy council clerks. Since being knighted, he had risen to a much more influential position. Winwood was Cecil's trusted representative at the truce negotiations.

In addition to discussing international politics and giving Isobel pamphlets, Winwood had written a Letter of Authority instructing his most senior officials in Amsterdam to give her their full assistance. Roseberry, Bowland and Tibbs ran the Customs Farm at the harbour, collecting taxes from English ships.

Clearly, Isobel was impressed with Winwood. He had also provided advice on how to set up a charity board, a necessity for such undertakings in the Dutch Republic.

"Did Winwood really say there would be a truce? Won't Spain expect unacceptable trade restrictions."

"Sir Ralph thinks it will be signed before next summer, possibly lasting nine or ten years. Neither side can afford to keep fighting indefinitely."

I had not believed a truce was possible, let alone such a long duration.

However, I was even more surprised by Isobel's next revelation. She had seen Julian Felde at the Hague, after her audience with Winwood. I did not realise she even knew Felde.

"I met Sir Julian once before, whilst visiting the Weekes to collect blankets."

Isobel had seen them together. Now, I had reliable evidence the two men had met. She was a more trustworthy source than Eva Witte or Gertrude Lemmens.

"What did Felde and Weekes talk about, Isobel? Did they seem to know each other well?"

"I felt I had interrupted something important. Felde's hand kept returning to the hilt of his sword. I didn't feel threatened, but was glad to leave."

The second sighting was more astonishing. When Isobel left Sir Ralph Winwood's office, Felde had been waiting outside to talk with him.

"Again, Sir Julian seemed anxious and impatient. He didn't recognise me."

"Did you hear their conversation? What did Felde want?"

"Winwood obviously knew him. He greeted Sir Julian warmly before shutting the door. I didn't hear any more."

Having such a wife was a bonus in more ways than I had expected. Isobel was observant and brave. She did not cower in the presence of powerful men, as others might.

Despite seeing even more patients after Isobel's return, I still found it hard to save money. Some plant bundles were nearly dry, but I did not have enough to start blending them yet.

Most often, Isobel and I saw each other on Sunday afternoons, initially walking out of the city towards *Overtoom*. I held Isobel's hand while she bent down to pluck plants from the water's edge. My future wife was more agile than me, even though she was three years older. Fortunately, she was forgiving when I slipped and she got wet.

Isobel liked my duck pond too. The babies had all grown. Adult birds swam over to inspect us. We threw ships' biscuit crumbs for them to eat.

Once the weather turned, the two of us would sit on Temperance's stools on Sunday afternoons, watching the rain come down. There was much to talk about.

I listened to Isobel's tales of hardship and hunger on the islands. The Dutch Reformed, Anabaptist and Jewish communities provided alms for their own poor. Isobel had convinced Sir Ralph Winwood that English exiles should do the same, although she planned to offer assistance more widely.

NAMING THE DEAD

During our conversations about the charity, I suggested Cornelis van Giessen might be a suitable candidate for her charity board. Grateful for the suggestion, she expressed interest in visiting him. Also, she was pleased to learn I was treating poor patients for minimal fees, "Your heart is good, Baxby."

Isobel tried calling me Alexander, but it did not feel right. Fortunately, Temperance had stopped using the name.

One Sunday, I took Jane's little Geneva bible from my pocket to show Isobel. She held it to her nose before unwrapping the shreds of Gainsborough leather that had kept it safe through numerous exploits. Isobel remembered buying gloves from Jane's shop in Lincoln. Tears formed in her eyes as I recalled the sad details of Jane's passing, on the same day as her young son Piers.

Staring at the underlined verses in the bible, Isobel said, "I had a child who only lived two days. My late husband never recovered from the shock."

She quoted psalm twenty-three from memory.

Though I walk through the valley of the shadow of death,
I will fear no evil

"Sometimes I try to imagine what Naomi would be doing if she had lived. My girl would be ten years old now."

It was a lovely name. After staring at the rain, I added, "Crackleton still misses his wife. I wish I could have helped him more after we returned from Nieuwpoort."

"I should have protected his wife Catherine from Sculthorpe and Pusey in Lincoln."

"You were no more responsible than anyone else."

"We all make mistakes," Isobel concluded, looking down at the book again, "We hurt others and they hurt us. When Jesus died on the cross, he paid the price for *all* the pain, suffering and self-centredness in our lives. His resurrection assures a fresh start to those who put their trust in him. Remember this whenever you touch Jane's bible in your pocket, Baxby."

Isobel offered to underline more verses after our wedding, then kissed my cheek handing it back. Irritatingly, it would take longer to marry than either of us envisaged.

When we visited the Town Hall, the registrar's office was shut. A crowd had gathered to read a notice which explained the reason in several languages. The city council apologised for the temporary closure whilst officials prepared for the forthcoming truce.

"How can you stop people getting married? When will you open again?"

The guard on the door refused to answer questions.

"Don't worry," Isobel tried to calm me, walking back to Temperance's home, "A few more days won't hurt."

The Town Hall was shut for much longer, with further delays caused by roof damage after heavy rain.

Listening to Paget's long sermons was not sufficient for Temperance and Michael. In addition, they started attending a bible study group at the English Reformed chapel on Sunday afternoons.

When the pair were at home, Isobel and I continued our pattern, conversing on the stools by the front window. Once they left, we raced up three stories to the attic room to consummate our relationship on Alice Weekes' enormous bed. How could we wait any longer?

My future wife was even more beautiful than I imagined. As I removed the clasp, her dark hair fell to her waist, relieved to be released. Her skin was soft. Her hands were not rough like other women's because she had often worn gloves.

Isobel loved me as much as I loved her. We will forever associate the smell of drying leaves with precious hours in that room. The rain hammered on the roof above.

Matthew once asked me if there were attractive women in London. There were none like Isobel, on either side of the Narrow Sea.

We both knew the risks we took. Neither of us cared at the time. Like the stag who was washed down stream, we had escaped. If only we could return to those carefree afternoons.

26

When I left the bakehouse yard, I expected another standard day, listening to my patients' woes, hearing about the pamphlets they had read. The sun broke through the clouds as I turned on to the Amstel pavement. I felt its warmth. However, my optimism was short-lived.

Earlier that morning, Raphael Barr's son had made a grim discovery, when crossing the Blue Bridge with his easel, hoping to capture the dawn. The artist never took his brush and palette from his bag. He was still shaking when I arrived.

A small crowd had gathered already, making it hard for me to see below. There was another body in the river, at the same spot where Peter drowned. Samuel Barr described details reminiscent of the scene the previous spring. Only the face had been visible at first. The man was clean-shaven and pale. He had been secured to the platform by a rope. The officials, who arrived later, cut it with a knife.

I pushed my way through to where Temperance was watching. Further progress was blocked by a portly Englishman carrying a musket and sword. Clearly in charge, he shouted instructions to two other greybeards below. Neither looked sufficiently strong to lift a body onto a stretcher. They rolled it instead, then manoeuvred the stretcher up the steps, refusing offers of help. As they passed, I was horrified by what I saw.

Julian Felde was dead. I could not mistake the crook in his nose. He was wearing an embroidered waistcoat with the colourful buttons he favoured, but not the customary matching cape. His cherished rapier was missing too. Felde would not have parted with it willingly.

Remembering the scent at the barber's shop, I was not surprised by his tidy appearance. Felde must have visited recently, never anticipating it would be his last time. I wish I had met him there, a better way to remember him.

Felde and Weekes were acquaintances who had died in the

same horrific manner. I did not believe their relationship was closer. Regardless, no one should have to suffer like that.

Feeling physically sick, I held my hand to my mouth. Temperance's face was white. She claimed not to know the English officials, then tried to dissuade me from following them. I wanted to know who they were and where they were taking Felde.

The leader cleared a route for the others, speaking perfect Dutch.

Given how slow they were moving, it was easy to follow them along the Amstel pavement, but harder once inside the crowded city walls. I kept some distance back. A burgher's wife was directing servants from the relative safety of a herring crate. Residents complained when I obstructed their efforts to brush floodwater from their homes.

The stretcher party passed the former Holy Place and New Church. They were taking the body to the harbour, using the quieter route Thomas favoured on our arrival.

I thought they might load Felde on to a ship. Instead, they turned left towards the *Haringpakker* tower. The leader knocked on a warehouse door. After giving a codeword, it opened and they all disappeared inside. Whatever lay behind, I could not follow.

The warehouse stood in a row of similar brick buildings, with no windows or further means to investigate. I stood staring out across the River Ij, trying to make sense of what I had seen.

A splendid fluyt was preparing to leave the port, the letters VOC emblazoned on her side. A cold wind blew from the west, with little to block its path from the Narrow Sea. When shouts abated, I heard the steady thud of the pile-drivers beyond the *Singel*, preparing the foundations of the new bastion wall.

The Dutch protected their own with concentric defences. In times of acute danger, they could thwart an advancing army by flooding farmland and marshes too. If the States General agreed an advantageous truce with Spain, was there any limit to how prosperous and secure Amsterdam's ingenious citizens could become?

Yet, immigrants were not protected in the same way. Two capable Englishmen had died in suspicious circumstances since my arrival last spring. Weekes' death had not been investigated properly. Felde's was unlikely to be either.

The city's tolerance was both our friend and foe. No one checked papers as in England. People could arrive and leave as they pleased. Spies and assassins could follow the innocent across the Narrow Sea and pay hungry neighbours to inform.

Whatever others believed, I was convinced Felde and Weekes were both killed in cold blood. One or more murderers were stalking Englishmen in Amsterdam. They might strike again at any time.

A whore approached me as I watched the fluyt depart, despite a sign saying it was illegal to solicit there. She knew the warehouse was used by English officials, but refused to tell me more until I paid her. I recognised the names. Winwood had addressed Isobel's Letter of Authority to Roseberry, Bowland and Tibbs. They worked for the Customs Farm.

Intrigued, I paid her more, "Did you see the man they carried inside? Has he been here before?"

"No, he asked questions in *De Wallen* about an acquaintance who drowned, whereas you and that bony girl from the far side of *Uilenburg* wanted to find a missing woman. I don't ask names, but remember faces."

She would have made a good spy.

Isobel was talking with Agnes outside Temperance's door. They had heard the news already.

Agnes assumed Felde's death was another accident. Matthew had not told her he believed Weekes took his own life. Surely, he would have to revise his verdict now.

Isobel was reluctant to draw conclusions, "I can't pretend I'm saddened by Felde's loss. However, it's strange that he and Peter should die in similar ways at the same location. Both were intelligent, sensible men who knew to take care in bad weather."

"Perhaps they were drunk," Agnes suggested.

"That's unlikely in Peter's case. He was an esteemed member of the English Reformed Church."

Paget and numerous other English exiles remained convinced that Weekes was a godly, upright man. I had started having doubts. In particular, his relationship with Felde aroused my suspicions.

When working for Cecil, Felde committed crimes with no regard for who he hurt. Although I admired the former deputy's ability and ambition, I would never count him a friend nor wish him to enter my home. Surely, an astute individual such as Weekes should have recognised Felde's true nature.

27

Not only had Isobel met Roseberry, Bowland and Tibbs, she had visited the warehouse at the harbour. Sir Ralph Winwood instructed her to take his letter there. The customs officials lived in the rooms above. There was a grander entrance on the other side of the building. She had never known them use it.

"If the three men are responsible for collecting customs, why did they remove a body?" Isobel questioned.

"They may do more besides."

It was hard to imagine they were capable of enforcing their demands, being more elderly than any customs officials I had known before.

Although impressed by my future wife's courage and resourcefulness, I was worried about her safety, "Why didn't you ask me to accompany you? They could have hurt you, or arrested you as an illegal emigrant."

"I trusted Sir Ralph. He works for Robert Cecil who King James relies on."

"That means he's used to lying and manipulating people for his own ends."

Once I was similarly ignorant of the underhand tactics used by powerful men. Each relies on cohorts of pliant spies, informers and agents to propel his career. I wanted to protect Isobel from such men. Perhaps I was too late.

My second trip to the harbour with Isobel was more sedate than the first. We took the same route. The burgher's wife had left her herring crate to chat with a neighbouring milliner.

Isobel raised her skirts to clear the puddles, laughing, "Amsterdam's fairer than Lincoln where the rich live higher up the hill. Here everyone gets wet when it rains."

Turning on to the waterfront, we were surprised to see Michael Knowsley remonstrating with the whore I saw earlier. I had never seen him so animated before. Why was he here? What would his fellow church members say if they saw them together?

Isobel and I crouched behind a pile of sacks to watch the drama unfold. We did not have to wait long.

Temperance emerged from the warehouse, holding her handkerchief to her face. The door slammed shut behind her. Michael rushed to console his tearful mother. She was not as distraught as on the day I arrived in Amsterdam, but flustered nevertheless, "They won't let me organise a funeral, or bury him with the respect he deserves."

"They may wish to take Felde back to England," Isobel whispered, "After all, he was a knight of the realm."

Given his history of spying, I thought it more likely Felde would be tossed overboard with weights, to join countless others whose grave is the Narrow Sea.

While we waited for the Knowsleys to leave, I explained my plan to Isobel. Taken aback by the strength of her conviction, I knocked a sack off the pile, "God will punish the killers in the next life. For now, we must do everything we can to bring the victims justice here on earth."

She helped me lift the sack back, stronger than she looked.

After knocking and giving the password, Bowland opened the door, "Dearest Mistress Greenacre, what brings you here again?"

"Please call me Isobel. Baxby is a physician. He knows a way to prove if Sir Julian Felde was killed by the same hand as Peter Weekes."

Bowland shut the door again, without speaking. Roseberry reopened it and beckoned us in, "Tell us what you know."

Felde's body was still lying on its stretcher, under a sheet. Isobel did not seem unduly alarmed by its proximity while I explained what I had seen in Cornelis' loft. Tibbs and Bowland blocked our exit to the door.

"Would I be able to recognise such marks if I examined the body?" Roseberry asked, "Can you describe them more fully?"

"A friend drew a sketch. We could fetch it from *Vloonburg* for you."

"That will take too long. You and I will look together now,

while Mistress Greenacre waits outside."

Isobel and I protested for different reasons. I was not happy for her to linger outside, despite having walked to the warehouse alone before. She did not want to be excluded from proceedings which interested her.

"I will hold the sheet," she offered, moving closer to the body. Having read Sir Ralph Winwood's letter, Roseberry should have understood her better.

Felde still looked smart. The barber had done a good job. We turned his stiff, wet body on to its right side. None of us had any doubt about the marks. There were four on Felde's left buttock, identical to the three on Peter's.

"Do you know what caused these, Doctor Baxby?"

"Not yet. I intend to find out."

"Let us know when you do."

"I fear there may be more deaths."

Harrying Puritans out of England no longer seemed to be sufficient. Archbishop Bancroft was pursuing dissenters in the Republic too, determined to eliminate the threat they posed. Although England was many miles away across the Narrow Sea, it sometimes felt very close.

I did not mention Puritans or Separatists to Roseberry and his colleagues, not wishing to draw attention to my friends. Instead, I asked, "Was Felde's rapier with him when you found him?".

They shook their heads.

Isobel added, "Please inform Sir Ralph Winwood. He knew Felde, and will be concerned that Englishmen are dying here."

Roseberry indicated to Bowland to open the door. Tibbs stepped aside. I turned for one last look, knowing it was the last time I would see Julian Felde.

As we turned away from the harbour, Isobel asked, "How well did you know Sir Julian?"

"I scarcely knew him at all."

It was true, yet not the whole truth. Despite not knowing Felde personally, I understood his trade, the murky underworld of spies and secrets from which we both came. He knew the risks, as did I.

Despite loathing Felde's cruelty and guile, I had been unsettled by his disappearance. Since saving him on the ship, I had felt a strange premonition that his destiny was entwined with my own, which made his brutal death even more disturbing.

Felde had survived the storm at sea, only to drown in the River Amstel. Was my own life in similar danger?

I asked Isobel, "Did Felde have his rapier with him at the Hague?"

"Yes, it looked expensive."

"He was very proud of that blade. I don't think he would have left it behind if he had a choice."

"His murderer must have taken it."

Isobel was not unduly influenced by her own feelings and prejudices in the way others had been. I knew I was marrying the right woman.

28

London 1613

The vicar sinks into the straw, moaning, "Felde's dead. He died in Amsterdam. What will become of me now? How will I survive?"

His cell-mates assume he is delirious, a consequence of his damaged leg. Why else would a London cleric associate his own demise with the death of the former Lord Lieutenant of Lincolnshire's deputy? They do not know that during Geoffrey and Redfern's interrogation, he implicated Felde in a previous crime.

The vicar believes Redfern is currently looking for Felde in London. What will Redfern do when he discovers he has wasted his time? Having already suffered a kicking, the prisoner fears the worse. His leg still throbs. The shackle is too tight. If a physician does not authorise its removal soon, the vicar will lose his foot.

In reality, Redfern has already exhausted locations in the capital. In festive mood ahead of the wedding, many citizens were prepared to talk in the inns. Redfern is sorry to leave London at such a joyous time.

Geoffrey has given Redfern permission to search Felde's former Lincolnshire estate. He does not know Redfern has an additional motive for travelling north, nor that he sent a letter to Sculthorpe before he left. Both the secretary and his subordinate are anxious about what Geoffrey's errant hireling may divulge next.

Baxby does not trust spymasters. Strangely, they sometimes trust each other.

29

Amsterdam 1608

When Temperance reappeared at her home, she claimed she had been at the English Reformed chapel since I saw her at the bridge.

"It's so sad to learn of Sir Julian's death," Isobel said, "I believe you knew him."

"Sir Julian visited our church, once or twice, that was all."

"You met him on the night Peter Weekes died," I contradicted.

"Yes, of course."

"Don't you wish to know where they took his body?"

"Not now. I need to go upstairs."

Temperance moved quickly to avoid further questions. Michael followed her up, claiming he needed to peel vegetables.

Isobel and I sat on the stools, staring out the window. We were confused by what we had witnessed and Temperance's reaction when challenged. Had she lied to us deliberately?

Isobel suggested otherwise, "Temperance was clearly upset today. Perhaps Felde's death reminded her of Peter's. We know she was fond of him."

Certainly, women of her age could be erratic and easily fuddled, especially once their monthly blood stopped. They complained that it was hot, even on the coldest of days, then forgot people's names and where they put things.

"And Temperance could be worried about her husband," Isobel added, "The herring fleet hasn't returned yet."

"Have you ever seen him?"

Isobel had not.

Helen Kent was waiting with Matthew when I arrived at his home the next day. It was impossible to talk with him about Felde with Helen there. She had offered to help by listening to patients' concerns, predicting this would give the two of us more time to attend to their medical needs.

Matthew expected even more patients once a truce was agreed,

"Protestants will arrive from the Spanish-held territories, bringing more destitution and disease. My son Luke can help when he's old enough, but we need Helen now."

Having supported her husband for many years, Matthew said she understood how stressful ill health could be. Although sceptical, I agreed that Helen could accompany me to Raphael Barr's home.

Despite his son having found Felde's body, Raphael seemed more anxious about the truce than the drowning, "My son's painting a regent's wife. She said we shouldn't worry. How can we stop? If Jews are sent back to Spain, I'll jump over the side of the ship."

It seemed unlikely Amsterdam's council would surrender its foreign workers without protest, but the States General in the Hague might disagree.

Helen intervened, "Your family needs you. Please don't contemplate such a thing."

Raphael said the regent's wife wanted dogs in her picture, but they refused to sit still, "How can anyone fret about such trivialities at a time like this? We could all be dead by the end of next year."

"Baxby has sung your praises, Mister Barr. Please can I try one of your sweets."

He seemed to relax a little once the leech was full. I was pleased to leave Helen to apply the dressing and listen to his laments. She tried to reassure him, while eating more sweets. Raphael gave her some for her children, a kind gesture.

Samuel arrived home to fetch brushes. He was keen to talk about the truce like his father. Rather than being concerned about his clients' pets, he questioned their future ability to pay for works of art, "Maurice of Nassau-Orange must secure favourable terms for trade with both east and west. That's the source of Amsterdam's wealth. We all suffer if burghers lose money at the Exchange."

On my way out, I took the opportunity to ask Samuel about finding Felde. Samuel confirmed the body had been tied to the *stilletjes* platform in the same manner as Weekes'. Roseberry, Bowland and Tibbs had arrived on the scene quickly. Someone must have alerted them.

Gertrude and Stefan Lemmens were arguing about the truce when I arrived at their home.

"Stefan thinks we should return to Ostend," Gertrude huffed, "But any land Spain cedes could revert back in ten years' time, or whatever period they decide."

"In Ostend, we lived in a three-storey house with a maid. It's hard to make a living here. I have to weave every hour of the day."

"I have lots of friends in Amsterdam. The children have settled too. I don't want to move again."

"You don't understand how hard it is to pay our bills, including physician fees."

"If you want me to come less frequently …"

"No, Doctor Baxby. I need you to see me each week. Did you hear what happened to Julian Felde? He died in the same way as Peter Weekes. We told you what they were like."

If Helen had been there, she could have listened to their arguments and gossip instead of me.

Jan Munter was waiting in the flour store meeting room, having heard about the second death. After offering condolences, we discussed possible scenarios and motives together.

"Why would the English Church target Weekes and Felde, rather than Separatists?" he queried when I shared my theory, "Surely, Independents pose a greater threat to the Church's authority."

Although logical, this argument brought no comfort. Jan's next admission worried me too, "Pastor Smyth's been discussing believers' baptism with leaders of my church. He's increasingly interested in the subject."

This was disturbing news. Such conversations might seem harmless to some, but Archbishop Bancroft would not tolerate this subversion. He abhorred the practice above all others.

Jan Munter apologised for scaring me. He too would be affected by the truce. If the Dutch made peace with Spain, the navy might cut his biscuit quotas or even cancel the contract completely, with implications for members of our group and the other immigrants who worked for him.

30

Eva Witte was my only patient who welcomed the idea of a truce. Having seen considerable suffering in her early life, she did not believe anyone should fight. Edwin took an opposing view when he arrived with her shopping. Like many young lads, he had an unrealistic view of what war was like.

Edwin had already been to the harbour that morning. Matthew and Agnes would be angry if they found out. Producing a pile of crumpled pamphlets from his pocket, he beamed, "The sailors let me have these."

Edwin was more knowledgeable than I expected, having read so much.

Amongst pamphlets variously praising the Pope, King Philip, King James or the Holy Roman Emperor for their near-miraculous peace-making powers, a different type of headline had caught Edwin's eye. Often writers criticised James' propensity for handsome young men, declaring this weird, depraved or a risk to national security. This pamphlet was about his son.

Prince Henry to marry Spanish Infanta

Edwin protested, "The writer must be mad. Prince Henry won't accept such a marriage, neither will his Danish relations on his mother's side."

He had strong opinions about the future monarch of similar age, "Henry is a true Christian prince, like Maurice of Nassau-Orange and Elector Frederick of the Palatinate. He has his own court, where great men discuss the latest ideas about science, trade and religion. When his ludicrous father dies, Henry will unite the Kingdoms of England, Scotland and Ireland in splendour and glory."

"You shouldn't refer to the King in that way," I warned.

Personally, I did not believe James would be foolish enough to pursue such a match. Despite his Scottish origins, he must understand England's antipathy towards the Catholic Habsburgs. King Philip had sent an Armada to destroy us. What more evidence did he need?

Reading on, Edwin's pamphlet claimed James also planned to marry his daughter Elizabeth to a Protestant Dutch or German prince, thus bridging Christendom's religious divide and bringing peace to Europe. What conceit and ignorance! Those who formed the Protestant Union would not permit this if Henry married a Spaniard.

Hopefully, James' thoughts would return to hunting, his favourite pastime, before he damaged England's reputation further.

As Supreme Governor of the English Church, the King saw himself as God's ultimate representative, but one trip to Amsterdam would prove his folly. More wise and wealthy than his subjects, the Dutch did not even have a monarch. Trade, finance and industry mattered more than marriage diplomacy now.

Reading through Isobel's pamphlets later, I spotted inconsistencies. Her Dutch ones declared the Republic to be England's greatest ally, whilst Edwin's English ones claimed the same for Spain. Some praised Maurice of Nassau-Orange's military prowess and his Reformed Protestant faith, whereas others deplored the same beliefs if held by English Puritans.

By the end, I was surprised none advocated Princess Elizabeth marry a Spaniard and Prince Henry a German, such was the confusing mix of contradictory opinions claiming to be fact.

When Isobel returned, I quickly forgot about such matters. Fortunately, Temperance and Michael were out. She cleared the pamphlets from Alice's bed and sat beside me to tell me her news.

Of course, we knew the risks we were taking whilst the Town Hall was shut. None of the methods couples use to prevent conception are reliable. Nevertheless, it was still a shock. I did not listen properly. She had to tell me twice.

Isobel was pregnant. How did I miss that? What glorious news!

"Are you alright? Do you feel sick or need to lie down?"

"I'm perfectly well. Please don't worry. Remember, this isn't my first pregnancy."

I kissed her and felt her forehead. Isobel was not too hot. I had watched other women suffer during pregnancy and childbirth.

NAMING THE DEAD

Isobel must have the best medical care.

Our baby was due in the summer. We prayed the registrar would start licencing marriages again soon.

Soon after, I visited the harbour. Growing up near Boston in Lincolnshire, I had often trekked to the coast, finding relief from my childhood fears whilst staring out to sea. Here, the walk to the waterfront was shorter.

After following the familiar route, I was stunned by the extraordinary sight. Little bus boats filled the Ij estuary and rim of the *Zuider Zee* beyond, bobbing up and down in the sparkling waters, as far as the eye could see.

The herring fleet had returned from its summer fishing grounds in the North Sea. Although I had been told it was the largest on earth, nothing prepared me for the spectacle. The bus boats were accompanied by larger factory ships which processed the catch at sea, and men-of-war which guarded them all.

Dutch families had gathered to admire the view. Parents pointed out little boats to their children. Some waved at long-absent loved ones. They bought herring to eat.

One day, I would bring Isobel and our children to watch the fleet's return. We would converse politely like the families around me, dressed in warm clothing to keep out the wind. Then we would return to our fine canal house, surrounded by paintings and shelves filled with books. We might even keep a dog.

Our children would be born in the Dutch Republic, the United Provinces of opportunity and wealth. Its wrights built the world's largest ships from timbers cut with windmill-powered saws. The East India Company sailed to faraway lands returning with spices to flavour sumptuous meals. Assured of their own places in heaven, upright members of the Dutch Reformed Church even allowed diverse immigrants to pursue their own beliefs.

Now Isobel was pregnant, it was even more important that we find our own home. We would be safer inside the wall, where the Watch patrolled each night. Peter Weekes and Julian Felde would not have died within its protection.

However, landlords charged exorbitant rents for even the smallest properties. I needed to increase my income, by finding rich patients and perfecting the ointment recipe. Michael's first pots had been too large. I had insufficient plants to experiment as I wished, but could not pick more until the spring.

Once I had saved enough for the fee, I resolved to ask Cornelis to sponsor my application to become a burgher. Hopefully, he would introduce me to similarly well-connected men. I might even invest in a mercantile venture at the Exchange. According to Jan Munter, Cornelis had been an impecunious immigrant before making money there.

31

London 1613

"Congratulations," the printer exclaims, "I became a father in similar circumstances. Our first child lived until he was three. Did yours survive?"

"She will be five years old in the summer."

"Hopefully, you'll be released in time to celebrate."

Baxby remains silent, despite disagreeing. Whatever fate awaits his fellow prisoners he expects no mercy from Sculthorpe.

"Did you spot Felde's name on any pamphlets?" the printer asks.

"It was on an obscure one about the Catholic League, which was not formed until after his death. Felde could not have written it."

"How bizarre. Ghosts don't write pamphlets. I fail to see why anyone would impersonate either man. I've never known it to happen here, in all time as a printer."

32

Amsterdam 1608-1609

Although Isobel often felt sick in the morning, she continued to pursue her bread charity plans. Increasingly worried her condition would show, I kept praying the Town Hall would open.

When I saw a different notice in Dam Square, I almost cried with relief. The Town Hall roof had been mended. It would reopen the following day. If Isobel and I came back tomorrow to register, we could marry in two weeks' time.

I ran back to the Knowsleys' home. Temperance was delighted by the news. She let me climb the loft ladder to tell Isobel, rather than wait on the stools.

Isobel whispered, "Do you think Temperance knows about the baby? I think she can hear us up here."

We heard a noise below as if to confirm her suspicion. Temperance did not need to eavesdrop. We lived beneath her roof.

"One of my pamphlets is missing," Isobel said, "Do you think she could have removed it? She doesn't seem to approve of them."

"Temperance prefers people to read the bible and contemplate godliness."

"She has been kind to us. Nevertheless, I don't feel I know her well."

"Have you seen her husband since the herring fleet returned?"

"Not yet."

When I showed Temperance another Dutch pamphlet at my lesson, she scoffed at the idea King James was responsible for brokering peace. Temperance had left England during Queen Elizabeth's reign, so I did not credit her with particular knowledge on the subject. However, she was still better at translation than me.

"Don't believe everything you read," our landlady echoed her earlier sentiments.

"I don't believe everything I read or hear. Why did you visit the Customs Farm warehouse after Felde's death?"

"I offered to organise a funeral, as I did for Peter. He deserved a proper one."

"I think they both were murdered by the same hand. Roseberry, Bowland or Tibbs may know more. Felde owned land in Lincolnshire. No one has mentioned a will."

"Felde was English, that was sufficient reason. I would do the same for you."

I preferred to contemplate marriage and fatherhood than my funeral, knowing danger was never far away.

The canal pavements were dry when Isobel and I registered at the Town Hall, but hidden by a covering of snow on our wedding day. No one remembered it falling so early before. Each winter was colder, according to those who had lived in the city longer.

We asked Matthew, Agnes and Crackleton to accompany us. Although only two witnesses were required, we wanted them all to join us. They were delighted to be asked.

I visited the *Marken* barber again, and wore my favourite grey capotain hat and cloak which I bought in London, after the Earl of Essex's execution in the Tower. They were still in good condition despite their age. Crackleton remarked how smart I looked.

Isobel insisted on wearing her best dress despite the cold weather, pleased it was not too tight. Fortunately, she also possessed a long, thick cape with a hood. It looked perfect leaving the bakehouse, but was drenched by a snowslide passing under the *Munt* gate. Matthew and Agnes gripped Crackleton's arms to ensure he did not slip.

Despite the *Rokin* being partially frozen, boats were still sailing to *Overtoom* Dam. Merchants continued their business in Dam Square. Fortunately, we did not have to queue outside the Town Hall for as long as I did with Nicholas and Margaret earlier in the year. Once inside the entrance, we brushed off the snow.

In addition to mending the roof, the council had hung paintings of Johan van Oldenbarnevelt and the city regents, positioned at regular intervals on either side of the long wood-panelled room. Isobel and I were excited, as any younger couple would be, while we waited for our names to be called. We savoured the walk to the table, smiling as we went. Matthew and Agnes took so long helping Crackleton up the stairs that they only arrived just in time to witness our signatures and add their own.

"Well done, Mister and Mistress Baxby. You're married," the registrar pronounced, after turning the book to check our names and handing us our certificate.

My wife beamed when I kissed her. Crackleton was asked to move away from the table after cheering. Guards escorted him downstairs, ignoring his protests.

Back outside, he muttered, "That lacked charm. There was apple blossom in the churchyard on the day I married Catherine. I kissed her beneath the lychgate."

I disagreed. It was Isobel I wanted, not traditions and fruit trees. I had waited for so long. Now she was truly mine. I loved her with all my heart.

Padding back to the bakehouse together through melting snow, we admired the fine canal houses within the walls. An elderly watchman was braving the cold to fix a wreath to his door. My wife knew why, "It's an old Spanish tradition associated with a bishop called Sinterklaas. His feast day is soon.".

"How strange the Dutch wish to remember him."

"Sinterklaas is said to bring presents to children, a custom even the most ardent Protestants are reluctant to shed."

Hopefully by next winter, we would be able to give little presents to our own child in our new warm home.

As with Nicholas and Margaret's wedding, Jan Munter provided generous quantities of food and drink. Plates and bowls filled the central table in the flour store meeting room, an impressive spread.

Stefan Lemmens gave us a woven table mat he had made as a present. Raphael Barr sent a large box of sweets. Cornelis van Giessen provided wine and a delightful gift for us both.

Neither Isobel nor I had seen such an exquisite writing set before. Its base was made of wood, with different size holes for ink bottles and quills. A carpenter must have taken a long time to fashion it.

I fell over Margaret's mother's foot, taking it to the window for a better look.

"Baxby's trying to generate business by injuring his guests," Crackleton joked.

"How else will I ever afford the burgher fee?" I laughed back.

"He's drunk too much," the old lady snorted.

Isobel took the writing set away for safe keeping, "We must visit the van Giessens to say thank you. It will be good to meet them at last."

Nicholas and Margaret had moved to a one-roomed house on *Vloonburg* island after their wedding. Now they were looking to rent a larger one, in preparation for their baby's birth. Although I did not begrudge the younger man his success, I would have like to be able to provide for Isobel in a similar way. We would have to stay longer in Temperance's loft.

"Do you think she's listening?" Isobel whispered as we collapsed on to Alice's bed, "Should we pretend it's the first time?"

Temperance was a capable woman. Reverend Paget would struggle to cope without her help. However, I no longer trusted what she said.

Temperance had said her husband was staying with sick relatives. Neither of us had seen him yet.

33

I woke early the following morning, knowing what I wanted to write. Isobel helped by finding paper. I practised using the smallest nib by candlelight. It had been a long time since I had needed to write neatly. She was impressed with the result.

Although I loved seeing friends on our wedding day, many were missing. Some still lived in England. Others had departed this life. My mother would have been proud to see her son marry a gentlewoman. Even Sir Julian Felde should have been there.

I resolved to write the names of those who had died on the empty page at the back of my bible from Jane, a practice I had seen others follow before. The list would help me remember them. One day, I would show it to my children too.

I worked carefully, starting with my mother at the top of the list, followed by Catherine Crackleton, and the baker Buckler who was murdered in Lincoln. Then Agnes' sister Susannah, Matthew's first wife Eunice, Jane Sudwell and her son Piers. I included the Nieuwpoort surgeon Lupton and Scrooby's thatcher who died at sea.

The process took longer than expected. Memories resurfaced as I added names.

Should I include the second Earl of Essex, whose bloody execution in the Tower still troubled me? I decided to exclude those disgraced publicly in case the book fell into evil hands.

Instead, I concluded the list with Weekes and Felde. I suspected Alice was dead, but it was too soon to add her name.

There was space for more names at the bottom. Who would be next? Aggrieved by a sudden sense of my own mortality, I moved to the window for fresher air. Although I could not see the Amstel in the dark, I could hear the water rolling past on its relentless journey to the *Zuider Zee*.

As often happened, the drying plants made me sneeze. Isobel put an arm round to reassure me. She understood.

My wife was keen to visit the van Giessens to thank them for our gift, "Cornelis might know more about the truce, and I can ask him to become a member of my bread charity board."

"I won't have time this week."

"I can go on my own if you prefer."

"No, I don't think that's a good idea."

It was unfortunate that she had visited the harbour alone before. Now she was carrying our child.

My wife persisted, "They live in a stylish part of the city. The New *Achterburgwal* is one of the prettiest canals. I would like to visit it."

"We'll go together."

Arriving at the van Giessens' house, Isobel was impressed by its height and the width of their door. Sophie opened it wide, resplendent in a red gown with lace collar. Giant ruffs were no longer so fashionable.

From the argument emanating from the reception room inside, I concluded that Amalia had refused to answer the door. I had not met Cornelis' daughter when visiting before. It would be interesting to see her at last.

Sophie smiled down at Isobel, "You must be Baxby's new wife. Nicholas and Margaret have told me all about the wedding. It's a delight to meet you."

She swung her hips as we followed her in, accentuating her curves, then addressed Amalia as we entered the elegant room, "Mister and Mistress Baxby are paying us a visit. Please would you be kind enough to fetch more wine?"

Her stepdaughter promptly refused.

"Please don't worry on our behalf," Isobel said, "We just came to say thank you for your delightful wedding gift."

"My wife chose it in a shop near the Exchange," Cornelis grunted, rising from a chair by the fireplace, "I work hard to earn money. My wife and daughter spend it."

"This is a delightful room. Whoever chose these colours and furnishings has outstanding taste. And what a delightful portrait of you all."

Cornelis beamed, clearly proud, "My first wife died when Amalia was a baby. I'm fortunate to have such an attractive replacement."

"And I'm fortunate to live here with you," Sophie responded, without a hint of gratitude in her voice.

She indicated we should sit, before leaving to fetch the wine herself.

While we waited for Sophie to return, Amalia leaned forward to address us, in admirable English given she was only fourteen years old, "My father told me you intend to open a charity to feed poor people on the islands. Is that wise? You might catch a dreadful disease."

"I think it's a superb idea," Cornelis contradicted, still standing by the fireplace, "My wife will assist you in any way she can. However, I think you should wait until after the truce. Much may change then."

Isobel had been hoping Cornelis would join her board, but did not show her disappointment.

While we waited for the wine, Amalia provoked another argument by asking us, "What do you think Maurice of Nassau-Orange will agree? Papa is worried he'll concede trading rights to Spain. I think Johan van Oldenbarnevelt will champion Amsterdam's interests."

"My daughter doesn't understand Hague politics. All seven provinces must agree the deal."

"But Johan is Stadtholder of the wealthiest."

"Yes, my dear, but the Spanish will negotiate with Maurice. They don't understand our system of government. Few do."

I asked, "What about King James of England. I've heard he is playing an important role."

Cornelis laughed, "I expect the French think their King's doing the same. Everyone underestimates the Dutch."

He explained why Amsterdam's trade and finance were superior, stressing the importance of the Exchange. Amalia interrupted regularly. At the end, I still did not understand what a derivative was. Wisely, Isobel kept quiet throughout.

As we rose to leave, Cornelis warned us to be careful. His men were lowering chests from the loft above. We watched from the relative safety of the top step as they lowered them on to a waiting cart. The pavement was unusual in being wide enough for one. All the chests were inscribed with the letters VOC.

"That's a long way to fall," Isobel remarked, looking up to the open loft doors.

"What's in the chests?" I asked.

"A range of different goods for customers in the Hague."

His answer surprised me. The chests all looked to be of similar weight as we watched his men manoeuvre them into position on the cart.

Walking back, Isobel shared my sense of unease about the visit, "Although their house is beautiful, clearly it is too big for their needs. If Amalia was my child, she would not speak to us like that. And I don't think he should have dismissed the English contribution in that way. Sir Ralph Winwood is a skilled diplomat, one of our finest."

I told her how Matthew and Margaret had been disappointed by Cornelis' behaviour too. He had provided the names of two printers who might produce their book. When they eventually found the addresses, there were no presses there. A tilemaker thought the building might have been used by a printer before he started renting it, two years ago.

"What did Cornelis say when they told him?"

"He apologised and said he'd find another name. They're asking others for recommendations now."

Despite this and the family's arguments, we both came away convinced the Republic and Spain would agree a truce within the next twelve months. Our child would be born at a historic time, not just for those two countries, but for the whole of Europe.

34

It was a cold, wet winter, the worst my older patients remembered, with the weather worsening each day. Many sat in the dark, not wanting to waste precious pay on candles and fuel. Several remarked about Isobel's belly size, and wondered whether the baby would be born earlier than we thought. My aching wife was grateful for Sophie's help with the bread charity board.

Speculation about the truce continued into the new year. Spring arrived later than usual, still wet. The second batch of ointment was better than the first, giving me hope I could perfect the blend once I collected more plants. At least the weather meant they should grow well once the temperature rose.

Every time the Amstel rose, I checked the *stilletjes* beneath the Blue Bridge, but no more bodies appeared.

Toby was the first to spot the new notice at the Town Hall. After receiving his message, I hurried there to see for myself. Many others were doing the same. Despite my height giving me an advantage, it was difficult to read the details. However, the main points became clear.

The Spanish and Dutch had signed a treaty in Antwerp, agreeing a twelve-year cessation of hostilities. Maurice of Nassau-Orange had made a fine speech afterwards. Henceforth others would recognise the Republic as an independent nation.

Amalia was proven to have greater insight than her father. Johan van Oldenbarnevelt secured a good deal for Amsterdam, enabling the VOC to exploit more trade routes.

Twelve years was longer than any of us expected. Others in the crowd felt similar relief. Regardless of religion and background, they welcomed the onset of peace.

Also, the notice stated the city would organise its own celebration on the fifth of May, culminating in a play in Dam Square to which everyone was invited.

Turning away, I saw a well-dressed man outside the Bank which had recently opened adjacent to the Town Hall. His wide eyes looked familiar. His pistol and sword were of English origin.

"What are you staring at Baxby?" Sophie van Giessen had been viewing the notice too, "This is great news for Amsterdam and the rest of North Holland. Johan van Oldenbarnevelt has done well."

After agreeing, I asked, "Are Englishmen allowed to deposit money at the Bank?"

"If they have sufficient wealth. The Truce may encourage more foreigners to bring their money here."

The man's pointed shoes and well-starched collar suggested he had plenty.

"Do you intend to watch the play?" I asked, "It should be a memorable spectacle."

"My husband will no doubt expect me to attend. I might prefer an evening at home by the fire."

Without thinking I added, "You should come. There may never be such a historic event again."

Before I turned away, I braved a further question, "Someone told me Cornelis is Flemish despite his Dutch name. Is that true?"

Sophie sighed, "Things were harder for him than people realise. He wasn't always rich. However, that's all behind him now. My husband is a very wealthy man."

She made me feel inferior. Despite all my efforts, I had only managed to save a small amount. We parted at the Holy Place. Sophie returned to her fine home on the New *Achterburgwal* canal. I walked back to Temperance's loft room.

Although the islands' inhabitants had predicted far-reaching consequences, their lives barely changed as a result of the Truce. No one was expelled to Spain or anywhere else. Now patients talked about the play instead.

"Is Dam Square big enough?"

"What will the players perform?"

"Will it be suitable for children?"

"Will I be expected to stand?"

"Do you think they'll be fireworks afterwards?"

"Will it all be in Dutch?"

The islands bubbled with increasing interest as the day

approached. Some were sceptical, others excited. Isobel thought fireworks would be a waste of money. Neither she, Matthew or Agnes wanted to attend.

Edwin and Toby protested, "You must take us, Baxby. This is the best thing that's happened since we arrived in Amsterdam."

Remembering *Macbeth*'s fearsome witches at the Globe, I replied, "You'll have to ask Matthew. Plays can be scary. I don't think it's wise."

"He's more likely to agree if you come too."

Eventually persuaded, the Mobleys permitted Nicholas and I to take the boys.

The bells of the Old and New Churches rang for most of that day. The leeches were oblivious, the patients easily distracted. Nicholas and the boys called on me early, eager to get a good spot. Agnes had given them food and drink.

"Hurry up, Baxby. You're taking too long."

I nearly changed my mind when we met Amalia van Giessen, who informed us the play would tell the story of Lucius Tarquinis Superbus, the last King of Rome. I knew some details having heard a poem about him.

Bewitched by this confident young lady, both boys refused to turn back. If Amalia could see the play, why not them? Once in Dam Square she ran off to greet friends. They were mistaken if they thought Amalia would be interested in them.

The stage in front of the Town Hall was higher than Toby. Statues of soldiers and sailors, with unfeasibly large swords and anchors, topped pillars on either side. Above, in the centre, sat Neptune, Roman God of the sea.

No one could doubt the message this construction conveyed. As soon as anyone stepped into the Square, they would know. The Dutch Republic ruled supreme, militarily and commercially.

The curtains were drawn. We waited while the Square filled. Dutch burghers and their wives wore warm clothing, capotain hats being popular with the men. None of them wanted to miss this occasion. Stadtholder Johan van Oldenbarnevelt and the city regents would be there.

There was a separate seated area for dignitaries, with sides and a roof which gave some privacy and protection from the weather. The regent families filed in to applause but waited to sit.

The man I saw earlier outside the Bank followed them, with another face I recognised instantly. Sir Horace Vere's chiselled nose was distinguished like his brother Sir Francis'. Together they had commanded our English regiments at Nieuwpoort, where I had met them in a requisitioned farmhouse.

Heralds raised long trumpets, quietening the crowd. Then an announcer climbed the steps to introduce Amsterdam's most important citizen. Although no longer a young man, Johan van Oldenbarnevelt was clearly in good health. The crowd cheered as he strode on to the stage to bow.

"Fellow citizens of Amsterdam, we have achieved that which we intended. Even mighty Spain has been forced to concede. Despite our smaller size, we are a mighty nation under God. The whole world will see what the Dutch can achieve."

Once the Stadtholder sat, the regent families and other dignitaries followed suit. The heralds played again. The curtains opened to further applause.

35

Although the script was in Dutch, the four of us understood most of the brutal story of Lucius Tarquinius. As if killing one's own father and brother were not horrific enough, other scenes featured kidnap, rape and suicide.

Smoke rose on either side of the stage. The servants and slaves were black. The man who played the part of Lucretia looked astonishing in both day and nightwear.

Edwin and Toby watched aghast, drawing the same conclusions as everyone else from this bloodthirsty tale from antiquity. The days of slack-spined kings and crowns were over. The Dutch Republic was in the ascendancy now. Wherever we were born and raised, in that moment watching the play, we wanted it to be true. Those of us who had found a sanctuary in Amsterdam stood alongside those whose families had lived there for generations.

Smoke rose again when the cast bowed. They retreated, then returned for a second time and a third. We cheered them all. We cheered Stadtholder Johan van Oldenbarnevelt who came back on stage. Like many, I did not know the words or tune of the Dutch national song, but tried my best.

As the curtains closed for the final time, I was distracted by Sir Horace Vere. Clearly, he was enjoying himself, laughing and joking with neighbours before rising to leave.

Sir Horace knew the efficacy of Geoffrey's ointment. He had been with his brother when I delivered the jars. The pair never revealed the intended recipient, or recipients. Both expressed gratitude.

On his return to England, Sir Francis had recommended the ointment to the Earl of Essex for his servant Crespin. Could Sir Horace be persuaded to recommend mine to friends or associates whilst residing in Amsterdam. The latest batch was still curing. It should be ready in a couple of days.

Nine years had passed since the Battle. I looked different, even though Vere did not. The commander might not recognise me. If I was going to approach him, I would have to move quickly, before he disappeared into the Town Hall with the other distinguished guests.

Toby was arguing about fireworks. Nicholas wanted to get back to Margaret who was due to give birth soon. Edwin was distracted by Amalia who was chatting with female friends. I tried to take my leave of them, saying there was something important I needed to do. Intrigued, they ignored me and followed behind.

My head filled with conflicting anxieties approaching Vere and his companion. In London, I treated bishops and other wealthy patients, but had only conversed with commonfolk in recent years. How should I address Vere? My Lord? Your Excellency? There were numerous rules associated with rank, which I had not needed to concern myself with since leaving England.

"Sir Horace …" I started.

"Baxby! How good to see you here. What a lovely surprise."

Despite my pencil beard, he claimed I had not changed at all, then sung my praises to his companion, "Young Baxby removed the foot of an injured soldier at Nieuwpoort, after our dear old surgeon Lupton died. According to Crespin, your father also appreciated his service whilst incarcerated in the Tower."

My shock must have shown on my face as Sir Horace introduced us. The man I saw outside the Bank was Robert Devereux, the third Earl of Essex, son of the people's hero whose beheading I watched at the Tower. Despite being shorter than his father, less handsome and more plainly dressed, there was a likeness in the face.

When they asked me what I was doing in Amsterdam, I mentioned the ointment hoping to rouse their interest, "The meadows here provide a ready supply of ingredients. Do you think your brother or Crespin might wish to buy more?"

"Sadly, Francis has been forced to retire from active service due to ill health. He would have liked to be here to celebrate the Truce today, something we've both worked tirelessly for."

"Perhaps we could purchase some for the troops," Essex suggested.

Sir Horace agreed. He wanted an exclusive contract, seeing this as advantageous for our regiments. After some discussion, they agreed to buy an initial ten pots, with an option to buy more if the results were satisfactory. What fortune! A fruitful conversation indeed!

My benefactor said I should bring the pots to the English Reformed chapel on Sunday. He was looking forward to seeing Reverend Paget, who had once been his chaplain. I would have to endure another long sermon, but that was a price worth paying in the circumstances.

The boys had been listening to the conversation, clearly impressed to be in the presence of English nobles. They were not dumbstricken, though. Edwin demonstrated his courage too, "Excuse me, Sir. Do you know Prince Henry? We want to serve in his army."

"Indeed, I do young man," Essex smiled, "Prince Henry is one of my closest friends. He would be delighted to hear this. You can enlist at any time by visiting the Trade Mission at the harbour."

That was the official title of the warehouse where Roseberry, Bowman and Tibbs took Felde. Matthew and Agnes would not be pleased to hear about the content of the play, nor the boys plan to enlist.

I was overjoyed by the results of this visit to Dam Square. As we watched the two men disappear into the Town Hall, I could scarcely believe my luck. Now I would need to work even harder.

I woke Isobel when I returned home, then had to apologise to Temperance for disturbing her too.

Although concerned about the boys, my wife was delighted to hear my news, "You've worked hard, Baxby. This is thoroughly deserved. Does it mean we will be able to move to our own home?"

"Yes, once Sir Horace orders more. We need to finish preparing the current batch and have plants ready for the next. Michael will need to produce more pots too."

Jan Munter had told Isobel about a new row of one-room

houses, conveniently situated between the *Zuiderkerk* site and St. Anthony's gate. With time, I might even entice some patients beyond the city walls. Grateful for the information, I promised to investigate further.

It was hard to sleep that night. Isobel was troubled by her back. I had new plans to make. A year after arriving in Amsterdam, the future looked brighter for me and my family. At last, I had escaped from Geoffrey's shadow, making a bold move on my own initiative.

36

London 1613

Engrossed in his story, Baxby does not see the cell door open at first. The captain has brought Doctor Farron to inspect the vicar's leg. As Sculthorpe was busy elsewhere, he interrupted Geoffrey's schedule to authorise this.

Concerned that nothing untoward happens during the visit, Geoffrey is listening outside.

Baxby remembers Farron. They discussed scientific methods at a Strand party when he was working in London. The older physician still wears a bulging pomander round his neck. Despite professing an interest in modern theories and practices, Farron trusts his own experience and instincts more, still believing gaol fever is caused by bad air.

Doctor Farron pretends not to recognise Baxby. It is easier that way. One never knows who will fall out of favour at court. He has visited patients in palaces, only to next see them on their way to the block.

After examining the vicar's leg and applying a soothing balm, he agrees the shackle must be removed. Otherwise, the medical consequences will reflect badly on his custodians.

The captain steps outside to inform Geoffrey who signs the necessary paperwork. Why did Redfern have to kick the vicar so hard? Minimal force usually works best in such circumstances.

Geoffrey did not foresee Redfern would take so long to find Julian Felde. The King wants to change the royal wedding itinerary again. Redfern should be assisting Geoffrey with the security arrangements.

Sculthorpe made the decision to employ Redfern, without consulting Geoffrey. Increasingly, the spymaster believes this was a poor choice. His own recruit Baxby proved a much better resource. Hearing the younger man's voice in the cell, has reminded him of happier times.

NAMING THE DEAD

37

Amsterdam 1609

The anniversary of our escape from England was particularly difficult for the Scrooby men, separated from their wives and families. They had to wait, knowing their loved ones' lives were in Bancroft's hands.

I was concerned for Crackleton too, who still missed Catherine. He rarely travelled beyond the bakehouse walls. Although my friend enjoyed his work for Pastor Robinson, I tried to encourage him to venture further afield for the sake of his health.

Conversely, Nicholas and Margaret were doing well. The proud parents of baby Mabel now owned a two-roomed house.

One Sunday soon after Mabel was born, we heard knocks of the outside door downstairs as Pastor Smyth was concluding his sermon. Memories of Church enforcers in England still caused us anxiety when this happened.

Nicholas looked out the little window and screeched in amazement, "Fetch Mister Brewster quickly. Mistress Brewster's here."

Looking down, I could not believe my eyes. Mary Brewster, her daughters, Scrooby servants and cook were striding through the bakehouse gate. Patience gripped little Fear's hand as they crossed the yard. The tiny baby, born just before we escaped, could now walk.

Having been released from gaol, they had crossed the Narrow Sea at the first opportunity, after the winter storms. We would scarcely have been more shocked if they had risen from the dead.

Nicholas lifted Constance Mobley to see her childhood friend. Jonathan Brewster, William and Mary's son, was already at the bottom of the stairs.

"Praise God, you're safe," his mother gushed, gripping him tight.

The women had been worrying about us while we were worrying about them.

135

Although tired and hungry, most climbed the stairs unaided. William Bradford pushed to the front. The Brewsters' ward loved them as a son.

Margaret Barton showed her former mistress her baby. The Brewster's cook hugged Nicholas. Constance smothered Patience with kisses. The noise grew steadily.

Only William Brewster hesitated. He had waited patiently for this day, encouraging others to pray and trust God. Overcome with emotion, we had to help him across the room.

"Please keep the noise down," Jan called up from the store, "You're only tolerated in Amsterdam, not loved."

When he realised the source of the commotion, he went to fetch wine.

More screams of delight rose later, when Bridget Robinson, her sister and the rest of the Scrooby women and children arrived. Pastor Robinson leapt across the room on hearing his wife's voice. Holding her and the little ones tight, he repeated, "Praise God, Praise God," until persuaded to let them sit and eat.

Thomas Helwys was the last to climb the flour store stairs. Praise God indeed for his return. His eldest children huddled round, delighted to see their father again, but were nervous encountering their youngest siblings who they did not recognise.

Pastor Smyth found an opportunity to hug Thomas too. Their friendship, formed many years before when Smyth convalesced at the Helwys' home, had not diminished. Neither had their radical understanding of Christian faith.

Smyth suggested the women wait before sharing their story. Mary Brewster disagreed. Having become the women's leader in gaol, she started to describe their ordeal in a clear, strong voice, "We wailed as we watched your ship sail away, doubting we would ever see you again. After waiting so long to escape from England, how could God abandon us now? In York we faced more immediate problems. The cells smelt of bad air, which seeps through grills and cracks underground. One Separatist had died before we arrived."

"Not Joan Helwys?"

"No, Joan knew what to do. We covered our mouths and noses whenever we could, and let the children sleep in the driest corners. Although they cried most nights, none died."

"The rats were enormous," Patience indicated their size.

"We thought we'd rot down there, forgotten by the world. Joan reminded us that God would not forsake us, even if others had. She taught us to follow her daily pattern of exercise, bible readings and prayer."

"Praise God."

"Our confidence grew as we took turns to preach on Sundays."

Alongside his relief, her husband William was shocked by Mary's self-assurance. It was hard to believe this was the distraught mother who gave birth just before we left Scrooby.

"As time went on, the guards took pity on us. One told us the patrol had been searching for other fugitives that day. Lincolnshire didn't betray us. It was a coincidence we were caught."

Nevertheless, the guards would have informed Archbishop Bancroft.

"How did you escape?"

"Whenever the churchmen interrogated us, we said we only boarded the barge because our husbands told us to. This confounded those who expected their own wives to follow their orders at all times."

The clerics did not know how Separatist practices differ from those of the English Church in this respect. All believers are allowed to voice their opinions and vote at Separatist business meetings, not just men.

Also, the gaolers needed more space. Many are imprisoned for trivial offences. They kept running out of room.

Captivity had strengthened the women's faith and resolve. Pastor Smyth asked Mary Brewster to speak at our service the following week, clearly impressed.

The flour store meeting room was too small for all the adults to sit. Songs and prayers lasted longer than before. Noisy children chased each other round, as existing members welcomed newcomers by shaking their hands.

At last, Pastor Smyth reestablished order. He invited everyone to link arms to say the words of their covenant together, a banned practice the believers had followed since constituting themselves as a Separatist church in England. So much had happened since I first heard this covenant at Gainsborough Old Hall, on the Sunday after Joan Helwys' arrest, but the words still had a powerful effect. Many had tears in their eyes, such was the emotion they felt. I could not imagine such a scene in Paget's church, or any parish back home.

Squeezed between Isobel and Agnes, I joined in this time.

We as the Lord's free people
join ourselves by a covenant of the Lord
into a church estate
in fellowship of the gospel
to walk in all his ways, made known and to be made known
according to our best endeavours
whatsoever it should cost us

It was wonderful to be together again, free at last. This was a sobering moment. We had sacrificed so much. Bridget cried whilst praying for Joan, imprisoned in York. Pastor Smyth still coughed, many years after contracting consumption whilst imprisoned himself.

38

I was grateful for the opportunity to speak with Thomas Helwys in the yard, having missed his wise counsel while he was in England. Thomas confirmed what I suspected about his wife. Incensed that Thomas had evaded arrest by going into hiding, Archbishop Bancroft had imprisoned Joan instead, and still refused to release her, a great injustice.

"My wife is resilient, but found it hard to say goodbye to our youngest two who have been with her since the start."

I stared glumly at the floor, mindful of my own failings. Although I had done other grievous things in my life, betraying Joan troubled me more. I had inadvertently mentioned her whereabouts when riled.

Thomas smiled, "Don't worry, Baxby. No bishop will deter Joan."

"What is really happening in England, Sir? Some pamphlets say King James will join the Protestant Union, others that he will marry Prince Henry to a Spanish Infanta. Both can't be true."

"People don't speak openly. It's still not safe to do so, given the number of informers and spies."

However, Thomas trusted information from his cousin Gervase, an alderman at the Guildhall.

Gervase had told him about disquiet amongst the guildsmen and councillors in the City of London. They were unhappy with the way James gave monopolies to his favourites. While other nations' merchants were benefitting from the Truce, ours were crippled by royal interference.

Also, James had antagonised the country's senior lawyers, including Attorney General Edwin Coke who had previously prosecuted Guy Fawkes.

"Coke is challenging the King's assertion that he is above the law, along with the legitimacy of Bancroft's High Commission Court which James uses to circumvent it."

"Will that help Joan, and other Separatists in hiding?"

"Hopefully yes. The High Commission provides an easy way for the King and Archbishop Bancroft to prosecute us."

It was reassuring to have this update from Thomas, after many months reading pamphlets and listening to patients' opinions. Although Gervase Helwys was not a Separatist, he understood our needs.

Thomas was horrified to learn Felde had died in a similar way to Weekes. Whilst admitting they had never been close, he appreciated Felde's help arranging voyages. Thomas did not believe either man died as a result of an accident.

"It sounds plausible they were killed by the same murderer, or murderers. A second killer might copy the first by positioning the body under the bridge. However, he would not make the suspicious marks."

"I fear Bancroft has followed us across the Narrow Sea, and is targeting us one by one."

"Although possible, you have no proof. Besides, Coke is keeping Bancroft busy with church court legalities. He won't be able to leave London for some time."

"Bancroft doesn't need to travel personally. He has an extensive network of pursuivants, spies and informers to do his bidding. Must we wait for another Englishman to die, watching the waters rise?"

Walking past, Nicholas and Margaret stopped to ask if everything was alright, my anger having caused me to raise my voice. Thomas reassured them whilst admiring little Mabel. She was an adorable baby with a rosy face.

After the Barton family exited the gate, I whispered to Thomas, "I think Felde spied for Cecil in England so was effectively a rival. Bancroft might have had him killed for that."

Thomas smiled, "Yes, but not Peter. Again, you have no proof."

He knew Felde had met Cecil in London, but had no reason to suspect their association continued once Felde left the country.

When I told Thomas how Roseberry, Bowman and Tibbs took Felde's body, he agreed to visit them. Also, he would make enquiries about Alice Weekes, assuming someone must know where she had gone.

Logical as always, Thomas calmed me down, then returned to supervise his seven children in the flour store meeting room.

Despite seeing Matthew most days, it had proved difficult to talk with him in private. Helen Kent was always with us when we met in the mornings, Agnes and the children at his home. I was surprised and pleased when he offered to pick plants with me.

Matthew and Margaret still had not found a publisher for their autopsy book. None of the names Cornelis suggested had proved fruitful. My old master was interested to learn about my ointment plans, but primarily wanted to talk about Weekes.

Previously, Matthew had been reluctant to revise his suicide verdict or draw other conclusions from our autopsy findings, until determining the cause of the marks. Following the path to my favourite duck pond, he explained what he had found in one of his medical books. Matthew had managed to bring several with him from England, whereas I fled without mine.

"An Italian physician conducted an experiment, whereby he tried to dispense a medicine by puncturing a patient's skin."

Immediately, I saw the link with what we discovered at the autopsy.

"Was the Italian successful? What did he inject the medicine with?"

"He tried different implements, including a hat pin, needle and stiletto blade. The patient lived longer than was usually the case. Someone could have punctured Weekes and Felde in a similar way, to help or harm them."

"You were Weekes' physician. Wouldn't he have told you if he was undergoing a novel treatment?"

"I don't know. Peter was desperate, in serious pain. I'll see if I can find any more clues in my books."

I thanked him. This was an intriguing idea.

However, my mind was soon preoccupied elsewhere.

39

Desperate to leave Temperance's attic room before our baby's birth, I managed to arrange a visit to one of the one-bedroomed homes Jan had recommended. Isobel wanted to join me. I insisted she rest.

Although tired after a busy day, I was excited crossing the Blue Bridge. The sun was shining. Hopefully, this summer would be dryer than the previous one.

Numerous questions filled my mind. Would the house be big enough? Would the landlord expect a deposit, and if so, how much? Would our cess empty into a pit or common channel? I did not wish to live in a home riddled with shit-stench, as some of my patients did.

The *Zuiderkerk* workmen were finishing for the day when I walked past on the way to my appointment. It would grow to be a magnificent building, the first Protestant church since the Alteration. The outline was already visible.

As I passed the building site, I noticed a stocky man purchasing a spade from a labourer. His back was towards me and I did not hear him speak, so carried on regardless.

Despite its small size, the house would be ideal for our immediate needs. The fireplace warmed the whole building adequately. There was room in the loft to dry plants. I still hoped to move to a larger home eventually. This one would work well for now. It was astounding to think our child could be born on its alcove bed.

When I returned to the *Zuiderkerk*, the man was still there with the spade. He stood between me and the bridge back to *Vloonburg* island. I recognised him once he put his beaver hat back on. There was no doubt. Leonard Redfern was in Amsterdam, perilously close. Sculthorpe's vile lieutenant had tracked me down. The city was no longer safe for me or those I loved.

My old instincts returning quickly, I doubled back knowing I should not take a direct route home. It was difficult to move at speed, against the tide of weary hawkers returning to the islands. Perhaps I could lose him in the crowds.

I heard him shouting, calling me names I will not repeat, but I kept on running, trying to remember Temperance's map. If I followed the wrong canal, I could easily become trapped. Which way should I go?

Despite difficulty weaving my way through, I followed the route the immigrants were taking, in the opposite direction. They showed me the way to St. Anthony's gate, where hopefully I could cross the *Kloveniersburgwal* and lose Redfern inside the walls. *De Wallen*'s maze of alleys would be even more disorienting.

Fortunately, the bridge was narrow. I might get away from Redfern there. His spade slowed him down as he followed me across, but not sufficiently. Apologising, I knocked a woman's half empty basket of fish in his path and gained a few yards.

My pursuer did not desist, though. Despite being stouter and less agile, Redfern was still behind me, almost keeping up.

Once through the gate, I had to make a decision quickly. Which way should I run? How well did Redfern know the city? Was this his first visit, or had he sailed into the harbour before, to murder exiles or for other nefarious purposes?

Previously, I had only seen Redfern in London. In my experience, he rarely travelled, preferring to live in relative luxury near Fleet Street, whilst others performed his evil deeds. The beaver hat was evidence of his expensive tastes.

In truth, I feared for my life, imagining my adversary would prick me with a stiletto or other blade if he got close. Although a spade could be used as a weapon, it was an unlikely choice.

Would anyone notice if Redfern hit me in *De Wallen*, once, twice or more? Its patrons' attentions would be focused elsewhere. If I turned into a quieter street, those admiring the view from their high canal house windows would not notice me collapse.

Farmers were clearing produce from their stalls in St. Anthony's market. I could not spot anywhere to hide. A fat man, leading a donkey in the direction of Dam Square, caused a new plan to form in my mind. If I crouched alongside, I could use the beast to block Redfern's view. Thus, I reached the centre of Amsterdam with a few more yards between us.

Traders were still doing business in Dam Square. Piles of cloth and sacks of beans provided some cover. I chanced a look back from the relative safety of the corner of the Exchange.

Redfern had stopped on the edge of the Square to catch his breath. He was likely to attract undue attention running across with a spade. He looked unsure how to proceed, surprised by the scene before him. Perhaps he was not as familiar with the city as I had previously feared. Redfern could have sent a more junior member of the team to kill the others, then decided to come for me himself.

Whichever was true, I needed to escape.

The Town Hall and Exchange had shut already. Nicholas might have helped me if I ran into the latter otherwise, although I might have endangered him too. Instead, I darted into the Weighing House, just before it closed for the day.

Pausing behind a pillar, I was relieved to hear someone address Redfern in Dutch, "The *Waag* shuts promptly at six o'clock. You can't come in."

Its punctilious officials barred Redfern's entrance. Their profession demanded accuracy.

The last goods of the day were arranged in a neat row, with chalk numbers indicating the order in which they should be weighed. Once they had done this, they wrote the details of the transaction on an enormous board. Then the type of goods, weight, buyer, seller and each one's nationality were copied into a large ledger.

These men knew more about international trade than any king or statesmen. They captured pertinent information in their book.

Despite being in charge of its operation, there was no sign of Cornelis van Giessen at the Weighing House. The officials did not need his supervision to do their work. The older ones looked like they had been doing this job for decades.

Did Peter Weekes share their fastidious traits? If so, it was ludicrous to believe he would have tangled himself in a rope by accident, or killed himself it such a way.

NAMING THE DEAD

In different circumstances, I would have asked his former colleagues about him, but
Redfern was cursing and shouting outside. They refused to let him in, but I could not stay on the weighing floor all night.

Irked by the commotion, the buyer and seller of a wool consignment were happy for me to exit with them. I left via the back door, hiding between their bundles. Redfern was still arguing at the front. Thank God. That was close. I did not see whether he was carrying the spade when I left.

I still needed to be careful walking back. Redfern was not waiting at the *Munt* gate, as I would have done, which strengthened my supposition he did not know the city well.

Temperance was cross that I was late, having cooked a meal for us both, "Where have you been, Baxby?"

"I bumped into someone I knew."

"You should be more considerate. Your wife's back is hurting again."

Isobel asked, "What was the house like?"

"It wasn't right for us," I lied.

It would have been ideal, but we could not risk moving there now.

Although relieved to have survived, the encounter confirmed my worst fears. The English Church had widened its net. Not content with pursuing Puritans in Paget's congregation, Sculthorpe's enforcer Redfern was trying to catch me. My wife and friends were not safe either.

Leonard Redfern was not a man to be crossed. When on a mission, he would persist unless forcibly stopped. From previous experience, I knew I would require equal resolve.

40

Isobel could not get comfortable in bed. I fell asleep assuming this was on account of her back pain, as on previous nights. It was a shock when she prodded me before dawn, "Wake up, Baxby. I think the baby's coming."

"Are you having regular contractions? How frequent are they?"

"This isn't my first labour. Get out of bed!"

I knocked over a pile of ointment jars searching for my shoes. Redfern's appearance had distracted me. I should have been better prepared.

"What are you doing, Baxby? Go and fetch Matthew, now!"

I had never heard my wife swear before. We had agreed that Matthew would help with the delivery. Although experienced, I felt it would be problematic to assist my own wife. How right I was. Already, this was unbearable.

At least the noise woke Temperance, who called from below, "Is everything alright up there?"

"I'm in labour," Isobel shouted back, "It won't be long."

"Go and get Matthew," Temperance ordered me, "I'll help Isobel down to a bed on the third floor."

What would happen if the baby came before we returned? Sometimes the cord wraps around the neck, once, twice or several times. Temperance was accomplished in many ways, but I doubted she could cope with a midwifery emergency. I had seen the anguish couples faced when their babies died. Please God, keep our baby alive.

Isobel screamed at me again. I ran out into the night, still fastening my cloak, splashing through puddles as I went.

The Blue Bridge looked enchanting in the moonlight, its black arches outlining the twinkling waters, but I could not linger to appreciate the view. I held the rail tight, mindful of the uneven planks. The rats were enjoying the solitude, even if I was not.

"Matthew, come quickly. Isobel's in labour," I banged on the

Mobleys' door.

Matthew did not panic, having supervised many births before. His bag was already packed. However, he surprised me by knocking on Nicholas' door, requesting he come to supervise me. Nicholas and I were to wait on the ground floor with Michael, while Matthew and Temperance assisted Isobel upstairs.

Whenever we heard her scream, I jumped off the stool and paced the room. How could anyone sit in such circumstances? It was hard to breathe.

"You must be patient," my former servant reminded me, "Babies come when they're ready."

Suddenly remembering Redfern, I insisted on bolting the door. Nicholas knew more than me about fatherhood, not the specific threat. I could not tell him without explaining my shameful past.

"It won't be long," Matthew called down.

"Is Isobel alright?"

"She's doing very well. Your wife is a brave lady."

I did not doubt it. The others were not as convinced about me.

Nicholas fetched breakfast. Michael showed me how he turned pots. I was impressed by his skill, yet found it hard to concentrate.

"It won't be long," Temperance came down to tell us.

She was right this time. Soon after we heard a baby's cry. Hallelujah! Exhausted, Matthew descended the stairs to declare, "It's a girl. Come and meet your new daughter, Baxby."

Nicholas and Michael followed a respectable distance behind, excited too.

Isobel was sitting up in the Knowsleys' spare bed, with our new baby in her arms. No artist could ever paint such a delectable scene. She smiled, passing the little bundle across for me to hold, "Say hello to Grace Jane."

How tiny she was, with ten perfect little fingers protruding from the blanket. Previously, Isobel and I had agreed the name after long discussions. It seemed to suit her well. Those who remembered Jane in Lincoln, agreed it was fitting for our girl to take her name.

Grace Jane was small enough to rest in the hollow of my hand, delightful from the start, with her mother's thick dark hair. I adored her from that first glimpse in Isobel's arms.

After kissing her forehead, I handed her back. Isobel let Nicholas and Michael take turns holding her, before Temperance shooed us out of the room.

Matthew was pouring himself a drink downstairs. He stopped to pat me on the back, "Well done, Baxby! You're a father now."

Nicholas poured another for me, "It's good our daughters are close in age. They will be able to play together when they are older."

Crackleton hugged me, "Congratulations Baxby. You moved quickly."

It was gratifying to see him there. Nicholas had sent Michael to request he join us, assuming my old comrade would help calm my nerves. Grace Jane was born before he arrived.

Crackleton retold the tale of how I saved his life at the Battle of Nieuwpoort by removing his injured foot. Despite having heard this several times before, the others did not mind. They understood the operation had formed a bond between us, stronger than other friendships. This was a day for drinking and joyful relief.

Matthew reminisced about his daughter Constance's birth in Lincoln, "I wanted to protect her from Secretary Sculthorpe and the Church, yet could only do so by leaving the city."

I could not admit I feared the same, since seeing Leonard Redfern. Instead, I told them how William Brewster paced the room whilst waiting for baby Fear to be born, a couple of days before our escape from Scrooby. Now, I understood his anguish better.

When I reached the bakehouse, already a little drunk, Jan Munter had heard the news. He passed on his congratulations, and expressed satisfaction at the name we had chosen, "May God always be gracious to you and your family."

When I went upstairs, the mood in the flour store room was more sombre. Seated round the table, Pastor Smyth, Pastor Robinson, Thomas Helwys and William Brewster had just finished a serious meeting. They all wore similar black tunics, and black capotain hats which were becoming increasingly popular.

Brewster rose first, delighted by my news, "May God bless you, now and always."

The rest followed suit, seemingly pleased by the distraction. Robinson found beer in Crackleton's room. I enjoyed my time with the four men I admired greatly. It was hard to leave. I even wondered whether it was time for me to join the church as a believer-member, such was the bond I felt.

The Lemmens were complimentary, as was Raphael Barr. He suggested we move to a vacant home near his, then accompanied me to meet the owner. I did not mind how slow he walked. This was a fortunate development indeed. Redfern was less likely to search an area inhabited by Jewish immigrants.

Isobel would be pleased by its location too, close enough to *Marken* and *Uilenburg* islands to distribute bread.

I paid a deposit and agreed to move in on Saturday.

However, my fears returned when I reached Eva Witte's home in the *Begijnhof.* It was hard to fool Eva. She listened well, and noticed things others missed. Peter Weekes liked to visit, as did Edwin.

"What is it?" Eva asked, after we had talked about Grace Jane, "Are you alright Baxby?"

It was tempting to unburden myself, but it would be foolish to disclose too much.

"Yesterday, I saw a man who worked for the English Church in London."

"A cleric?"

"A spy master and bully."

"Did he see you?"

"I lost him in Dam Square. He doesn't know where we live."

Despite being relieved to hear this, Eva shared my disquiet.

Walking back through the *Munt* gate, I felt the same sense of dread as before. Redfern could be lying in wait. I checked the other doorways in Temperance's row, before opening hers and fixing the bolts. There were only a couple of days to wait until we moved to *Vloonburg*. Hopefully, we would be safer on the island.

41

Isobel and I settled in quickly. The total space was smaller than Temperance's attic. This did not stop us loving our little house. Grace Jane slept in a cradle next to our alcove bed.

By the time she was a month old, Edwin Helwys was living in our attic too. After falling out with his father, Thomas agreed he could stay with us, providing he promised not to visit the harbour or try to enlist. As I was out visiting patients much of the day, it was reassuring to know someone else was there to protect my wife and child if necessary.

Edwin helped with chores, showing the same willingness he showed towards Eva. Sometimes Toby visited too. They liked rocking Grace Jane's cradle. Both learnt how to grind dried plants and stir the resultant mixture.

Sophie van Giessen suggested we set up a bread distribution stall outside our home. I was too busy to contemplate such matters, still troubled by thoughts of Redfern.

Towards the end of the summer, I visited Raphael Barr again. His house was close to our own.

The terms of the Truce had allayed Raphael's fears. His artist son Samuel was making a comfortable living. Their rabbi was trying to open a synagogue building. Although there was no certainty the council would allow this, the idea pleased him in his old age.

Raphael Barr was a private gentleman who conducted his business indoors. I was surprised to see him arguing with a man, as I came round the corner. When he tried to shut the door, the visitor blocked it with his spade.

Trembling, I pressed back into a doorway, uncertain whether to intervene or run away. Leonard Redfern had returned, perilously close to my home this time.

Raphael shouted for neighbours to come to his aid. Several Jewish gentlemen appeared, closing in, clearly braver than me.

NAMING THE DEAD

My old spymaster removed his spade from Raphael's door and edged away. Even with minimal Spanish, he understood the locals' intent. After muttering English profanities, he headed off in the direction of the Blue Bridge, without noticing me.

When Barr had finished thanking his neighbours and offering sweets, I emerged from my hiding place. Once inside, we bolted the door. Not knowing Redfern, Barr was less anxious than me but still cautious. He would not speak until convinced the house was secure, "That man was trouble. He asked cunning questions like the spies in Spain."

"What about?"

"He asked about *you*, the English physician. He wanted to know where you lived. I refused to answer in any language. I wouldn't help that man."

"Thank you."

"You're not safe here, Doctor Baxby. *Vloonburg* people are good but poor. Informing helps to pay the bills. The temptation can prove too great. Do you understand?"

I understood well. The island was no longer safe, for me and my family. Where could we go?

While the leech was filling, Raphael told me how Jews had resided in Spain and Portugal for centuries in relative peace, until the Inquisition demanded they convert on threat of death. I showed him the frontispiece in my little bible, depicting Moses and the Israelites' escape from Egypt.

Raphael smiled, explaining how Amsterdam's Jews ate a special Passover meal each year, remembering the way an angel of death had killed the Egyptians, enabling their ancestors to go free. In Spain, they had not been able to celebrate in this way. Their rabbi had reinstated the annual tradition.

I needed an angel of death to slay Redfern and save me.

Too anxious to visit more patients, I decided to walk to the meadows to pick plants. It was time to deliver another box of ointment jars to the agreed location, and prepare for the winter.

Edwin was watching boats near the Blue Bridge, clearly bored. He missed his trips to the harbour, but appeared to be obeying his father's rules. When I suggested he accompany me, he was grateful.

Walking along the usual track, I showed him which plants to pick. He liked the duck pond with its tiny waterfall, insisting it was sufficiently dry for us to sit there. As we watched a duck avoiding the attentions of a drake, he unburdened his soul.

Edwin missed his mother. It was hard for a lad of his age to admit this openly. He remembered how Joan used to read him stories, sitting on his bed at Broxtowe Hall. The ground had been covered with bluebells on the last occasion they walked together in nearby woods. She had told him they would have to move away. His father left the next day.

There were tears in my eyes as Edwin spoke. He had not seen his mother since the cart took him and his two oldest siblings away to stay at the Mobleys' home in Gainsborough.

The clouds were darkening. I suggested we return. Edwin wanted to show me his latest pamphlets first. He produced a ragged assortment from his pocket, whilst expressing concern for Prince Henry.

"Edwin, you promised your father you wouldn't visit the harbour again."

"Toby found these. Neither the Dutch nor English pamphlets mention Henry. They just rage about Jacob Arminius, whoever he is."

"Let me see."

Jacob Arminius, a principle at Leiden University, was criticised for not attending an important conference at the Hague. Although he was ill, most thought this scandalous. The conference had been called to settle an important religious matter.

I could see why Edwin was disappointed. The pamphlets focused on this obscure topic, whilst ignoring Prince Henry's matrimonial state.

"Could you ask your father or Pastor Smyth what this means? They understand religious matters more than me."

"I don't want to understand. I want to know if Prince Henry has thwarted his father's ridiculous plan."

Some thought King James was motivated by noble sentiments,

trying to bridge religious divides. Given the way he and his Church chased down Puritans and Separatists, I found this hard to believe.

Isobel was busy with Grace Jane when we returned, but sensed my anxiety nonetheless. As we lay in bed, I asked her what Leiden was like.

"That's a strange question. Why do you want to know?"

"Edwin showed me a pamphlet about a religious controversy there."

"It's a beautiful city, smaller than Amsterdam."

She knew Jacob Arminius had caused uproar by questioning Reformed beliefs, but little more.

"Would you consider moving to Leiden?"

"Of course not. I'm very happy here, and will be leading our first bread charity board meeting soon. Let's just enjoy Grace Jane's first year."

She had the child she longed for. There were tears of joy in her eyes. How could I shatter Isobel's happiness by mentioning Leonard Redfern?

42

Some evenings Crackleton and I sat on the flour store step, drinking beer and reminiscing together, whilst his children played with others in the yard. On one such evening, he was the first to inform me about our leaders' disagreement.

When I asked him if he thought we would ever see England again, Crackleton shook his head, "No, I will move with Pastor Robinson to Leiden and continue working for him there."

After wiping dregs from his wooden leg, which I had spilt in shock, I stuttered, "What are you talking about, Crackleton?"

"Leiden University has offered Pastor Robinson an important position. I don't understand the theological arguments. I just know the professors are eager to employ him."

"What arguments?"

"I told you I don't understand them."

"Then why are you moving to Leiden?"

"I've already said that too."

Crackleton sipped more beer, staring at his children playing in the yard, only speaking when their rag ball landed close to our feet, "I will follow Pastor Robinson anywhere. He has been good to me."

I understood my friend's loyalty. Without Robinson, and others who taught him to read, Crackleton and his children would have been taken by the poor law commissioners, never heard of again.

"Do the others know about this move?"

"William Brewster will come to Leiden. Pastor Smyth and Thomas Helwys intend to stay in Amsterdam. You must choose which group to belong to. If you speak with Pastor Robinson, he will help you decide."

Was this the miracle I had been praying for, an opportunity to leave Amsterdam without losing face? Crackleton was often confused. I needed more information.

I found Pastor Robinson emptying a trunk from England, surrounded by books on his floor. He confirmed the university had offered him a tutorship, without smiling for once.

"Congratulations, Sir. I'm pleased your talents have been recognised. Do you know what this means for the rest of us?"

Anticipating this would be a challenging conversation, I picked up a tract and stared down, unable to meet the pastor's eyes.

"A schismatic Dutch pastor called Jacob Arminius has retired from his professorship at Leiden University due to ill health. Arminius challenged the very foundations of our faith. Now, his followers want to employ equally errant Conrad Vorstius in his place."

Trying to sound knowledgeable, I asked, "Is Arminius an atheist? Does he deny God exists?"

"No, Arminius denies the *omnipotence* of God."

Pastor Robinson often used illustrations and stories to convey complex theological ideas in simple terms. However, this was particularly difficult to follow. He explained slowly, "We Calvinists know salvation comes from the Lord, but Arminius says God gives people free will to decide for themselves instead, as if salvation depended on human endeavour."

"We're saved by the *grace* of God," I stated, having listened to numerous sermons on the subject, affirming His generous love.

"Correct. We haven't come this far just to return to Rome."

Why mention Rome where the Pope lives? This was too difficult to understand. Free will did not sound contentious to me, yet Robinson had studied piles of theological books, those on the floor and more besides.

Fortunately, Bridget and her sister returned with the children, saving me from further confusion and embarrassment. Realising the tract in my hand was upside down, I discarded it quickly, hoping they had not seen. Robinson must have noticed my foolishness, without commenting.

Matthew found me at home, grinding medicinal plants with unnecessary vigour. Trying to help, he started, "According to Arminius, God gives us free will so we can choose whether to accept or reject His salvation. Arminius' view is called *general* salvation because it's offered *generally* to everyone, whereas Calvin's is called *particular* salvation because it's just for a *particular* few."

"Robinson mentioned Rome," I replied, "Is Arminius a Catholic?"

Matthew looked more serious, "No, he is definitely Protestant, as is Conrad Vorstius. General salvation isn't about receiving sacraments. People don't secure it by good works, penance, attending mass or any other prescribed behaviour. We need true *repentance* inside."

"A change of heart?"

"A complete change of heart *and direction*."

"Why doesn't Robinson agree with that?"

"Reformed Calvinists believe in predestination. To me, it makes most sense if we consider time as a river. Being eternal, God sits outside of time. He sees the decisions we've already made upstream in the past and those we will make downstream. He knows who will be saved and who won't in the future."

"Pastor Robinson didn't mention a river. This is very confusing."

Certainly, I would need to understand the arguments better, if I was to persuade Isobel to move to Leiden. Matthew suggested I listen to the speakers at the next business meeting and then make up my mind.

I broke a bowl before he left, which did not augur well.

The business meeting was tense from the start. Smyth and Helwys faced Robinson and Brewster across the table. The rest of us sat in silence waiting for our leaders to speak.

Pastor Robinson rose first, "Arminius has claimed God gives people free will to decide, as if salvation depends on individual effort when we know it comes *from the Lord*."

"God longs for *all* to repent and return in faith to him," Pastor Smyth countered, "The Anabaptist practice of believers' baptism helps us understand. Anabaptists immerse new believers in water, an external sign of inner repentance. In repentance and faith, we die to the old life and rise to the new."

They discussed the various doctrines for two hours, until unable to contain herself any longer, Agnes raised her hand to speak. Her contribution surprised us all. Having previously questioned conventional wisdom about *natural* conception in Lincoln, insisting it was not dependent on women being fully aroused, Agnes now shared her novel theories about *spiritual* rebirth.

"It's different for those of you who grew up in caring homes with Christian parents. It's easier to believe you're predestined for eternal salvation when you've known God's love from birth. What about the rest of us? Are we excluded? Or predestined for damnation, just because of the circumstances into which we were born? My late sister Susannah and I only came to know God's love later, because believer-friends cared for us. We've had to choose our own path in life, as has Doctor Baxby."

How did she speak so powerfully? Why did she mention my name? I wanted to move to Leiden as a matter of expediency, although agreeing with Agnes who had taken the Arminian side. After Brewster thanked Agnes for her contribution, I put up my hand. It was hard to wait for my turn. This would be the first time I had spoken at a business meeting.

"I agree with Agnes," I managed, "My early life was problematic too. I've done things I regret. Yet God rescued me when I cried out to Him in the storm."

Frightened and distraught at the time, I had no longer believed I deserved to live.

"But we can't deny the omnipotence of God," Robinson interjected.

"No," Agnes called out, "But why can't God set aside his power to give people like us a chance? Jesus was killed on a cross. He accepted that limitation on our behalf."

William Brewster returned the meeting to order. All contributions had to be addressed through him, the chairman, not argued directly across the room.

Isobel whispered, "I'm proud of you, Baxby," whilst clutching my arm to prevent me from saying more. My heart was thumping inside my chest. Having never voiced an opinion in this way before I was surprised by the quickening effect. I had spoken from the heart, rather than arguing the sensible option.

43

At the meeting's conclusion, Isobel and I chose to stay in Amsterdam, along with former Gainsborough believers. Nicholas, Mary and her mother were the only other former Scrooby residents who did not move to Leiden. Agnes stayed, so the professors never had an opportunity to contest her theories there.

Henceforth Pastor Smyth and Thomas Helwys would be the leaders of our bakehouse church. Without Pastor Robinson and William Brewster, the old friends were free to explore more Arminian and Anabaptist ideas.

Crackleton still did not understand the theological differences. He was impressed by Agnes' and my contributions at the meeting, but his loyalty to Pastor Robinson outweighed all else.

I helped him carry the family's luggage to the *Rokin*, and boarded the boat bound for *Overtoom* Dam where we would part. We sat in the stern together, watching Amsterdam's spires disappear. The *Zuiderkerk*'s now rivalled the older ones.

"We've come a long way since Nieuwpoort, Baxby."

"I remember when you had two legs."

"I was terrified watching you draw the saw from that bucket. Do you remember the woman who fell in the River Witham after we returned?"

"What a sight."

When I took my little bible from my pocket, and showed him Catherine's name on the back page, Crackleton quietened. Although he did not share my convictions about their murders, he was pleased to see Weekes and Felde at the bottom of the list, keen to respect their memories too.

"You've been a good friend, Baxby. I'll miss you. Thank you again for saving my life."

The little boat had reached *Overtoom* Dam. It was time to alight. Someone stepped aside to let him disembark. He walked across the plank remarkably well with his wooden leg.

While my friends waited for the Leiden boat, I shook hands

with William Brewster and his family, "I owe you so much, Sir."

"It's been a pleasure. I wish you and your lovely wife were coming with us, but respect your choice."

"I will always remember the remarkable way you led us from Scrooby, and your sermon about pilgrims in the barn."

"Our pilgrimage isn't over, Baxby. None of us know where God will lead us. Pilgrims' paths must part sometimes. Perhaps we will meet again one day."

The Brewster's ward Bradford promised to write. I was interested to know how this promising young man's life would unfold.

Pastor Robinson's eyes were smiling when we said goodbye, despite his sadness.

"Just remember," he said hugging me, "Everything good ultimately comes from God."

It had been hard to disagree with the man I loved and admired, but there was no bitterness when we parted.

Crackleton and his children were the last to board the larger boat.

"One word before I go," he said, "Do you really need to work so hard?"

"I want to become a burgher once I can afford the fee, and buy a better home for my wife and family."

"That's understandable. However, there's little point if you don't spend time with those you love."

"Is this about you or me?" I rebutted cruelly, knowing how he left Catherine before we met.

"It's about us both. I made a dreadful mistake when I joined the militia. Catherine had every right to be cross."

"Write and tell me about Leiden."

"I will."

After embracing him and his children for the last time, they marched off to catch the boat. As his former surgeon, I was delighted by the way his leg had healed. As his friend, I was inconsolable.

If Crackleton had known about Redfern, he would have admonished me for not leaving with him.

I watched until their ship disappeared from sight. It was awful turning away, not knowing if I would see any of them again.

I decided to visit my duck pond on the way back, hoping the peaceful spot might bring some consolation. My patients would have to wait a little longer.

Back in Scrooby, Pastor Robinson had underlined some verses in my bible, during one of the times we drank Brewster's delicious wine by Scrooby Manor's fire. I found comfort in them by the pond.

I saw a great multitude, which no man could number, of all nations and kinds, and people, and tongues, stood before the throne and before the Lamb, clothed with long white robes and palms in their hands

And they cried with a loud voice, saying Salvation comes from our God who sits on the throne and of the Lamb

Robinson had explained that the people in robes are those who had suffered on earth. Their cry echoed his maxim *Salvation comes from the Lord.*

I imagined the martyrs in Foxe's book would all be there, worshipping God in heaven, singing their favourite psalms. Perhaps John Calvin and Jacob Arminius would be singing too. How many of us really know how much of our path depends on our own intent, that of others, or a greater deity?

Sometimes, I dream I am sitting with Crackleton and Robinson again, by Brewster's enormous fireplace. I smell the burning logs from the adjoining hunting forest and hear them crackle. The fire warms my heart and extremities.

My dream will not come true, of course. I will not return to Broxtowe, Gainsborough Old Hall or Scrooby Manor. Yet if Arminius' insights are true, we might meet again in heaven.

Turning to my bible, I read the list of names again.

I planned to pick more plants on the way home, deposit them with Isobel, and Edwin if he was there, before visiting Raphael

Barr and a new Jewish patient with a rash. There had been several similar cases on the islands recently. Fortunately, most spots seemed to disappear as mysteriously as they came after a few weeks. However, it was best to check, and offer a lotion if the rash was causing discomfort.

I remember closing my bible and wrapping the first leather strip around. It slipped from my fingers. A sharp pain lanced the back of my head. Then I was tumbling too, toppling sideways, unable to move my arms to cushion the impending impact.

Time seemed to slow as I fell. My brow hit the ground. I cried out in vain. What was happening to me? Was I dying? There was no one to save me that far from the city.

Worse than any I had experienced before, the blow left me breathless and unable to think properly. I hit the ground, then darkness, only darkness. Long, long silence. Not a whisper or a prayer. No plants. No rain. No bog or tufts of spike sedge. No despair or hope. Silence.

I remember stirring, hearing Matthew's voice, "Baxby, can you hear me?"

I blinked but could not speak.

"Baxby's alive," he shouted, "We must move him somewhere warmer and dryer, or he'll die of cold."

I heard other voices too, but did not recognise them. The pain was unbearable as they tried to move me. I slipped into darkness again.

44

London 1613

The captain ordered a guard to reopen the cell door while Baxby was speaking. He has brought the blacksmith to remove the vicar's leg-iron. Geoffrey has signed further paperwork authorising the procedure. He will take responsibility if the prisoner tries to escape, which is unlikely given his desperate state.

The noise reverberates around the tower. The guards hear it in the gatehouse, also passengers and boatmen on the quay below.

Geoffrey shudders on the stairs. Unbeknown to the prisoners, he has been listening outside again.

The blacksmith is good at his job. The shackle breaks apart on the stone slabs, leaving the blithering cleric even less intelligible than before. He gobbles the food the guard has brought, despite seeming uninterested in anything else. If the captain had not intervened, he would have eaten Baxby and the printer's shares too.

Geoffrey is pleased his plan is working, his old instincts proving correct. Placing the vicar and printer in the cell with Baxby has enabled him to gain useful information about his past. He did not know Alexander was attacked whilst in Amsterdam, let alone by whom.

Hopefully, one more day will suffice. Then he will interrogate one or both of Baxby's fellow prisoners. If Redfern does not return in time, he will do this on his own.

NAMING THE DEAD

Sunday

45

Amsterdam 1609-1610

Lying down, I had no sense of time. Was I in the realm of the living, the dead, or the grey nether world Catholics call purgatory? I cannot describe the numbness I felt each time I stirred from sleep. Previously, darkness had helped me think. Now, it was difficult to form a fleeting thought.

Occasionally, pain shot through my head. Thank God, it was not permanent. At Nieuwpoort, I saw soldiers pleading for death after twenty-four agonising hours. Others, robbed of their dignity, dissociated from everything and everyone around them. Some thought they were back home, calling out for their mothers. Was this to be my fate? How long would I survive?

Sometimes, I heard noises in the room above my head, as if something heavy was being dragged across bare boards. Then, a rhythmic click which reminded me of Cornelis van Giessen's winch. I guessed I was in a canal house, on the floor beneath a store room.

Once I longed to live in such a dwelling. These were not the circumstances I had in mind. I could not move any limb, finger or toe, but not because I was bound.

Although I felt abandoned, this was not the case. Later, I learnt that Pastor Smyth had organised a vigil from the start. My friends were taking turns to sit by my bed. Without them, I doubt I would have revived.

One day, I opened my eyes at the sound of gentle snoring. The light from the window warmed my face. Despite not being able to turn my head sufficiently to see her, I woke the guardian angel sitting in the chair to my right.

Agnes jumped up and came nearer, "Baxby! You're awake. Can you hear me? Can you hear me?"

Somehow, I convinced her. She ran out of the room, shouting for Matthew to come upstairs, "Baxby moved his eyes when I asked him a question. He understood what I said."

She brought her face close enough for me to feel the warmth of her breath.

"What happened? Where's Isobel?" I mouthed, frustrated that no sound emerged.

Recognising my distress, Agnes moved back to her seat. I must have fallen asleep again.

Through moments of such lucidity, I learnt I had been attacked by an unknown assailant and left for dead.

When I did not return home, initially Isobel assumed Matthew and I were staying late with a patient. The Mobleys had already finished eating when she called at their home. Despite the late hour, they knocked on several doors. Nicholas and Agnes joined the search while Margaret looked after the children. Raphael Barr and other regular patients confirmed they had not seen me that day.

Pastor Smyth had not seen me either. However, he had witnessed a strange event earlier that day, which now acquired a sinister significance. Someone had thrown my bible over the gate into the bakehouse yard. They did not stop or show their face, so Smyth could not describe their features, but thought it was probably a man.

Wrapped in its leather strips, the bible was protected from damage, but my wife and friends knew this was an ominous sign. I had always kept it safe in my pocket, since the day Jane died. The treasured gift had travelled from Scrooby with me, shared the winter in hiding and survived a storm at sea. Several friends had underlined favourite verses as Jane once did. I would not part with it by choice.

There was another nasty surprise within. After Pastor Smyth gave Isobel the bible, she looked inside the back cover and screamed. Someone had added my name to the list of those I mourned. *Alexander Baxby* was written below the others in an untidy hand.

Ever the logical lawyer, Thomas had advised caution, "This

does not prove Baxby is dead, merely that someone has maliciously written his name beneath those of other departed friends."

Pastor Smyth led a prayer, refusing to believe I was dead.

Edwin and Toby found me the following evening, having demanded to join the search. I was lying in a ditch near my favourite duck pond, caked in blood. Toby went to fetch Matthew, whilst Edwin stayed by my side not knowing if I was alive. I will always feel gratitude towards both boys, as Crackleton does towards me for saving his life.

Cornelis van Giessen leant the use of his cart, then seeing the extent of my injuries offered a bed in his home. Isobel and my friends could visit and care for me, confident I was comfortable.

So, the vigil had started. Matthew provided my medical care. Isobel, Agnes, Margaret and Helen looked after each other's children, enabling them to take turns sitting with me. Margaret's mother and Mary Smyth helped occasionally too. Matthew refused to let the Pastor attend himself, because of his cough.

Smyth wrote to tell our friends in Leiden what had happened. They sent kind regards and offered prayers for my swift recovery.

When Isobel brought Grace Jane to see me, I was amazed by how much she had grown. Our daughter could sit if supported. She was interested in everything she saw. Isobel brought her close enough for her finger tips to touch my face. Her delightful smile warmed my heart.

"Grace Jane," a whisper left my lips, the first sound I made.

"Isobel put her arms around my neck, clearly overjoyed to hear my voice again, "I love you, Baxby. We're going to be alright."

For the first time, I believed it might be possible, although it was some time before I could form meaningful sentences.

Why had I worked so hard? Crackleton was right to challenge my priorities. Widowerhood had made him wise. I should have cherished each day with Isobel. An impressive family portrait on the wall was no substitute for my wife's warmth and touch. I missed our alcove bed, with the plants drying overhead and the little crib alongside.

I would have made any bargain to have my old life back, despite knowing this was futile.

"God does not make deals with humankind," Pastor Smyth had said, "He works for the good of those who love him, according to His greater plan. Even though we rarely understand this, we must keep trusting Him."

Slowly, I was recovering. My mind began to work again. I struggled to make sense of what had happened to Peter Weekes and Julian Felde in the light of my own attack. They both died in the River Amstel. I had been left in a ditch but survived. Was this an oversight on the part of our common assailant? Had someone interrupted his heinous act? Perhaps the other men had been lured to a more secluded location before being hit.

The longer I reflected, the more I became convinced their drownings could not have been staged by a single actor. If like me they were hit from behind, the attacker would have needed someone to help transport them to the riverside and bundle the bodies down.

How little I knew. I could not remember more about what happened at the pond however much I tried, apart from the absence of ducks. Perhaps my attacker had scared them away.

There was an outstanding question I needed assistance to answer. Were there marks on my underside too, similar to Weekes' and Felde's? As soon as I was well enough, I should ask Matthew or Isobel to help me find out.

46

Gradually, I regained sensation in my upper body. Although my back ached at times, I knew this was a good sign. My fingers began to tingle, then I could move the tips. There were still long nights without sleep, but the pain in my head was subsiding. It was easier to think.

"What is the prognosis, Matthew?" I asked.

"You were badly bruised and swollen when we found you. Your spine was injured too. In such cases it's hard to make predictions. Alongside the physical effects you've had a horrendous shock."

"I'm too young to lie in bed like this. Eva Witte's the oldest person I know. Even she takes a walk each day."

"From now on, you need to keep moving whichever parts of your body you can to make them stronger."

I promised to do everything I could to recover, not just for my own sake, for Isobel and Grace Jane's too. Despite everything that had happened, I was determined to muster whatever strength I could.

Margaret's mother was sitting with me, when we heard a tap at the door. She disappeared, then returned to ask, "Do you feel well enough to see Thomas Helwys and John Murton? They have information about Alice Weekes, but will wait if you're too tired."

I was eager to see them both and intrigued about what they might say. Generally, neither man engaged in idle chatter. It would be a pleasure to converse with them both.

Thomas explained, "I made enquiries about Alice as I promised. I'm sorry this has taken so long. She was arrested soon after her husband's funeral and has been in the *Spinhuis* since her trial."

"Arrested?"

"We think she stole something, possibly from Temperance. Members of the English Reformed Church are reluctant to talk.

This is embarrassing for them all."

The *Spinhuis* was a prison where female offenders were expected to work long hours. Those who refused were confined in a watery dungeon until they changed their mind. The Dutch had novel ideas about punishment. They did not hang everyone who committed a petty crime.

Temperance must have known all along. She either forged Alice's letter instructing others not to look for her, or made Alice write it under duress. I was not surprised she would want to keep criminality a secret, yet felt betrayed. Temperance had deceived me, caused unnecessary grief and wasted Thomas' precious time.

I asked him if it was possible to visit Alice. If so, we could discover more about her and Peter's origins in England, which might give more clues about his death. It was frustrating not to remember where I had seen him before.

"People are allowed in the *Spinhuis* at certain times. Parents take their children to warn them what will happen if they misbehave. However, I don't think it will be necessary. Murton knew her family in Gainsborough."

I had never asked the ex-tanner about Alice. There was no reason to suppose he would know her or her family's background.

The two men switched places, Murton taking the chair. He looked tired. Bombazine work is demanding.

"I knew Alice's godfather in Gainsborough. He saved her life by hiding her in a cowshed, then paid for her passage out. That lass was trouble from the start."

"Was he one of the believers at the Old Hall?"

Murton laughed, "Good Lord, no. The man was a drunkard and thief himself, but cared enough about Alice to not want to watch her hang. I think she stole some peas, not a horrendous crime in my opinion."

The judge would disagree.

A thought crossed my mind, "Do you know if she sailed from Boston?"

Its townsfolk had helped others, not just our Scrooby group. Many fled into exile from its port for disparate reasons.

NAMING THE DEAD

Murton did not know where she had departed from, but it did not matter, for as he reminisced, other memories returned, about Alice's escape from England and Peter's too. Also, I realised the reason why his face was familiar but hard to place.

The adult Peter resembled his uncle, who lived on the far side of Boston during my childhood. They were the Wilkes family not Weekes. My mother warned me to keep away. People said they retained Catholic sympathies.

Certainly, Peter's grandfather had been hanged for his role in the Lincolnshire Rising during King Henry VIII's reign. His mother was rumoured to have had Peter baptised by a Jesuit priest.

Nevertheless, the landlord Edmund Sibsey had employed Peter as a servant at the Red Lion inn. The lad was working there when I returned from London, after meeting Geoffrey for the first time. Generous as ever, Sibsey ignored others' advice, until Peter argued with one of the local vicars. After that, the landlord had no choice but to sack him, or lose his licence for sheltering a Catholic.

To his credit, Sibsey had paid Captain Atherton to smuggle Peter out on his ship the *Mary-Anne*. I had overheard them arranging this in the Red Lion kitchen, on the night before the ship sailed. Sibsey had also asked Atherton to take a girl on the run for stealing peas. She would hang if caught. Peter would more likely be burnt for heresy.

How remarkable that I should remember this now, after suffering such a serious blow to my head. There was a stronger bond between Peter and me than I had realised. We shared similar roots.

Each person on the islands had had their own theories about Weekes' death. None of them knew his background as I did. Peter had not always been a stalwart Calvinist, as Paget assumed at his funeral. Like me, Peter probably arrived in Amsterdam eager to start his life anew, subsequently changing his name and eschewing his Catholic past by joining the English Reformed Church.

Perhaps Alice found it harder to mend her ways, evidenced by her subsequent arrest for stealing again. She was harder to comprehend. Her reaction to news of Peter's death had been muted, as had her sympathy with his pain. Their home was cold and bare, compared to our own. They never had children. Agnes did not believe this perturbed her in the way it would other women.

In truth, I pitied Peter in his choice of wife. It was always a delight when mine visited, especially if Isobel brought Grace Jane.

It should have been a relief to solve the mystery, yet something did not feel right. I was exhausted after Thomas and Murton left, then slept most of the following day.

Gradually, more memories resurfaced. I recalled meeting Peter at the coast as a boy. The waves were rougher than usual, due to the strong wind. We had tossed pebbles into the sea together. Although smaller and younger than me, he was better at making them bounce. I blamed the weather.

I could remember this as if I had been there yesterday, yet still no details of my attack.

47

When Isobel next visited on her own, we talked about Murton. She remembered him from Gainsborough, and was impressed with the way he had learnt a new trade. Also, Murton had helped her erect a shelter outside our home to distribute bread.

Still puzzled by Peter's membership of the English Reformed Church, I asked her whether people could change their faith. My wife was more knowledgeable about religious matters. She fed the hungry regardless of their backgrounds and beliefs.

"Peter could have changed as he grew older," Isobel concluded, "After all, Pastor Smyth's beliefs have developed over time. He was a Puritan preacher in Lincoln, a Separatist leader in Gainsborough, and now he's writing a book about believers' baptism."

"He's been spending too long with Anabaptists."

"Don't mock Smyth, Baxby. His theology may be too radical for some. That does not mean he's wrong."

"But can a Catholic really become a Protestant? Isn't that a bigger chasm to cross?"

"Anyone can be baptised as a believer according to Pastor Smyth, even former atheists who profess that Jesus is Lord and join with other believers in an independent church like ours. Believers' baptism is the true outward sign of the New Testament covenant relationship between God and us."

More pertinent to my own situation, she added, "The circumstances of one's birth don't matter nor the manner in which one's lived since. Anyone can be baptised in water and embark on the journey of faith."

Despite not professing belief like my wife and friends, I was grateful to God for having survived my attack, where poor Weekes and Felde did not.

Isobel was proving capable with practical matters. After I provided instructions, she delivered more jars to the prescribed location, then deposited the money at the Bank for safekeeping. Although it seemed ambitious given her other responsibilities, she was determined to make more ointment too.

"You could ask Edwin to help. He proved useful before."

"Thomas has sent Edwin back to London. His cousin has enrolled him at Gray's Inn. Edwin will train to be a lawyer like his father."

"He wanted to be a soldier."

"Thomas decided otherwise. I think finding you by the duck pond made Edwin even more determined to enlist."

I was disappointed to learn I would not be able to thank Edwin, and was concerned for his well-being too. Thomas had his son's interests at heart, but Edwin's character was very different.

"Toby fetches Eva Witte's shopping now. He misses Edwin, and seems to have grown more reserved since he left."

"Toby is a good lad. Susannah would have been proud."

"He's growing tall. His hair is darkening too, so he looks less like her and Agnes."

I wondered if Agnes had told Toby who his father was yet. The two sisters were the only ones who knew his name. Toby might have started asking questions.

As time went on my appetite returned and I grew stronger. Matthew was impressed but still limited my number of visitors. Raphael sent sweets at regular intervals. Isobel tried to persuade me to eat healthier soups.

With lots of time to think, I became obsessed with the idea that whoever had made the mysterious marks on Weekes and Felde must have done the same to me. I could twist my shoulders and arms a little, but not enough to check.

I plucked up courage to ask Isobel to look. She would recognise them, having seen Felde's, albeit after death.

After struggling with my weight, my wife concluded, "We need help with this."

I suggested she ask Nicholas who had once been my servant.

Isobel rearranged my bedding before replying. Why hesitate? Given my nervous state, I assumed an awful fate had befallen him too. It was a relief when she answered, "Nicholas won't come here. He's upset, as we all are, but that's not the reason. He senses something strange about this house."

"I used to feel uneasy here too. Now I realise my foolishness. I would not have recovered this well without the van Giessens' hospitality."

Isobel suggested asking Margaret instead. I agreed with the choice, having been impressed with Margaret's character since first meeting her in Scrooby Manor's buttery. She had calmed Brewster's cook, despite being the one who was injured after falling in his hunting forest. Her autopsy sketches were excellent too.

Having given up waiting for Cornelis to find them a suitable printer, she and Matthew were now intending to use the same one as Pastor Smyth. Their book should be ready in the new year.

It was difficult for Isobel and Margaret to visit together without the girls. By the time the day came, I could sit up in bed. However, I remained nervous about the procedure and the implications of what they would find.

Their arrival coincided with a sneezing fit, an inopportune moment. When they were certain it had past, Margaret helped to roll me over while Isobel examined me.

"No marks," she proclaimed.

"Are you certain? I thought they would be there. Could you check again?"

Margaret protested, "I can't hold you like this for long. Doctor Mobley won't be pleased if he learns we've done this."

Isobel released me, "We've finished. There are no marks."

I should have felt relieved, yet as they lowered me back, I struggled to believe their verdict. Having found many other similarities between myself and the murdered men, I expected this to be the same. I was even more puzzled than before.

Additional inconsistencies between the other deaths and my own attack now seemed more significant. Why leave me in a ditch, instead of tying me to the *stilletjes* to ensure certain death? Why take my bible and add my name? Someone might recognise the handwriting. Was the killer growing more careless? If so, I was grateful that this had spared my life.

My thoughts were interrupted. Sophie van Giessen was standing at the door. Occasionally, I had heard her voice in the house before but not seen her. The van Giessens had left my friends to care for me since my arrival.

"Is everything alright?" she asked, "Baxby seems to be recovering well."

I had forgotten Sophie's charming accent and the smell of her perfume.

"Doctor Mobley's very pleased with his progress," my wife replied.

"There's no hurry. He can stay as long as he needs. If you need help at any time, just let us know."

"Thank you. We are managing well. We're fortunate to have lots of friends."

"Indeed."

While they talked about the bread charity, Margaret whispered in my ear, "I need to speak with you, alone."

Isobel had arranged to collect both girls from Mary Brewster, so Margaret could have more time to talk with me. Sophie escorted Isobel out. The van Giessens had still not employed a maid.

48

Margaret wanted to talk about two matters. Hopefully, this would not prove too tiring.

Firstly, she told me the true reason her husband had not been to see me, "Nicholas feels guilty. He should have told you that he saw Julian Felde before he died."

I made her explain this slowly, not believing I had heard her correctly. How could Nicholas have hidden such a thing from me? Margaret waited for me to calm down before continuing.

Nicholas had seen Felde at the Turkish barber's soon after Peter's death, the one on *Marken* island that he had recommended to me.

"Nicholas would be cross if he knew I was here. Felde swore him to secrecy."

"You're right to tell me now."

Temperance suggested the barber to Nicholas. After two weeks at sea, he had wanted to improve his appearance before proposing to Margaret.

"Felde told Nicholas about the job at the Exchange, then said we must visit Cornelis so people would assume it was Cornelis' idea."

At the time, it had seemed strange Nicholas had found the well-paid job when others struggled. I never suspected Felde's involvement.

"Felde said they wanted an intelligent young English-speaker, with the potential to learn Dutch. It was an ideal opportunity. They're pleased with Nicholas' work at the Exchange. He has been beside himself with worry since Felde died."

In Scrooby, Nicholas did not hesitate to share his thoughts with me. I never imagined my former servant could hide his feelings so well, despite keeping secrets of my own.

As Margaret talked, I began to spot similarities between Nicholas Barton and Peter Weekes. Both were ambitious, capable young men, as I had once been. Both were recruited to roles with access to information about influential individuals and international trade, for which governing councils would be willing to pay.

For the first time, I wondered if Felde had arranged Peter's job at the Weighing House too. A poor lad with heretical relations, on the run from the law, would be easy to trap.

Previously, Felde had given me the impression he worked for Cecil on a casual basis in England. What if he was actually a more senior member of the spy team than I realised, enlisting young men like Peter and Nicholas, on either side of the Narrow Sea?

If so, helping Thomas arrange voyages would have provided useful cover, an excuse for travelling back and forth. Generally, Thomas was a good judge of character but not in Felde's case.

When I asked if Nicholas had seen Felde again, Margaret said not, despite visiting the barber regularly.

"Felde's death was a terrible shock to us both. Nicholas has remained loyal. We needed the money from the job to buy our home. We were looking forward to Mabel's birth."

Felde must have died before he had a chance to use Nicholas in the way he intended, making it hard to deduce its true nature.

Nicholas was fortunate to avoid a similar fate to Peter Weekes. The Lemmens misunderstood his relationship with Felde. The spymaster would have extracted a high price in return for preferment. Peter had more worries on his mind than cancer pain.

I asked Margaret to fetch me some drink before continuing. The conversation having affected me personally, I needed time to recover.

Geoffrey had trapped me for years, as Felde had Peter, initially tempting me with tales of adventure and generous meals. After Cadiz, the work deteriorated quickly. Instead of serving Sir Francis Vere at Nieuwpoort, as promised, I was instructed to assist his overworked surgeon instead. On my return, Geoffrey expected me to spy on the Bishop of Lincoln, having switched allegiance to the Church by then.

Ultimately, Peter and I had worked for rival masters, Robert

Cecil and Archbishop Bancroft.

Margaret passed me the cup, "Do you want me to come back another day, Doctor Baxby? This must be hard soon after your attack."

"No, Margaret please go on."

Her second revelation was an even greater surprise.

Margaret had seen more than I realised near the duck pond, "After the boys found your body, I saw Matthew pick up a note. Your attacker removed your bible, rapier and dagger. He left a message tucked in your tunic. The boys must have missed it. Matthew has it now."

"Do you know what was written on the note?"

"It was short so easy to remember. It said *For Gilbert Grey.*"

I left Margaret in no doubt I recognised the name, falling back on the van Giessens' pillows in shock.

She remembered it too, "I met a man with that name before we left Scrooby. He approached me near Mattersey Bridge, when I was returning from visiting my mother."

"You fell over running away. The wound healed well."

"The man said his name was Gilbert Grey. He wanted to see you."

I never expected to hear the name again. After doing my utmost to safeguard my friends, I had pushed memories of Grey to the darkest corners of my mind. Margaret forced me to remember uncomfortable truths which had lain hidden for years.

"Do you remember anything else?" I asked, trying to discern how much I should tell.

"At the time, you asked me if he wore a beaver hat which seemed strange. However, William Brewster told me such a man had been seen acting suspiciously in Gainsborough. Do you know why Gilbert's name was written on the note? Do you think he's here?"

I shook my head. Although I felt sick, I did not want to concern Margaret by asking for a bowl. She did not need to know that dark humours were afflicting my soul.

Pleading tiredness, I thanked her for the visit and told her not to worry about Nicholas. Her information was safe with me.

I did not lie to Margaret but omitted much. As soon as she mentioned the note, there was no doubt in my mind. Leonard Redfern hit me at the duck pond. Despite outwitting him at the Weighing House and hiding near Raphael Barr's home, Bancroft's henchman had tracked me down.

If I had been more alert, I might have paid more attention to serious differences between Weekes' and Felde's deaths and my attack. After Margaret told me about the note, I assumed Redfern killed them on Archbishop Bancroft's behalf, not for religious dissent but because they worked for his rival Cecil. This would explain why more bodies had not been found since.

Of course, a man of Redfern's inferior intelligence was unlikely to devise such a complex method. He was more likely to murder someone with a single, decisive blow, than tie them up and wait for the River Amstel to rise. Fear and guilt were clouding my judgement, alongside ongoing weakness following my attack. Lying in the van Giessens' bed, I held Redfern responsible for all three despicable crimes.

When Matthew next came to visit, I would ask if he had discovered any more clues. Hopefully, this would prompt him to discuss the note he found, without the need for me to implicate Margaret.

However, when Matthew opened the door, I was too stunned to speak. There was a large clue in his hand. He lifted the spade on to the bed. It looked similar to the one Redfern had bought near the *Zuiderkerk* building site, apart from having blood stains on its blade.

"What's that?" I stuttered, foolishly.

"Toby found it on another walk near the duck pond. I think someone hit you with it."

Good Lord! Staring at my intended murder weapon, I found it hard to breathe. Now I knew. Redfern had intended to kill me with it, to avenge Gilbert Grey. He added my name to the list in my bible assuming success, without realising the spade was not decisive in ending Grey's life.

49

London 1613

The printer scratches his head, "This is too confusing, Baxby. I understand Felde recruited Weekes to collect information at the Weighing House. Leonard Redfern must have sailed from England to put a stop to this, but who is Gilbert Grey? And why was a spade significant?"

"Initially, I thought Redfern killed Weekes and Felde, acting on Bancroft's behalf. That was not the case."

The vicar stirs, having managed to listen more since his leg-iron was removed, "Our Lord Bancroft would never sanction such brutality. He should be canonised as an English saint. Where would we be without his authorised King James bible translation and scholarly defence of the Episcopate?"

"Bancroft did not kill either man. I had reasons for wanting to forget Gilbert Grey, but could do so no longer."

The vicar protests, "What are you talking about? Who is Gilbert Grey? I don't understand."

"Neither do I," the printer is equally puzzled.

"When Brewster called me to the buttery to treat Margaret, I pretended I did not know Grey. I did."

The vicar says, "Are you saying Redfern attacked you in Amsterdam, because of something that happened back then?"

"Yes, Redfern had not forgotten what happened at Mattersey Bridge. He came to Amsterdam for revenge. He did not kill Weekes or Felde."

After reminding his listeners of the route through the Manor's hunting forest, which the Scrooby-believers used on the night of their escape, Baxby takes them back to the shameful days when he spied on his friends.

50

Lincolnshire & Nottinghamshire 1607

Although I distrusted Geoffrey during the years I worked for him directly, nevertheless he advanced my career. I would have complained less if I had known who would take his place. When Secretary Sculthorpe promoted Geoffrey, they expected me to report to Leonard Redfern instead.

My new spymaster gradually reduced my responsibilities. He gave my best patients to other members of the team. My previous intelligence about the Bishop of Lincoln and other prominent clerics counted for nothing in his eyes. After I argued back, he demoted me again as a punishment.

Clearly, Redfern wanted to get rid of me. I was not surprised when he found a different role, but was furious he did not explain more. Redfern just ordered me this way or that depending on his current whim.

When he put me on a horse I discovered where I was going. Incredulous, I protested without success. Redfern was sending me back north to spy on my old friends, from the Nottinghamshire village of Scrooby on the Great North Road. The local physician had died recently, creating a vacancy.

Before leaving London, Redfern gave me my contact's name as part of my brief. He expected me to receive instructions and pass intelligence back through a novice called Gilbert Grey. We would only make contact infrequently due to the mission's sensitivity. The radicals of interest spanned both sides of the River Trent, the border between Bancroft's Canterbury province and York where his High Commission Court had no jurisdiction.

Redfern supplied me with a wooden box of ribbons. If I wanted to speak to Grey, I must leave a green piece in a crack in the wall on the Scrooby side of Mattersey Bridge. Likewise, Grey would leave a yellow piece for me to find. Then we would meet on the following Monday, at dusk when the bridge was presumed to be most quiet.

My servant Nicholas did not work on Mondays which made it easier for me to slip away. Unbeknown to Redfern, Nicholas' sweetheart Margaret Deryngton, the Brewsters' maid at Scrooby Manor, did not work on Mondays either. The meeting point was on the route she used to visit her mother.

The first time I met Grey he smelt foul. How could Redfern choose such a lout? Grey carried a rusty shovel, and wore a woollen cap although they were no longer compulsory. Did he not know the law mandating them was repealed in the last century? Gruff and clumsy in his manner, I assumed Grey was a grave digger or common labourer. One Monday, I followed him with the intention of finding out where he lived, eventually losing interest after trekking a mile through bog. I assumed Gilbert Grey was an alias. I never knew his real name.

Redfern made a poor choice from a professional perspective. Grey was unpredictable, a liability from the start. Not content to pass on what he was told, as other intermediaries would do, Grey tried to understand my intelligence himself. His ridiculous questions proved he was ill-qualified for the task.

Pastors Smyth and Robinson were our main targets. Since refusing to sign Bancroft's pledge, they had started leading illegal services of worship at the Old Hall in Gainsborough.

This was not a severe crime in my opinion. Why not chase Catholic priests instead? Some were trained in French and Spanish seminaries, with the purpose of undermining our country. Smyth had been a popular preacher. He developed consumption during a period in gaol, for which I sympathised.

Grey did not understand any of this, despite my patient comparisons of different religious beliefs.

"I listen while the vicar reads the prayer book on Sundays," he yawned, "That's enough for me."

Foolishly, the Monday after I visited the Mobleys' home in Gainsborough, I mentioned Joan Helwys' name to Grey. How could I have been so stupid? Thereafter, the clod-head became preoccupied with her and the Helwys family, rather than Smyth and Robinson.

Incensed, I must have given him sufficient information for Redfern to track her down. Joan was arrested shortly afterwards, a tragic injustice with long term consequences. I never repeated the mistake. It was too late for her and the family.

Grey raged after the Gainsborough-believers fled, "Why didn't you tell me they were leaving the country?"

"I didn't know what they were planning. They barred me and other sympathisers from the business meeting where they made the decision."

"It was your job to know."

William Brewster took precautions. Having worked for a privy councillor before inheriting his father's postmaster position, he understood security matters. Brewster used contacts in London to investigate my background before I arrived.

"You're a useless spy, Baxby. Why are we paying you so much?"

"Redfern was to blame. He crossed Gainsborough square during one of their Separatist meetings. That was the final straw."

"Leonard didn't tell me he did that."

"Of course he didn't *tell you*," I despaired, "Redfern only gives you the bare minimum you need to do your job. You need to prise information *from him*."

"I'm sure Leonard knows what he's doing."

"You need to find out what's really going on, for your own sake and mine. Keep him away from the Separatists. He mustn't scare more away."

Like me, Grey feared Redfern but he trusted him too much.

Increasingly disturbed by the Scrooby assignment and Grey's ineptitude, I reduced my visits to Mattersey Bridge, then ignored the yellow ribbon waiting in its crack. Hopefully, Redfern would be busy with more pressing business in London when Grey complained. I wanted them both to forget me, for as long as possible.

Each night, I opened my box and stared at the green lengths of ribbon, without summoning the courage to confront Grey.

Other matters took precedence as the year progressed. Patients died of famine and plague. Archbishop Bancroft's pursuivants were closing in on the remaining local Separatists, who had by now become my close friends.

I suffered from recurrent nightmares about drowning. Something had to be done.

After Grey identified himself to Margaret Deryngton and asked for me by name, I made up my mind. What was the idiot thinking of? Thank God, Margaret was not seriously hurt.

Brewster was suspicious despite my pleas of ignorance. He asked if Grey was one of my patients. I said no, but agreed to try to find out more. Brewster was satisfied, but for how long?

The confrontation convinced me. None of us would be safe with Grey so close. I could not let Redfern's lackey ruin our lives. It was time to face him.

51

As I trudged through the hunting forest in the drizzle that Monday, I knew it was time. Squirrels scampered up into the treetops. I could not hide forever. My friends' lives were in danger. I needed to protect them. The Scrooby-believers had showed me kindness where others had not. Crackleton was like a brother to me. Pastor Robinson was the kindest man I knew.

The snaking path seemed longer than I remembered. The damp chilled my bones. By the time I reached the river, my fingers were too cold. I dropped the green ribbon, then slipped on the bank retrieving it. Good grief, Baxby. Be careful. Don't make another mistake.

I lingered on the apex of the bridge in case Grey was watching nearby. The swirling waters beneath swept whole branches along. Eventually bored, I returned to my thatched cottage through the rain to wait.

How would Grey react when he found a piece of green ribbon in the mossy crack, after such a long interval? Would he be pleased to meet again or disappointed?

Once I had lit the fire, I could not stop thinking about the ribbon, plus a growing fascination with the topography of the location. Could I catch Grey unawares, on either side of the bridge? Would it be possible to tip a body over by pivoting it on the edge, or alternatively find a way to drag one down to the bank beneath? If so, would it be swept away reliably or tangle in the overhanging trees?

It rained heavily all week. The current would be even stronger by Monday. I did not know if Grey would reappear. If I was lucky, he might have moved on to a different assignment.

The forest path was saturated when I set off again. I tried to avoid the mud by edging through ferns. They seemed twice as large as they were before, soaking my cloak. Rain dripped from my brim and beard.

Despite my qualms, I must not relent. I needed to settle this matter, once and for all.

Gilbert Grey was punctual despite the damp. He was waiting on the far side, scraping mud off his shoes with his spade. Seeing me, he brought it in front of his body like a shield. The light was fading fast.

"Is that you, Baxby? It's been a long time."

"Why did you involve the girl?"

"I needed to attract your attention. It worked. Leonard wants you back in London."

"We need to wait longer. Robinson's still here."

I turned away, as if the matter was decided. Grey ran towards me and pulled my arm, "You're not giving us enough intelligence. Leonard isn't happy."

I shook him off, "He never is."

Grey still smelt bad. His cap provided poor protection from the weather. Strands of wet hair dripped down his face. When he tried to sweep them away with his sleeve, they just fell back.

"No, Leonard *really* isn't happy this time."

"Neither am I. Have you asked him why he visited Gainsborough, scaring my targets?"

"It's not my place to question strategy."

"It's not your place to risk my cover by approaching an innocent girl," I shouted in his face.

Grey stood his ground and laughed, "Why do you protest so much? If she's your trollop, I thought you had better taste."

My anger boiled over. How could Redfern have chosen this witless worm? Although not sharp-witted himself, the spymaster could have found someone with more intelligence than Grey.

As Grey swung his spade, his cap fell off revealing a bulging birthmark on his bald patch. Presumably, this was the reason he always wore it. How stupid to lunge like that. Grey had spent his life digging Nottinghamshire clay, whereas I was a veteran of Cadiz and Nieuwpoort trained by Geoffrey. He should not have challenged me.

As he bent down to pick his cap up, leaning on his spade, Grey's face and clothing changed before my eyes. He was no longer a labourer, but a Spaniard in the Nieuwpoort dunes with a slain soldier-boy at his feet. I had had similar strange experiences since returning from the battle, without hurting anyone on those occasions.

It was easy to pull the spade away from Grey. I hit him with it whilst he was still off balance. When he rose to mock me, I hit him again. His moves were easy to anticipate. He banged his head on the side of the bridge, a blow which could have killed him yet did not.

Lying in its bloody pool, the body became Grey once more. The Nieuwpoort dunes disappeared as quickly as they had come. I leant on the parapet for support, trying to slow my breathing, assessing what to do next.

Was Grey dead? I needed to be sure. If he recovered and told a local constable, I would hang. If he told Redfern, I feared worse.

After wiping the sweat from my palms, I knelt down. Grey was still breathing. I felt the warm against my cheek. I needed to act, quickly.

Whilst working for Geoffrey in London I had bought a stiletto blade. It was hard to find but worth the effort. The shopkeeper's Italian supplier only visited once a year. This was the last one he had. I bought it ahead of a trip to Southwark, knowing it was difficult to wield a rapier blade in the borough's alleys. Once I walked through a cockfight by mistake and had to run for my life.

Stilettos can be hidden out of sight, sometimes for years, then used in a brief propitious moment to deadly effort. They are like spies in that respect. Deniability is a bonus. Mine served me well.

Having checked that no one was coming on either side of the bridge, I pulled Grey's clothing from his left side, and calculated the best angle before plunging the blade in as far as I could. More blood spurted out. His breathing faltered, then stopped. Gilbert Grey was dead.

If my believer-friends injured someone they would feel remorse. Having taken Grey's life, I felt both relieved and anxious. I had killed before, at Cadiz and Nieuwpoort, and might do so again, but here I might be caught.

I pulled the body to a ditch, then collected the teeth I had dislodged and threw them in too. The spade proved useful for shovelling soil on top. Finally, I squeezed it in, and used my hands to add more soil, before smothering everything in greenery.

Although not perfect, the burial would suffice. Rain was already washing the blood from the bridge. It was likely to persist all night.

Every door knock scared me in the following weeks. I refused to walk through the forest alone, expecting Redfern to be waiting there to exert revenge. Gilbert Grey's blemished head returned to haunt me. I ran away if I saw a spade.

When the comet streaked across the sky, I thought I would die. I had no one to blame but myself.

My friends saved me. Without them I would not have survived. Robinson and Crackleton sat and talked with me by Brewster's enormous fire. I even delivered the Brewsters' baby Fear, shortly before we fled from Scrooby.

Grey's body lay undiscovered until then, when William Brewster's son Jonathan stumbled on it under the ice. As the group's physician, I was able to keep everyone away. Pastor Robinson said a prayer and we continued our journey, finally reaching the Red Lion in Boston after several exhausting days.

Grey no longer posed a threat. He did not jeopardise our escape.

52

London 1613

"How deluded to think you could escape English justice by hiding overseas," the vicar scoffs, trying to stand, "Your judges should show no mercy."

The printer agrees that Baxby deserves to be punished, but adds, "I'm sorry it has to end like this. You worked hard to make amends."

"Have you been bewitched by Dutchmen too? Baxby's a bastard, murderer and traitor. I'm ashamed to share this cell with him."

"He persuaded the captain to remove your iron."

"That maybe so, but it's no defence in law. He should be quartered for killing Grey who was keeping this realm safe from Separatist fanatics."

"How can a man of the church be so heartless?"

"How can you dismiss Baxby's abominable crime and ignore the traditions of our nation?"

They argue whilst the bells of St. Peter's Westminster summon Londoners to church.

When the guard brings their next meal, he informs the prisoners, "You won't have to wait much longer. Your trials will take place once the royal wedding celebrations are over."

The vicar grabs the food first, and takes a larger share, before handing bowls to the others.

53

Amsterdam 1610

Matthew saw the tears running down my cheeks as he showed me the spade, "I'm sorry, Baxby. I thought you were well enough to see this."

"It's not your fault, Matthew. I've made many mistakes in my life."

"Please don't blame yourself."

He told me I had woken after he reached the ditch where the boys found me. I had been lying on my side in a few inches of water. Face down, I would have drowned.

"You muttered something about Secretary Sculthorpe and a beaver hat, before falling back into sleep. I made enquiries afterwards. The harbour clerk said a stocky man, with such a hat, boarded a ship for London soon after your disappearance."

Although I could not be certain this was Redfern, I was relieved to hear this news.

"Was that all I said?" I asked.

"Yes, but there was also a note, tucked in your tunic. I didn't want to trouble you by mentioning it before."

Matthew handed me the single sheet, inscribed with the words *For Gilbert Grey.* They were written in the same hand as my name in the bible. Leonard Redfern must have written both.

"I don't know anyone called Grey," Matthew said, "But fear your attacker may have been an agent of the Bancroft's High Commission in London. We think the court still has active arrest warrants for Thomas, Robinson and Brewster, but seems to be targeting younger professional men."

"They didn't succeed in my case."

"Baxby, I'm sorry. I've been a fool. Memories of Eunice's last hours clouded my judgement. Peter Weekes did not commit suicide, despite the cancer. He was attacked, as you were. Neither of you deserved to suffer."

I found it hard to sleep. My throat tightened in the night. I sensed Archbishop Bancroft's hand, reaching across the Narrow Sea and crushing the life from me. Those keeping vigil said I called out Sculthorpe, Geoffrey and Redfern's names.

Ultimately, I knew I could not blame anyone else for Gilbert Grey's death. I hit him with his spade and spiked him with the stiletto. Redfern had tried to exert revenge by killing me in the same way. If he had known about the tiny blade, I would not be alive now.

Despite feeling battered and bruised, I kept exercising as Matthew prescribed. Redfern did not defeat me. He made me more determined. Anger helped to fuel my recovery. I battled invisible enemies, willing my legs to move.

Slowly, I managed enough steps to look out the window for the first time. The workmen had finished building two sections of bastion wall. Windmills pumped water to drain new canals. Amsterdam was growing. Soon there would be more canal houses, pavements and bridges.

As the sun dipped below the horizon, I cried again.

Matthew brought a copy of his anatomy book to show me. Margaret's pictures were impressively detailed. The printer had done a good job. Hopefully, this book would help other physicians understand cancer better.

Matthew told me more about Pastor Smyth's book too. He had been intending to call his *The False Constitution of the Church,* but was now considering *The Character of the Beast* which might attract more readers. Many are fascinated by the apocalyptic imagery in the Book of Revelation.

"People should read his book whatever the title. Smyth's as talented as any member of Bancroft's bible translation committee."

"They'll be shocked if they open it, Baxby. Smyth's advocating believers' baptism, rather than the infant kind."

When Isobel told me Thomas Helwys was also writing a book, I was sceptical at first. Pastors Smyth and Robinson were ex-clergymen, who studied Hebrew and Greek at Cambridge

University. Thomas was a lawyer, albeit an accomplished one.

Isobel was with Thomas when he brought some pages to show me, exclaiming, "I've found the key, at last. The first line of our covenant unlocks the truth. *We are the Lord's free people*."

"God created us *free*, to find faith for *ourselves*," Isobel agreed, "No one else can decide on our behalf, not even the King, however godly he may be."

Calmly, Thomas read more sentences.

For we do freely profess that our lord the king has no more power over their consciences than over ours, and that is none at all. For our lord the king is but an earthly king, and he has no authority as a king but in earthly causes

Isobel enthused, "A king doesn't have *spiritual* authority over his subjects. He can't create true faith, melt a heart in repentance or reform it with love. We must each decide for ourselves."

"I don't believe King James and his bishops think of religion in those terms. They don't even tolerate the most harmless Puritan ideas."

"That's why Thomas is writing this book."

The theological debate in the Republic had grown more heated since my attack. Vorstius' Arminian supporters had published *Five Articles of Remonstrance* detailing points on which they disagreed with orthodox Calvinist Reformers. Every day more pamphlets appeared, arguing for each side.

Pleased with my progress, Matthew decided I could return home once I could climb a few stairs. Although nervous Redfern might return, I longed to curl up with Isobel and Grace Jane. My heart dared to believe it was possible again. After being confined to that room for so long, canal houses had lost their appeal.

I pondered Thomas' assertions while I practised walking. If a man's religion was solely between himself and God, was there hope for someone like me? I would never be godly like Temperance and other predestined members of Paget's church, yet God had rescued me when I cried out in the storm.

191

Isobel started tidying up, ready for my move. She brought a cloak, and another paragraph from Thomas' book whose contents worried me more.

For men's religion is between God and themselves. The king shall not answer for it. Neither may the king be judge between God and man. Let them be heretics, Turks, Jews, or whatsoevers, it appertains not to the earthly power to punish them in the least measure

"Heaven help us, Isobel. Thomas is asking too much. He wants freedom for Jews and Turks, not just Independents like us."

"And Roman Catholic heretics," she added, "Isn't Thomas amazing? He plans to present his book to King James."

We were used to living amongst immigrants with different beliefs. King James had never visited Amsterdam to my knowledge. He would not approve. Archbishop Bancroft might burn such a book before letting him read it. Even if Thomas smuggled a few copies into the country, pursuivants would hunt their owners down.

"Thomas will call his book *A Short Declaration of The Mystery of Iniquity*. Iniquity dulls men's minds and clouds their judgement. He's explaining prophecy about the Last Days too, which should prove popular."

54

On the last occasion Matthew visited, he helped solve another mystery. He had bought a book about herbs and medicines from a shop near Dam Square. It listed toxins which witches use to paralyse victims, or make them believe they are more powerful than they really are, without actually killing them.

"Could these poisons be purchased in Amsterdam?"

"Probably, or made from toads and other local ingredients. Someone could have inserted Henbane or Mandray in Peter Weekes and Julian Felde."

Since watching Macbeth at the Globe many years before, I had been intrigued by witches' powers. Could one have inserted such a substance into the men's buttocks, whilst chanting a magic spell?

The van Giessens rarely came to my room during my stay, preferring to leave my care to my friends. Once I had asked to see Cornilis to thank him personally. Fortunately, he refused to take any payment. Although Isobel and Toby were continuing to make and sell ointment, there was little money to spare. In contrast, Cornelis' girth continued to increase.

Occasionally, Sophie would enter my room to replenish my drink or water flowers. Drenched in perfume, she smelt more fragrant than any in the vase, and rarely wore the same gown twice.

Despite the family's considerable wealth, they still chose not to share their home with a maid. Often, I heard them arguing with each other on the lower floors.

Above me in the loft, the workmen moving chests kept their voices low. I could not hear what they said.

One night the voices were louder. A dispute had broken out. I heard a loud thud, which sounded like a chest falling from a height, before the steady click of the winch.

No friend was keeping watch that night, as John Murton was

marrying Jenne Hodgkin. I had told them I would be alright on my own. After all, Matthew predicted I would be well enough to go home soon.

I levered myself out of bed carefully. It was harder to balance in the dark. Keeping my fingertips in contact with the wall, I made my way to the window without incident.

Against the starry backdrop, I could see a chest being raised on the rope. Watching it swaying in the wind, I was concerned it might drop. Cornelis' men were winching it past my window to the loft above. I opened the window slightly, making it easier to hear what they were discussing as they worked.

Cornelis' men were discussing their schedule in Spanish, a surprising development indeed. I had thought I heard the language once before in the house, when Sophie was saying goodbye to a man I did not recognise. I could have been mistaken, though. They had only exchanged a few words. This was a lengthy conversation between several participants.

Strangers were conversing in our former enemy's language, a few feet above my head.

What could this mean? Cornelis was unlikely to employ Sephardic Jews. Jan Munter told me he was originally Flemish. Could they have come from there?

I waited, too apprehensive to sleep.

Once convinced the loft was empty again, I took a few hesitant steps towards the door. I had not left the room in months. Matthew would not approve of me trying the stairs alone, but I wanted to find out what was going on.

The top flight was the narrowest and steepest. The treads were worn and slippery. At times it was easier to use my hands and knees, rather than trying to walk.

I rested on the tiny landing where once I paused before Peter's autopsy. Younger and more able-bodied then, I had reached the top before Margaret and Matthew. Now they would beat me easily.

The door seemed stiffer and heavier. I feared the creaking hinges might wake someone on the lower floors, but no one came. The room was quiet, deserted as I had discerned.

NAMING THE DEAD

By now the moon was high enough to shine weak light through the loft window. There were more chests than before, stacked around the central table. Otherwise, the room was bare. I tried to lever the lid off the first with partial success. By balancing it on the furthest edge, I revealed the astonishing contents.

The chest was full of pamphlets, not goods the VOC typically traded. It was too dark to read them properly, but all appeared to be the same. I kept one, then carefully replaced the lid, before moving to the next chest.

I looked inside six in total, ostensibly the same. Although nervous about descending the stairway again, it would have been wiser to return to bed sooner. However, I was glad I looked.

Five chests contained seemingly identical tracts. I dropped the lid of the sixth in shock. It contained a weapon I never expected to see again. Praying no one had heard the noise, I stared in astonishment. Even in the poor light, there was no doubt. The chest held Felde's beloved rapier, lying in its sheath on straw.

Felde was proud of his blade, regularly demonstrating its flexibility and strength for others to admire. He had threatened me with it in the past. It was considerably more expensive than my own, which was still missing along with my dagger.

I lifted the rapier out. How light it felt. I never expected to hold this beauty in my hand. Had one of Cornelis men found it? Why was it here?

Felde would never have lost his rapier, or intentionally left it behind. I shuddered, as another scenario came to mind. Someone had stolen it from him, possibly in this house. Could I steal it from them? It was too big to hide under my nightshirt. If Cornelis found it in my room, what defence could I make? Likewise, if someone found me with it in the loft.

I needed to return to bed. The Spanish speakers could reappear at any time. I replaced the rapier in its chest and headed down.

The stairs were dark and dangerous to descend. I moved slowly. Not only would I alert the household if I fell, I would delay my departure needlessly. With only a few steps left, I heard a noise below.

Someone was ascending the lower flights towards me. Could I get back to my room in time? Although I could not see her, I smelt her perfume. Sophie was coming up from the floor below. She reached my door first, and leant on the handle barring my entrance to the room.

Sophie was wearing a night coat, with a line of ties down the front. Her candle illuminated the low neckline. My first thoughts were inappropriate, a sign of recovery.

She smiled, "I heard something. Were you walking in your sleep?"

A woman of her intelligence was unlikely to be fooled. Nevertheless, I pretended she had woken me.

"Come now, Doctor Baxby. Let me help you back to bed."

I refused her invitation, knowing how easy it would be to be seduced in such circumstances. When Agnes was my landlady, she welcomed me to her bed, but neither of us was married at the time, and I loved Isobel now.

What a relief to collapse back on my mattress. How tired I felt.

"Let me know if there's anything you need."

Sophie left the candle on the table before returning downstairs.

55

When I stirred the candle had burnt out. Given the light from the window, it was nearly dawn.

Amalia was sitting on the chair to my right, where my friends had kept vigil. Her flute was in her hand. Sophie was to my left by the table. She had changed into her blue silk gown.

"Amalia has come to play for you."

They gave me no choice. Nevertheless, the music was soothing. Turning my head towards Amalia, I could easily have fallen back asleep, but sensed a movement just in time. Although it made no difference to my fate, witnessing the deft procedure solved a mystery at last.

Sophie was standing over me wearing gloves, wielding a needle which she had dipped in the open bottle on the table next to her. There was no way to avoid it. She grabbed the nearest arm to roll me to face Amalia, immobilising the other one beneath me in the process, obviously an accomplished practitioner.

I cried out in agony as I felt excruciating pain in my buttock. How easily this woman fooled me. What an indignity! Although considerably more attractive than Shakespeare's witches, Sophie was equally devilish.

As the pain subsided, I remembered the marks on Weekes and Felde. Sophie must have administered three doses to immobilise one and four the other. I could no longer recall which was which. My mind was becoming confused. The poison was taking effect. Whatever else happened, I must avoid a second injection.

The sun was higher in the sky when I saw Cornelis sitting in the chair. Although his lips were moving, I could not hear anything. I must try to regain my senses, but how?

Once I could count to eight, I heard him say, "I don't know how you could be so stupid, Sophie. Why did you do this today? You know I have a meeting at the Town Hall, which may finish late."

"Baxby visited the loft."

"I don't believe you. He wasn't well enough."

"It's time you trusted me."

"Give him another needle. I'll try before I leave."

Cornelis wanted to converse with me. What about? Had he talked with Weekes and Felde, before transporting their paralysed bodies to the Blue Bridge? Amalia had disappeared. Sophie moved towards the table.

The pain was less the second time, and brought me to my senses for long enough to hear Cornelis' demands, "Who is directing English operations in Amsterdam? Winwood would never trust Roseberry, Bowden or Tibbs. Tell me, who is in charge?"

Geoffrey taught me to remain silent if questioned, never to confirm or deny. However, in this case I had no answer to give. I was too confused to know what Cornelis was referring to.

Was this accursed form of torture connected to the pamphlets in his loft, or the result of a misunderstanding? I was terrified, knowing what happened to Weekes and Felde. I must not give up.

Cornelis instructed his wife, "Prepare a third one, ready for when I return. Whatever the hour, I will persuade him then."

I doubted I would be able to respond after another dose. This was an effective threat. Somehow, I must stay alive.

When I opened my eyes again Sophie had gone. She had left me on my own. The room was tilting back and forth gently, like the deck of a ship in a mild sea. I could only count to five. A herring gull screeched outside.

Why was Geoffrey sitting in the chair? He should be in England, with Bancroft and Sculthorpe. I prayed neither of them appeared.

Geoffrey's hair was streaked with silver. The last time I saw him it had been lighter. I was hallucinating, imagining my former spymaster as a younger man. Witches' poison affects victims in stranger ways than those listed in Matthew's book.

After smoothing his moustache from the centre to the edges, as was his habit in England, Geoffrey echoed words I remembered from my youth, before my apprenticeship, "This is a wonderful opportunity, Baxby. You should be more thankful. You need to work hard."

Geoffrey helped me understand. I spotted the similarities. Cornelis was interested in covert English operations because he was a spymaster too. He sought intelligence on his rivals, as any spymaster would.

However, I was not a naive young man any more. Redfern's attack had changed me. Riches had lost their allure too. I wanted to go home to Isobel, alive. Nothing else mattered more.

I could count to twenty, twenty-five, maybe more. This was my best chance to escape. It was too painful to put weight on my left buttock. I had to turn towards the chair.

"Hurry up," surprisingly Geoffrey encouraged me, "Sophie will return soon. You must go now."

Isobel had already taken most of my possessions. I grabbed the cloak and the pamphlet I had found in the loft. Fortunately, the van Giessens had not noticed the pamphlet while debilitating me.

Raphael's sweets helped. I stuffed three in my mouth before proceeding towards the door.

If only I had trusted my intuition about the house. Whether Weekes had fallen for Cornelis' promises or Sophie's guile, I should have spotted clues long ago. His death could not have been achieved by a single perpetrator, even an experienced one like Redfern. He would have needed accomplices to lower the body down from the bridge. Also, Redfern was too ham-fisted to hold a needle.

Cornelis owned a cart, one of the few in the city. It would not have been possible to transport the body by boat in such weather. I should have realised before.

Hearing voices arguing below, I aborted my original plan to head down towards the ground floor. Having no sense of time since being drugged, I did not know how long it had been since I last climbed to the loft. This time I kept counting as I made my way up. Forty-one, forty-two, my faculties were improving.

Again, the door creaked opened to reveal the cramped space. There was no sign that anyone had been there since my last visit.

I lifted Felde's rapier from the straw, and fastened the sheath around my waist beneath my cloak. If I had to defend myself, I would have the advantage of surprise. Although unlikely to wield the weapon proficiently in my current state, I would do my best if threatened.

However, I had a more immediate problem. The rope was the only way down. I inched open a loft door and peered out, keeping a sensible distance from the edge. The sun would set soon, beyond the new bastion walls.

It was a long way to fall. Could I take such a risk? Yes, I must. I desperately wanted to live. Hitting the canal pavement would be better than waiting for the River Amstel to rise sufficiently to drown me. Others would have the satisfaction of knowing I had tried.

I let the winch drum turn slowly, releasing the rope to its full length. It made its familiar clicking sound. I heard another noise whilst securing the mechanism. Someone had opened the door and entered the room behind me.

Unsheathing the rapier as I turned, I prepared to confront the intruder and kill him quickly. No one would stop me now.

56

Sophie van Giessen was standing before me with her arms raised above her head. Steadier on my feet than I had expected, and relieved by the absence of the needle, I lowered the rapier to my side. Thank God, it was not Cornelis or one of his men. The hem of her night coat revealed shapely ankles, "Forgive me, Baxby. I surrender. Please take me with you. I cannot bear to live here another day."

Did Sophie take me for a fool? Or think the drug was affecting my judgement more than was the case? Of course, I did not trust this enchantress.

She tilted her head to the side, and looked up into my eyes, "Cornelis made me do it. It was his idea. He is a tyrant in this house. My husband presents a jovial disposition to those outside the family, but terrorises Amalia and me."

Sophie was a good actress. In other circumstances, I might have been beguiled by the heartfelt pleas of a comely woman, but whatever the nature of her marriage, Sophie should have showed more remorse.

"Did you inject Peter with the same toxin?"

"Yes, Cornelis told me to lure him here which was cruel. The poor lad's wife wasn't interested in consummating their relationship, and he was clearly in pain."

The family had lived a lie in their beautiful home. The affability, gifts and portrait obscured a deadly pact. If the van Giessens had employed a maid, she would have seen them for what they were.

"Did you help Cornelis move Peter to the Amstel?"

"Yes, and Felde too. Felde came here asking questions, suspicious after Peter's death. In my defence I tried to refuse. Ultimately, I had no choice. You have no idea what it's like to be a woman married to such a beast."

Allowing us to conduct Peter's autopsy in the same house seemed particularly brazen. Sophie had not protested then.

"Why, Sophie? Did Cornelis torture them for information too?"

"My husband has been indebted to Spanish masters since first arriving in Amsterdam. They loaned him the money for his first investment, from which all this stems."

She tapped the nearest lid to emphasise her point, "Without their money we'd be as poor as any bread charity customer."

"Cornelis is a Spanish spy?"

"He hasn't spied on anyone personally for years. He makes others do his bidding now. Cornelis wants to know who runs the equivalent English enterprise. He can't bear to be outwitted. I think he's jealous."

It would have been hard to believe such a seemingly respectable burgher could be living a double life, if he had not menaced me. Was this what I would have become, if I had not escaped from Geoffrey? Or Felde or Weekes in Amsterdam?

Cornelis had tortured and killed, without a splinter of guilt or shame, devising novel forms of cruelty and terrorising family members. One lie begets another, then a third, the original sin polluting everything in its wake.

Although I was intrigued to learn more, every second of delay increased my likelihood of capture. Cornelis would be returning from his meeting soon.

Sophie pleaded with me again, "Don't leave me, Baxby. I reduced your dose, and deliberately chose a time when I knew my husband was going out. I've saved your life."

It did not feel like that.

Mistress van Giessen was a hard woman to gauge, the only French one I knew. According to Isobel, Dunkirker pirates had killed her Huguenot parents on their voyage to Rotterdam. Sophie was younger than my wife. The two women worked well together distributing bread. However, that did not mean I should take her with me now.

Geoffrey stepped out of the shadows to emphasise the point, "Go Baxby. Go now. Barricade her outside the door."

Sophie did not see or hear him. Geoffrey was not really there in the loft. My mind was tricking me again, proof of the poison's ongoing potency.

Sophie did not protest when I gripped her arm to force her back to the landing, then made no sound after I pushed chests against the door. There was no way of knowing if she had gone back downstairs to raise the alarm. It was time to leave.

After pulling the rope to test it was secure, I stepped out. It took enormous courage to go over the edge. The house was six storeys high. I dare not look down for long, nor admire the extensive view beyond the city walls.

Leaning out at a preposterous angle, I prayed my arms would be strong enough to keep hold, and my nerves would not falter.

Having spent so long indoors, I failed to anticipate the strength of the wind. This high up there was nothing to block its path from the Narrow Sea. The Dutch used windmills for good reason. If my flapping cloak caught on one of the plaster decorations protruding from the building, I might still be stuck there when Cornelis returned home. Alternatively, the Night Watch might spot me and sound the alert.

Moving one hand over the other slowly, I took my first tentative steps down the red-brick wall. Already perspiring and tired, I found it hard to breathe. When I lost count, I did not know if it was due to fear or the poison seeping through my veins.

If Sophie looked out, I did not notice. Although her desperate pleas had touched my heart, I could not trust a woman who stuck a poisoned needle in my backside, regardless of the amount. Sophie and Amalia could be descending the stairs even now, ready to confront me on the pavement or watch my fatal fall.

Hopefully, the chests would bar anyone entering the loft. My life depended on the winch, over which I had no control.

My bedroom window was the first obstacle. How could I manoeuvre around the ledge? I achieved this by twisting my body, but the rope began to sway, a little at first, then more alarmingly. A human pendulum might amuse casual onlookers. This could end catastrophically for me.

With enormous effort, I managed to reduce the movement by hooking my foot on the next sill down. I was grateful for the short rest. My head was spinning, disconcertingly. It was a long, long way down.

I wished I had eaten another of Raphael's sweets before descending. It was too late now. I must concentrate. The alternative was too awful to contemplate.

"Baxby, keep counting," I told myself out loud.

Three more storeys. Two more storeys. The ground was coming towards me. I was exhausted. The rope burned my fingers and palms. Slipping would be unbearable, not quite close enough.

As a young man sailing to Cadiz with Geoffrey, and later whilst working for sweet wine merchants, I had watched apprentices climb the ropes with awe. The youngest were sent the highest. One rat fell to his death on the deck near the Brittany coast, his body tossed overboard. Most returned stronger, more resolute to face whatever befell. Hardened sailors faced storms and other perils at sea, which would destroy weaker men.

Would I manage to hold on, until the end? My courage was being tested, unlike any time before.

The temptation to give up came as a bittersweet surprise. My body ached. I wanted the ordeal to end. Why bother? We must all die one day. You are the bastard son of a peasant girl, who killed Gilbert Grey on Mattersey Bridge thinking you were at Nieuwpoort. Murderers cannot be part of God's Elect. You will never be good enough to go to heaven, however much you try.

Paget knew.

Whom he predestined he also called, and whom he called he also justified, and whom he justified he also glorified

Pastor Robinson was convinced.

Salvation comes from the Lord

What hope was there for me? The Devil takes his own.

57

The first-floor window appeared, followed by the front door lintel. Sophie was not standing on the steps watching me. There were no other onlookers on the canal pavement. Keep counting, Baxby. Nearly there.

My legs buckled as I touched the ground. What a momentous descent, an ordeal I never wished to repeat. My body felt as if it would never move again. I had to get away before Cornelis returned. Thank God, he was at his meeting, but this was taking too long. Slowly, I pulled myself up on a plant pot. Which way should I go?

My initial instinct was to head north and follow the *Achterburgwal* canal to the harbour. It was not far to the *Haringpakker* tower. Once there, I might find a ship bound for England, thus putting safe distance between me and my murderous host.

However, Amsterdam was my home now whatever the current threat. I longed to see Isobel and Grace Jane again. I loved them more than anything else, save life itself. There must be somewhere to hide locally.

With renewed determination I turned south, taking the route Matthew, Margaret and I had used after we performed Peter's autopsy. How grateful we were for Cornelis' generosity back then, never realising we were returning Peter to the scene of his defeat. Cornelis could have even used the same chest to transport his body.

Matthew had blamed himself for not heeding his cancerous patient's concerns, whereas in reality, his murderer and accomplice were sipping wine five storeys below us at the time.

Having come close to death at Cornelis' hands, I was even more incensed than before by the great injustice. If Sophie had told the truth, Peter Weekes and Julian Felde must have suffered far more than me, even before they left the house.

I was surprised by the intensity of the emotions I felt shuffling along the canal pavement. It had been a long time since I last walked there, admiring the attractive bridges and grand frontages. There were more pots of bulbs than the previous spring, or perhaps I was just too busy to notice back then. Although bent by each gust of wind, the little flowers always returned to their full height.

Being straight and wide enough for a cart, the *Achterburgwal* pavement provided little cover for a fugitive. Cornelis could emerge at any point along its length and spot me instantly.

Some of the adjoining alleyways were blind. I had to find the right one. Temperance's map had been a godsend before. Now the poison was impairing my mind.

Geoffrey was standing at a corner, a few yards in front of me. Strangely, I was no longer troubled by the sight. He suggested I eat another sweet, somehow knowing I had brought more from the house, before pointing to the familiar shape of the New Church spire. Geoffrey showed me the best way to go.

How amazing that after years of resentment and anger at the way Geoffrey had taken advantage of my youth to manipulate me, the poison conjured him to help me. Why not a guardian angel or someone I respected? Only witches understand how their spells work.

After I turned, I heard a whistle behind me followed by shouts and barks. Cornelis must have returned home and raised the Watch. They were coming for me.

Could I move faster? My legs ached. I edged my way past the New Church, knowing it was unwise to cross open ground. Panicking, I found myself outside the old Holy Place which once housed miraculous Catholic communion bread. Holy Mother of God, I needed a miracle now.

Begijnhof's drawbridge was moving. I recognised the sound. Could I get there in time to lose my pursuers? Would the island be a good place to hide?

"Wait!" I called to Smeets, who recognised my voice immediately, having often talked with me when I visited Eva. He knew Edwin too, and presumably Toby now he fetched her shopping instead.

Smeets stopped winding and waved. I knew I must ignore him, and concentrate on the arm. As it slowed, I tossed Felde's rapier across the gap. It was hard to part with it, but I could have injured myself otherwise. It slid down, out of sight. The weapon was safe. I was still in mortal danger.

By now, Smeets had heard shouting too. My pursuers were close. I waited, judging the best moment to hurl myself across. Unable to swim, I would have drowned if I fell in. Instead, I felt the edge of the arm cut into my stomach. It winded me but I did not care. I was alive, albeit balanced precariously.

Smeets knew what to do.

"Open it! Open it!" I yelled.

He was already winding furiously.

With enormous effort, I pulled myself up sufficiently to tip over and rolled down the far side. My head spun. Every bone in my body ached. I bruised my knees and elbows. My buttock still stung.

Coming to rest in a puddle, I prayed. Jesus Christ! Mother Mary! Luther! SinterKlaas! In that moment, I did not care who answered. I just wanted to survive.

In truth, many friends had helped me already. Where would I have been without Isobel, Agnes, or Matthew's medical knowledge? Although Crackleton annoyed me at times, our relationship had been significant. Likewise, I appreciated Thomas Helwys, William Brewster, and the pastors' wisdom and encouragement.

Now, there was another saviour in my life. Winchman Smeets was remonstrating with Cornelis and the Watch.

"I raise it every night, my last task of the day."

"No, I can't relower it this late. The residents would complain."

"I saw a man in a cloak, heading towards the *Munt* gate. He may be the one you're looking for."

They could not see me from their side.

Tears of relief and exhaustion streamed down my cheeks once

they had gone. I could rest at last, as safe as a defender in a castle with the drawbridge raised.

Smeets was delighted to see me, having previously heard about my attack. The poor man needed to rest himself, yet listened to my garbled story without noticeable impatience. Despite omitting the poison and Sophie's role, I am not certain he believed every detail.

After helping me up, Smeets passed Felde's sword back, "This is a beautiful weapon. Having solved troubling mysteries, you should be allowed to keep it. Cornelis van Giessen must be brought to trial. However rich and powerful he is, those Englishmen deserve justice."

I assumed I would need to stay hidden until then.

My escape answered another outstanding question. It proved I had recovered from Redfern's injuries. Matthew had wanted me to climb a few stairs before returning home, whereas I had scaled a steep flight twice, descended the outside of a building and leapt across the *Begijnhof* channel. Although I felt I would never move again as I stood there soaking wet, my recovery was complete.

58

Smeets said he would delay relowering the bridge for a few hours in the morning. I would be safe until then. He wanted to take me to the convent in the corner of the courtyard, claiming the nuns would be happy to give me a bed for the night, "They'll be taking their evening walk soon. We could talk with them then."

I stepped away in horror. Why would the winchman suggest such a thing? Having just escaped from Cornelis I did not want to be apprehended by Papists.

The first black-clad women emerged from their door, followed by more, until a whole conventicle of nuns walked back and forth across the courtyard, in twos and threes, with their heads bowed. If Smeets had not warned me, I might have assumed I was hallucinating again. He did not seem alarmed.

Some nuns moved more easily than others, but it was impossible to guess their ages. They all dressed alike. Embarrassed by my own scant clothing, I pulled my cloak across my legs.

In the year after the Gunpowder Plot, I watched the death of a co-conspiring priest who was hanged, drawn and quartered at St. Paul's Cross. Despite admiring his courage, I drew the same conclusion as everyone else. Anyone who fell for Papist lies would suffer a similar fate.

Did *Begijnhof's* Protestants not realise? How could they tolerate these heretics in their midst?

Smeets was persistent, "What are you afraid of, Baxby? My uncle was grateful for a blessing shortly before he died. Saint Gianna helped my wife in labour."

"They'll bewitch me with Latin spells, make me kiss relics and worship the Pope."

Cornelis had sold his soul to the Spanish. Once obligated, he could never escape. Smeets might think the convent a good place to hide. How could an Englishman like me trust Catholics?

The nuns were turning back, converging on the corner from

whence they came. Smeets tried to prompt me once more. It was too late. The door had shut.

Next Smeets suggested I try Paget's chapel, "There are side rooms where you could hide, or the Reverend might let you stay with him."

After climbing the steps to the big double doors, he was disappointed to find them locked. I was relieved. It was not just Paget's long sermons and certainty that bothered me. Sometimes, he seemed to enjoy the notion that he and his members were predestined for heaven whilst the rest of us would descend to hell. Offering hospitality to a reprobate like me, could merely increase his own sense of superiority.

Although Calvinists attributed the doctrine of Election to God's grace, preselection seemed cruel to me. It would be fairer if everyone was offered the same opportunity, regardless of their background.

However, I had a more immediate concern. I needed to find somewhere to sleep before the light failed.

Eva Witte had always been pleased to see me before. She was grateful for the way I had encouraged her to walk. Eva would not make me feel guilty or inadequate.

Was it too late to call on an elderly lady? Smeets encouraged me to knock. Hearing no response, I called out, "Eva, it's me, Baxby."

"The door is open, come in," came the familiar reply.

Although surprised, she did not hesitate to welcome me. Having heard about my attack from Toby, she saw my escape as an answer to her prayers.

That night, I slept in Eva's second room. Although less comfortable than the one in Cornelis' home, the bed was a welcome sanctuary nevertheless. I slept with Jane's bible and Felde's sword under my pillow.

In England Anabaptists were seen as inferior, not just in religious terms. Wealth and respectability gave other dissenting groups an advantage. Catholic noblemen might hide a priest in a palace or castle to conduct mass. City merchants could support a Puritan preacher through generous giving. Conversely, Anabaptists were predominantly poor. Excluded elsewhere, they appreciated belonging to the sect.

Despite her limitations, Eva was happy with her life. She had returned to helping her neighbours since her walking improved. They enjoyed each other's company. If I survived this experience, I vowed to be more grateful for what I had, like her.

During breakfast we heard Smeets shouting to those waiting to cross from the far bank. My fate would be decided when the bridge reopened.

Peeping out from behind Eva's curtains, I saw a queue forming outside. *Begijnhof's* residents were quieter, waiting patiently to cross.

Cornelis would be angered by the delay. He was used to getting his own way, both at home and in his business dealings. However, he had not obtained the information he wanted from me, namely who was in charge of Sir Ralph Winwood's operations in Amsterdam. The subject interested me too.

Clearly, Weekes and Felde had worked for a higher authority, someone who could arrange lucrative work at the Weighing House and Exchange. Cornelis had ruled out Roseberry, Bowland and Tibbs, but made the mistake of assuming I worked for the same boss. Who could he be?

Also, I still did not know the significance of the pamphlets in Cornelis' loft, or why some had been posthumously accredited to Weekes and Felde. Eva refused to have pamphlets in her home, without knowing I had brought one with me.

I did not tell her about Cornelis' longstanding allegiance to Spain, not wanting to scare her unnecessarily. The former occupying power had murdered her parents and countless other Anabaptists. However, I accepted her offer of prayer, nervous about what would happen when Smeets relowered the bridge.

59

As I watched from behind Eva's curtain, Temperance Knowsley emerged from the direction of the bridge. She must have been amongst the first to cross when Smeets lowered it, ahead of Cornelis. Obviously preparing the chapel for a service, she was carrying flowers.

Like me, Temperance had been convinced that Weekes and Felde were murdered. She wanted to organise funerals for both. Would she have demanded to supervise mine in a similar way, another Englishman?

On the day I arrived, Temperance had questioned my nationality and foolish boasts. She had since taught me Dutch, and let Isobel and me sleep beneath her roof. I was keen to share what I had discovered with her, but not now.

She put the flowers down to unlock the chapel door, before disappearing inside.

Cornelis arrived soon afterwards, carrying a pistol and sword, mercifully alone, "Get out of my way imbeciles."

The queue of timid residents scattered to clear his path, before reforming to watch what happened next. Whatever evil he accomplished, there would be multiple witnesses this time.

Instinctively, I moved behind the curtain to unsheathe Felde's blade. Eva was praying for safety throughout.

Cornelis did not call my name nor hammer on doors. Instead, he ambled towards the chapel and tripped on the bottom step. His curses attracted more onlookers as he struggled to stand.

Had the belligerent been drinking? If so, it might be easier to overcome him than I had feared. However, this did not prove necessary. By the time Temperance reappeared in the doorway, he had slumped on the ground. After failing to revive him, she called others across to help, without staying to assist herself.

As I watched them carry Cornelis away, I was reminded of my own confused state after Sophie injected the poison. Could she have stuck a needle in her husband too, enough to debilitate him? If so, I would never tell. Sophie's secret was safe with me.

NAMING THE DEAD

Eva was relieved when I put the rapier down. Her scar reddened when she was cross. Despite objecting to the weapon's presence in her home, she was adamant I could stay as long as I wished.

Toby was due to bring her shopping in a couple of days. He could let Isobel know where I was. We could communicate through the lad.

For all I knew, Cornelis might have already visited our home or the bakehouse, fawning concern for my well-being or making me the villain in a preposterous fraudulent tale. Would they be fooled by his disarming style? Hopefully, not for long.

Toby was delighted to see me when he brought Eva's shopping. I was surprised by how much he had grown. He was lean as well as tall. His hair had darkened more.

Agnes' nephew was young enough not to attract attention, yet old enough to understand the gravity of his task. He proved a perfect intermediary, well suited to undercover work. If I had thought he was in serious danger, I would have stopped immediately.

Using invisible ink, I wrote a letter on the back of Eva's shopping list, instructing Toby to destroy it once read. Thomas used cyphers when communicating with sympathisers in England. We had to rely on lemon juice.

During the weeks I stayed with Eva, Toby passed messages back and forth. He brought items of clothing for me, sometimes wearing them under his own. I learnt Grace Jane was crawling. Margaret was expecting a second child. Raphael Barr sent more sweets.

In contrast to her aversion to Felde's sword, Eva was fascinated by my little bible from Jane, especially after learning Jane had been an Anabaptist, "Too many have died. People make the Christian faith more complicated than it needs to be. Elaborate sacraments, eloquent sermons and precious art can obscure the basic truth. Jesus lived, died and rose again without any such embellishments."

When she spotted the names at the back of the book, Eva wanted to know who the people were and why they were there. I was reluctant to tell her at first. Geoffrey had taught me to refrain from divulging more details than necessary. It had always been easier to say less rather than more, yet with Eva the words flowed from my lips.

Each life, and death, on the list was unique. Talking about them in turn gave them the honour they deserved. We had shared joys and sorrows together, laughed and cried.

Eva was good at listening. She did not interrupt, nor suggest theories of her own. Instead, she posed thoughtful questions which helped me untangle my feelings as I spoke. Saying why others mattered to me, revealed a lot about myself.

When we reached more recent names, Eva recalled her own fond memories of Peter's visits to her home. I shared recollections of his family in Lincolnshire, yet found it hard to summarise his later years. Peter had hidden his Catholic roots and subsequent motivations.

Who helped him obtain his job at the Weighing House? Did he discover Cornelis was working for Spain whilst there, and foolishly confront him? Whatever transpired, it was sufficient grounds for the burgher to want him dead.

Cornelis' associates could have supplied the poison, or Sophie consulted a witch. After administering sufficient to disable Weekes, she would have helped her husband bundle him into the chest. The chest would not have attracted attention, identical to all the others with the letters VOC on its sides. No one would have noticed the cart in heavy rain.

The couple left poor Peter to his fate beneath the Blue Bridge as the waters rose. Whether Catholic or Protestant at the end, he did not deserve to die like that.

Did I feel sorry for Felde, the next name on my list? I had felt a strange connection with my former rival, since inadvertently saving his life in the storm. Having worked for Robert Cecil for years, he would have spotted the intelligence value of the Weighing House job. The daily list of buyers and sellers would build a full and accurate picture of European wealth and trade, invaluable to any nation in its possession.

Felde probably approached Peter at the barber's shop, as he did with Nicholas, although the pair could have known each other earlier in Lincolnshire. How attractive the job must have sounded to the unsuspecting lad. He was caught as easily as Geoffrey once trapped me.

Felde would have ignored Peter's protests once he discovered the distasteful side to his role. Hellish cancer pain and his wife's propensity to steal, added to his woes.

Both men had worked for a mysterious boss. I tried to formulate theories as to who this could be.

Eva noticed my name on the list. As I told the long sorry story of my murderous outburst on Mattersey Bridge, she rose from her chair to fetch a quill and ink. After placing the latter on the little table between us, she held out the quill for me to use, "You must add another name on your list."

I was slow to realise what she meant.

"Gilbert Grey died too. Others will be grieving his death in the way you mourn those you cared about."

His blood was on my hands, yet I had dismissed him as inconsequential, denying my culpability for too long. I dipped the tip in the bottle and wrote

Gilbert Grey

Now, I would never forget his name.

60

Eva did not chastise me. Instead, she saw my confession as evidence of a change of heart. Admission of sin and repentance were fundamental Anabaptist beliefs. Without them I would fail. According to Eva, people needed to accept their own inadequacy, repent and start anew.

Aided by an eyeglass over the following days, she tried to match the verses in my little bible with the Dutch ones in her own. Although she could not understand English, they were numbered the same.

"Look, this instruction from Jesus is clear," Eva pointed.

Go therefore, and teach all nations, baptising them in the Name of the Father, and the Son and the Holy Spirit

Her translation was slightly different, yet we both agreed. Teachers only taught those who were old enough to understand. Jesus commanded his followers to baptise disciples, not babies.

It was hard to imagine thousands doing this, in the way other verses alleged. Eva assured me similar numbers of Anabaptists continued to follow the practice in the Republic, Swiss and German states. Her Mennonite group travelled back to the Waterland region regularly, to immerse new believers in the *Zuider Zee*.

My elderly tutor knew about Smyth and Helwys' intentions from members of her own church. Jacob Arminius was not their only influence. Both had become convinced by the New Testament practice of baptising believers.

If they had shared the Mennonites' antithesis towards warfare, I might not have done what I did. After all, my family were aiding Vere's English regiments by producing syphilis ointment. Insisting on separation from state authorities, Eva's group would not even serve as magistrates.

After making me leave Felde's rapier in my room, she made a troubling suggestion, "Once you leave here, you should throw that abominable blade in the River Ij to stop it hurting anyone again."

How could I assign such a weapon to that fate? Felde had been rightly proud. Although I had never been able to own a horse or fulfil other childhood dreams, at least I had this now. Edwin and Toby were similar. Most boys are.

Toby started taking Eva out for walks in her wheeled chair on Sundays. Each time, she wore a shawl across her face and a blanket to keep out the cold. They ventured a little further each week. If anyone noticed, they did not say.

By the week before the historic bakehouse service, they had reached the *Munt* gate. Then it was my turn.

Unusually, it was not raining when Toby pushed me over the *Begijnhof* bridge. Even Smeets did not notice the difference. Felde's rapier was hidden beneath the blanket. I did not part with that.

Toby played his role well, never betraying my heavier weight. Despite the dire circumstances of his birth, he was growing into a reliable lad.

People pushed by on either side on the Amstel pavement, never realising our deception. I was grateful for the blanket, given the strength of the wind.

At last, we turned the corner into *Bakkersstraat*. I raised my eyes for the first time. Thomas and Nicholas were rolling a huge cauldron into the bakehouse yard. Pastor Smyth had decided to sprinkle water, rather than immersing believers, to ensure privacy.

As we followed the cauldron into bakehouse yard, there were tears in my eyes. My clandestine journey was complete. I was back amongst my friends, to share a remarkable day.

Once he had closed the gate, I rose to clamp Toby in embrace. Other friends crowded round. Tears of joy ran down my cheeks. John and Mary Smyth, Matthew and Agnes Mobley, John and Jenne Murton, and Margaret Barton descended the flour store steps to greet me in turn, along with numerous children.

Agnes hugged Toby, "Your mother would be proud."

Isobel appeared at the top of the stairs, carrying Grace Jane.

Our little girl was heavier now. She was beautiful like her mother, sharing the same thick, dark hair. The others stepped aside to let them through. I do not know who was smiling the most.

What a delight to hold them in my arms again, warm against my skin. I was reluctant to let go, having scarcely dared to believe this day would come, a miracle indeed.

Hand in hand we walked to the paved area between the flour store and the perimeter wall, where children were helping Pastor Smyth fill the cauldron. He showed them where to stand to watch. They must wait until they were old enough to decide whether to be baptised themselves. Parents should not dictate their offspring's beliefs. Wisely, Isobel had waited, not expecting this for Grace Jane.

The flour store congregation had grown since my attack. There were plenty of new faces interspersed amongst familiar ones. No one wanted to miss this day. How far we had come since escaping Bancroft's censure.

We clapped when Pastor Smyth rose to address us. His voice silenced us all, "When the Church introduced infant baptism, the original New Testament meaning was lost. Jesus commanded his followers to baptise disciples, not babies, in the name of the Father, Son and Holy Spirit, a sign of the new spiritual covenant. It wasn't magic water, just an outward sign of inner repentance. They simply professed *Jesus is Lord* and knew his blessing."

Several said, "Amen."

"Today we follow suit, declaring our commitment to follow Jesus and obey his clear command. No parent, priest nor bishop can decide on our behalf. Faith grows in the heart."

After Pastor Smyth dipped the jug in the cauldron, he held it high for all to see. Uttering the simple words *Jesus is Lord*, he poured the water over his head.

Having seen how much Smyth spluttered, Thomas confessed his faith before Smyth sprinkled him.

Jesus is Lord

Smyth baptised Thomas.

Jesus is Lord

Thomas baptised Nicholas, Margaret and her mother. Each dripped and smiled. Nicholas embraced his mother-in-law, declaring she was the best in the world.

Similarly, others before us were moved by their experience. They splashed in the puddles and sang. It was hard to wait in line.

At last, it was our turn. Isobel and I stood together, as Thomas poured the jug over our heads. Although the water was tepid, tremendous warmth seeped through my body, permeating down from the top of my head to the tips of my toes.

Isobel was crying with delight, "Baxby, this is amazing. Praise God and all his angels in heaven above."

The exhilarating experience was unlike any we had known before. We will never forget the joy that flooded our souls. The water streamed down our faces and soaked our clothes.

Why had I worked so hard to become a burgher? Money cannot bring happiness like this. I should have listened more on Sundays. Our preachers understood. Smyth and Helwys unleashed a profound yet simple truth, which many before them had missed. I wondered if any of us would ever be the same again.

61

London 1613

"What nonsense!" the vicar explodes, "The English Church mandates predestination in Article Seventeen, prohibits unlawful preaching in Twenty-Three and Anabaptist practices in Thirty-Eight. Your eternal destiny was sealed long ago."

"I'm not an *Ana*baptist. We gave birth to something new in the bakehouse yard, a different direction on the Christian weather vane, between Robinson's Leiden-believers and the Mennonites."

"That's impossible. Don't speak your heresies here. If you keep taking small steps towards a cliff, you will eventually fall over the edge. When you renounced your infant baptism, you didn't just reject our Church. Every Englishman *must* be baptised in their parish church and attend services on Sundays. That's the law and much more besides. It *is* Englishness. Suffering is just punishment for those who reject their divine birthright. They won't let you into heaven, Baxby."

As if to prove the point, a thunderous crack silences them both. The vicar moves to the window, just in time to see a second firework shower over Westminster. He describes the colours to his cell-mates. This is a rehearsal for the display, not the start of the royal wedding festivities as the prisoners initially assume.

"Time is running out," Baxby states when silence returns, touching the little bible in his pocket for reassurance.

If sentenced to death he cannot claim a glorious afterlife on account of his rank, deeds or occupation. He can only put his hope in the mercy of God.

Before sleeping Baxby prays for strength to face his last days on earth, whatever lies beyond.

62

Amsterdam 1610

There are days I will never forget. As we danced, sang and feasted in the meeting room, I did not want that one to end. Reminded of the wedding celebrations, I wished Crackleton and my other Leiden friends could have been there to experience it too.

Jan Munter joined in, "English Baptists seem to be as taken with believers' baptism as us Anabaptists. There's no point asking you to be quiet today."

Taking me aside, he told me Cornelis van Giessen had left Amsterdam. He had moved elsewhere to work.

Relieved, I wanted to hug Jan, but did not know whether Anabaptists approved of such a thing. Instead, I clamped his hand in mine, and shook it several times. This meant Isobel and I could live together, safe from fear of retaliation. Although our home was considerably smaller than those I had slept in since Redfern's attack, I longed to return there.

Toby wanted to push me home in Eva's chair. Matthew and Isobel thought this a good idea. I insisted on walking once on the island. Crowded *Vloonburg* had never looked so appealing before. People waved. Parents pointed me out to their children.

Our house looked grander now, with the porch Murton had built to distribute bread. When Isobel opened the door, I smelt the familiar scent. Our room was like a forest with the plants above our heads. I longed to pick more and fill jars again.

Once Grace Jane was asleep, Isobel and I agreed we never wanted to separate again. We climbed into our alcove bed. How wonderful to be back.

I no longer desired a grand canal house. This was my home, with Grace Jane and Isobel.

The rain woke us in the night. The Amstel waters were rising in the morning, when I crossed the Blue Bridge to return Eva's chair. A woman was waiting near the far side, with a shawl pulled over her head.

Drawing nearer, I realised it was Temperance Knowsley. She was standing at the spot where we lay Weekes' body and later watched Roseberry's team carry Felde's away. I was glad for the opportunity to talk with her. From the beginning, Temperance was convinced the two men were murdered. She deserved to know the truth.

"It's good to see you restored to health, Doctor Baxby. Did Cornelis van Giessen look after you well? He's a very wealthy man."

"I fear his riches have been ill-gained. Cornelis is not the man he seems."

Temperance listened in silence as I told her how the burgher gained his wealth, and the despicable way he murdered Weekes and Felde. She realised how clever Cornelis' choice of location had been. There was no proof Peter was careless, nor his relationship with Felde was intimate. People had jumped to conclusions, based on their own fears and concerns. Preoccupied with the dangers of unfenced waterways, or sodomites under the bridge, they had missed the true nature of two deaths.

Understandably, Temperance was distressed to hear about the young men's last hours. As before, I felt certain she knew Felde better than she admitted.

"It is a sorry tale indeed," she concluded, "You did well to solve these mysteries. I was impressed with the way you learnt Dutch too."

"Will you tell Roseberry, Bowman and Tibbs at the Trade Mission? You know them better than me."

"Leave it with me," she replied, without committing herself.

Disappointed not to have received a firmer commitment, I peered over the edge again. The swirling waters engulfing the *stilletjes* platform confirmed a thought which had taken hold in my mind. As soon as she saw him, a woman of Temperance's intelligence must have realised the man in the river was dead.

"Why did you rush to fetch a physician that night? Anyone strong could have helped you lift Peter's body."

Temperance smiled, "That's a good question, one that requires an honest answer, given all you have done to honour the memory of two of my best officers. Having heard Julian had returned from England, I wanted to warn him that Peter was dead."

What did Temperance mean? I did not understand who she was referring to.

"Your officers? Did you know Felde before that night?"

"Julian and Peter were both valued members of my spy team. Julian recruited Peter. Ultimately, they both worked for me. I ran to the bakehouse to warn Julian his life was in danger. He needed to hide."

When Matthew, Michael and I were lifting Peter's body on to the stretcher, I assumed Temperance had gone across to Felde because she wanted to keep onlookers away. In truth, they had been planning his disappearance.

"We knew Spanish agents were intending to intensify their activities in Amsterdam. That is why I was suspicious when I first saw you. Your colouring is not typical for your group. However, I soon realised where your loyalties lay."

"Were you the one who arranged Peter's job at the Weighing House?"

"Yes, although I can't claim all the credit. I had help from the Hague."

It took a while for me to realise the full implications of Temperance's revelation. She appeared to be an honourable member of the English Reformed Church. How incredible that this older woman was in a position of authority, working undercover for Sir Ralph Winwood and thus Robert Cecil.

"Poor Julian was distraught when he saw the pamphlet with Peter's name. I think Cornelis put it there to gloat, especially given the way the article lauded Spanish sentiments with regard to the Truce. Cornelis wanted to let us know he knew Peter's true trade."

After spotting the name, Felde had spent weeks following pamphlet salesmen and crates, until he identified the most likely sources.

"If only he had shared the names with me, before he disappeared. I might have saved him."

It was time to show Temperance the pamphlet from Cornelis' loft. Her knowledge of Dutch was superior to my own. This was as good a place as any. No one passing would know what we were looking at.

Temperance frowned, "What is this?"

"Cornelis' Spanish masters produced hundreds of these pamphlets. They advocate the Calvinist Reformed side in the Conrad Vorstius dispute, in a particularly biased way. The author predicts all sorts of implausible consequences if another Arminian is appointed professor at Leiden University in Jacob's place."

Temperance reaction was unexpected. A smile spread as she read down the page.

Unnerved, I continued, "I doubt Catholics in Spain really care about Protestant theological disagreements. King Philip must be trying to weaken his Dutch rivals through deceit and …"

Temperance erupted in convulsions of laughter, seemingly unable to stop. I had never seen her that unguarded before. Had she gone mad, overcome with grief and the responsibilities of her covert position? Sensibly, she moved to the parapet so passersby would not see.

"Baxby, this is marvellous. Thank you for showing it to me."

Had her superior knowledge of the Dutch language spotted a joke I had missed?

"Temperance, this isn't funny. The pamphlet says all seven provinces will flood and crops will fail, clear signs of God's wrath. Johann van Oldenbarnevelt is accused of nefarious practices, contrary to Old Testament law."

"Look, Baxby. Vorstius' Catholic origins are cited too, along with his childhood intention to become a priest. This is priceless."

Regaining composure, Temperance handed the pamphlet back and suggested we walk towards her home. Before leaving me, she remarked, "Do you remember the barber on *Marken* island? Why don't you visit him again? Your hair and beard need attention, after your prolonged stay with the van Giessens."

Now I was angry. Although Temperance seemed fonder of her agents than Geoffrey, her cryptic games reminded me of him. Why could she not explain her amusement in a straightforward way?

How little spies actually know about their masters' plans. Geoffrey, Temperance and Cornelis shared similar levels of seniority and longevity in the job.

63

Luke Mobley had been helping his father, but Matthew was delighted when I started working again. He gradually increased the number of patients I visited as I returned to full strength.

Several patients remarked on my appearance. My hair remained a frightful mess. Finally, I was persuaded to visit the Turkish barber again.

I found the shop more easily than I expected. Apart from being more crowded, *Marken*'s alleyways had not changed. The stink had not improved.

Once there, it was a relief to sink into the chair. I had not been so comfortable since leaving Cornelis' house. The hot towel felt soothing against my skin.

As before, the Turk did a good job. I was delighted when he showed me the pencil beard in his mirror. I looked more like myself again.

When I left the shop, Michael Knowsley was standing at the end of the alley staring at me. Instinctively, I followed him. He rounded a corner and negotiated the bank of a narrow channel. Now I had no idea where I was. There was no option but to continue.

Michael disappeared through a door that looked no different from its neighbours. Having come this far, I did not want to give up. I needed to know where Michael was leading me. He closed the door behind me. This was not a trap.

"Wait here," he said, whilst knocking on a second, inner door.

A small man in a dirty apron opened it and removed a glove to shake my hand. His palm and fingers were ink-black, stained through countless years at his craft.

The house did not follow the normal layout inside. There was a second room behind the first, with just enough space for three presses, each attended by an aproned printer and small boy.

In addition to supervising Cecil's spies in Amsterdam,

Temperance ran this print shop on his and Ralph Winwood's behalf. In addition to supplying material for local use, illegal pamphlets and books were shipped back to England too. In the past, these printers even produced Martin Marprelate tracts to rile Bancroft.

Michael let me wander around the room, watching the printers load their little shelves with letter blocks, spaces and punctuation marks. Time and time again, they applied the ink, inserted paper and turned the bar. What skill! What precision! Steadily, the piles of pamphlets grew. Some expressed outrage at King James' latest favourite, whilst others complained about the latest royal monopolies restricting trade.

Picking up a Dutch pamphlet I had not noticed before, Michael beckoned me towards the window to read it. This one warned of apocalyptic consequences if Conrad Vorstius was appointed professor at Leiden University.

"My mother thought you'd like to see ours. We only predicted Zeeland would flood. Otherwise, you'll spot plenty of similarities."

Although the style and sentence structure differed, the content of the first paragraph was almost identical to the one I took from Cornelis' chest. I took his out of my pocket to compare the two, but was slow to understand, initially assuming Temperance must have memorised mine.

Michael laughed, "No, one of Cecil's secretaries wrote the original English copy for ours. His team produces impressive quantities each year. Felde was one of our best couriers, smuggling them into the Republic for my mother to translate. Sometimes, she adds embellishments if she feels the author is insufficiently familiar with customs here. She didn't think it necessary in this case."

Temperance's pamphlet conveyed remarkably similar arguments to Cornelius'. Both took the Calvinist side, imploring the Dutch to reject Arminius' absurd notions of free will, whilst promising negative consequences if Vorstius was appointed in his place.

Given the historical enmity between England and Spain, and

their opposing religions, I found the similar pamphlets hard to comprehend. We had been adversaries since before my birth. Why were the two sides in agreement now, expending considerable effort and expenditure to influence Dutch religious matters?

English and Dutch regiments had captured Cadiz together, won the Battle of Nieuwpoort and defended Ostend. How could everything change so quickly? What could be more important than thwarting Spain? No other country had sent an Armada to destroy us. If Fawkes had succeeded, they would have usurped our throne. Cornelis had committed despicable crimes.

Michael assured me that before the Truce, England and Spain printed pamphlets with opposing arguments, each seeking to influence the terms and conditions for their own benefit. Weekes and Felde lost their lives during that period of intense rivalry.

Like many engaged in undercover work, Michael had tried to discern the true motives of his political masters. A spy's brief often obscures the truth, rather than enlightening him. Michael had reached two conclusions as a result of his investigations.

Since the Truce, Dunkirker pirates no longer posed a threat in the Narrow Sea, meaning Dutch ships could return from the East and West Indies unmolested. The Republic was growing richer at an unprecedented pace. England was trying to weaken its young competitor by causing internal division and strife.

Also, Michael suggested a more immediate financial reason for taking the Calvinist side. Johan van Oldenbarnevelt, and most others who argued for individual choice with regard to salvation, wanted the Dutch states to have more political autonomy too.

"English coffers are running low," Michael said, "Cecil wants to employ a sole ambassador at the Hague to negotiate with Maurice of Nassau-Orange, not haggle with seven provincial stadtholders who rarely agree on anything. We can no longer afford the expense."

I had never heard him talk so much before. The potter had hidden his intelligence well. Michael was good at his job, a valued lieutenant.

After persistent questioning, he admitted his father was

227

working for Cecil in Venice. The herring fleet job had been another deceit.

The print room was one of several on the islands, dedicated to producing tracts and books. Although an impressive undertaking, the insidious nature of the operation sickened me. How could anyone make sense of what was happening beyond their immediate locality, if they could not trust the source of the information they were reading, let alone the contents.

"How can you sleep at night?" I posed, "England and Spain shouldn't interfere in such an underhand way. People will read these pamphlets and assume they're authentic. Even those who instinctively distrust them, will still be affected by what they read."

I was angry on behalf of the citizens of the Republic. They had achieved so much since independence, surpassing other nations in engineering, finance, trade and more beside. The Dutch should be free to decide for themselves, especially in matters of religion.

As Thomas wrote in his book

The lord the king is but an earthly king, and he has no authority as a king but in earthly causes

64

Gradually, I settled back into a pattern of work, home and church life. It was a relief to have Isobel and Grace Jane by my side. Toby loved our little girl and often entertained her, giving the pair of us more time to produce ointment and distribute bread.

The jars proved popular with English regiments based in Europe. Sir Horace Vere increased his order several times. I decided to employ a couple of lads to help with basic tasks.

Gertrude Lemmens no longer wished me to visit. She found talking with Helen a more effective remedy for green sickness, especially after Helen convinced Stefan to reduce his hours at the loom in order to pay more attention to his wife.

Other patients welcomed me back. Raphael Barr gave me extra sweets for Grace Jane. Eva Witte forgave me for keeping Felde's rapier.

Isobel and I were able to move to a larger home, with two ovens and a separate room for preparing ointment. We stayed on *Vloonburg* island, surrounded by our friends. Crackleton wrote, making it clear we would be welcome in Leiden, but we wanted to stay.

Amsterdam had given us shelter when no one else would. Despite restricting our access to professional work, it welcomed all those escaping persecution and poverty elsewhere in Europe. If King James visited the city, he would see the benefits. The difference between Amsterdam and London's prosperity was stark.

I bought Grace Jane a picture book, similar to the one I once gave the Mobley children as a present. Sometimes sitting by the fire, showing her the lions and monkeys, I wondered how such a life could be possible for me.

We walked out of the city on Sunday afternoons, often choosing the path to *Overtoom* Dam. Isobel encouraged me to return to my favourite pond as soon as I felt able. Grace Jane liked the ducks.

Omitting names and codewords, I told Isobel about my past. She was not concerned to learn I was a bastard, whose parents never married, and was raised in poverty. More surprising, neither was I any longer.

"You're a whatsoever, Baxby. That's what Thomas wrote."

Let them be heretics, Turks, Jews, or whatsoevers
Men's religion is between God and themselves

Once he had finished writing, Thomas planned to send a copy of *A Short Declaration of the Mystery of Iniquity* to King James. Despite my misgivings, Isobel continued to believe this was a good idea, "One day, Catholics, Lutheran, Calvinist and Arminian Protestants, Anabaptists, Jews, Turks and even English Baptists like us will live in peace in our homeland."

"Do you think we'll ever return?"

"We're happy here."

My wife had her own theory why Cecil's pamphlet writers favoured the Calvinist side in the Vorstius debate, "King James and his bishops are scared of where Arminius' assertions will lead. If people are allowed to choose their own faith, what will they expect next? They might demand to choose their own political and religious leaders. In their eyes, the sooner the Dutch experiment fails the better. They want to keep control."

She cited me as an example of someone transformed by Pastor Smyth and Thomas Helwys' blend of Separatist, Arminian and Anabaptist ideas, "Once people taste freedom, they never go back. It brings new confidence and strength. Archbishop Bancroft can't put water back in a jug once it's been poured."

Certainly, when we sat by still waters or walked beside those flowing to the *Zuider Zee*, I felt a sense of peace I had not known before and gratitude for having survived.

Isobel said, "Although it's awful to contemplate what happened to you, I feel things have worked out well for us, and by implication for the hungry we feed and the patients you treat."

Neither Redfern nor Cornelis succeeded in killing me. Geoffrey had not appeared since I left Eva's home on *Begijnhof* island, the poison having left my veins. I was alive and well, with those I loved.

65

London 1613

The printer interrupts, "I doubt Thomas found someone willing to produce his book. It's unlikely to sell well. People want to read about controversy and royal intrigue, not religious toleration. He needs a better title too. King James' *Demonology* remains popular years after its release."

"Thomas included prophecy about the End Times."

"That may help. However, he's still optimistic, especially for a first book."

The vicar agrees, "I don't know what the *Mystery of Iniquity* means. I can't imagine many others do either."

"It's the lawlessness of those who oppose God's loving purposes in this world."

"Loving purposes indeed! I should never have been arrested or kicked in the shin."

"We haven't long to wait now, just a few more days before our trials."

Outside, many Londoners find it hard to settle too, even more excited about the forthcoming royal wedding having seen the fireworks.

Leonard Redfern saw them too, after entering the City through Bishopsgate. He is pleased to have returned to London in time for the festivities.

After visiting Julian Felde's former manor house in Lincolnshire, which the occupier claimed to have inherited after Felde died at sea, Redfern travelled on to Mattersey, in neighbouring Nottinghamshire, to visit Mary Grey. Her landlord let her stay in the cottage after her husband's death. Gilbert's grave digging spade still leant against the wall, where it was placed after his body was retrieved from the ditch.

Mistress Grey was delighted to see Redfern, although disturbed to learn that her husband's murderer did not die in Amsterdam as they previously believed.

"I don't understand, Leonard. You were certain that Gilbert's life had been avenged."

"Recent developments in London have proved me wrong. Don't worry, I won't make the same mistake twice."

"Will Geoffrey help?"

"Sculthorpe and Pusey are the only ones I trust now. They won't let us down."

"Thank you. It's what Gilbert would have wanted. He was a good man."

Redfern let her continue to believe the lie.

The wedding will be an even greater celebration with Baxby dead. After seeing the fireworks, Redfern travelled down Gracechurch Street to call on Pusey, keen to learn whether the deed has been done.

NAMING THE DEAD

Monday

66

London 1613

Geoffrey disembarks at the quayside mid-morning, having spent the night with an attractive gentlewoman near Leadenhall. Her wine merchant husband was away on business, a journey Geoffrey hopes he will repeat soon. Although he had intended to interrogate the vicar earlier, the time was spent well.

As Redfern has still not reappeared, Geoffrey intends to question the vicar alone. At least, it will be easier to ensure the guards do not use excessive force this time.

However, when Geoffrey enters the gatehouse, the men tell him their captain has been removed from his position. No replacement will be appointed until the investigation is complete. A prisoner has died, poisoned by unknown felons. Secretary Sculthorpe has overall responsibility, but the captain was in charge of the prisoners' food so must take the blame.

Geoffrey does not wait to ask more. He demands they follow him, as he heads for the stairs. They amble up, not sharing his sense of urgency. It is nearing the end of their shift.

Geoffrey calls down, still trying to regain his breath. How can he wait any longer? What will he find inside?

Although Alexander was a challenging recruit, especially in his youth, he became a good physician and spy, one of Geoffrey's best. Fondly, Geoffrey remembers the day he recruited him in the Boar's Head. It remains one of his favourite inns. Only last week, he bought dinner for another novice of similar age.

Unable to wait any longer, Geoffrey starts to unbolt the door. He sees a prisoner, shackled to the wall. As the door opens further, he sees Baxby too, unkempt and gaunt but alive.

The vicar's convulsions provided a warning to his two cell-mates. He died quickly, a grim end. Neither Baxby or the printer have slept or eaten since, too disturbed by what they witnessed.

The guards arrive just in time to enter the cell with Geoffrey. Weak and distracted, Baxby does not believe the evidence of his own eyes. Has someone administered another poison without his knowledge? Is he hallucinating again? No, this time Geoffrey is older and greyer. The guards and printer can see him too. His former spymaster really is standing above him, and reaching out to clutch his hand.

Geoffrey splutters, "Thank God, you're alright, Alexander. I thought they'd killed you."

Baxby rubs his eyes. Not only is it a shock to see Geoffrey, he now seems concerned for his well-being too.

"Is this your doing, Geoffrey? Why have you imprisoned me here?"

"No, Secretary Sculthorpe is to blame. I will speak with the Archbishop of Canterbury. There must be a way to get you out of here."

Baxby is not minded to trust Geoffrey nor forgive him. Not only has he been shackled for weeks, he has witnessed a horrific death in the cell.

"It was awful, Geoffrey. That poor vicar grabbed the soup, then shook uncontrollably after taking a few sips. We watched foam spew from his mouth and heard him screech out in pain, without being able to reach far enough to console him in any way."

Geoffrey does not seem unduly perturbed, "Don't worry, Alexander. I'll see what I can do to get you both released. In the meantime, I'll monitor your food. That vicar was not the intended victim. They want you dead. This has gone on long enough."

After Geoffrey leaves, the printer asks, "Do you think they'll give the vicar a funeral, or find another way to remember him?"

"They have more pressing priorities. The royal wedding festivities will start soon."

"They may postpone our trials in the light of what has happened, or even cancel them."

"Don't worry," Baxby seeks to reassure his cell-mate, "I'm sure your trial will go ahead. They'll probably make you pay a small fine."

Baxby's own future is less certain. He takes Jane's little bible from his pocket, and unwraps the leather strips which have kept it safe through the years. Turning to the back page, he glances down the list of names of those who have died.

His own name is there, ready for his inevitable death. Geoffrey's pronouncement confirmed his fear, "They want you dead."

"Please take this with you?" he holds the bible out for the printer to reach.

"I couldn't possibly …" the printer starts, realising the enormity of Baxby's request. The bible is Baxby's most treasured possession. Jane gave it to him before she died.

Baxby bows his head, "It will survive longer with you."

The printer takes the bible from him, and stares down at the names. Although he never met these people, he is pleased to have heard their stories.

"Yes, I'll look after your bible, Baxby. I can try to find Isobel and give it to her."

"You must be careful. Don't endanger your own family by helping mine. As long as someone remembers me when I'm gone, that's enough."

Ordinary people are not given lofty shrines in Westminster Abbey, or memorial plaques on ceilings or walls. Officials register our births, marriages and deaths. Otherwise, we rely on those who have known us to never forget.

KAREN HADEN

Author's Note

This is a fictional story inspired by historical characters and events. The ideas are my own, prompted by interest in the way printing technology affected earlier generations.

Naming the Dead is set in Amsterdam during the so-called 'Dutch Golden Age'. After winning independence from Spain and negotiating the Twelve Years Truce, the Republic grew to eclipse its neighbours in trade, wealth, engineering and art, underpinned by the dominant Calvinist Reformed faith.

While the Hague remained the political centre, Amsterdam was key to the Republic's economic success. The city was home to the world's first stock exchange and the headquarters of the lucrative Dutch East India and West India trading companies.

Also, Amsterdam was the most tolerant city in the Republic, absorbing those fleeing religious persecution and poverty elsewhere in Europe, including Jews, Muslims, Anabaptists, Huguenots and English Separatists mentioned in the novel.

Later, similar traits were seen in its most famous colony New Amsterdam, which was renamed New York after passing into British control.

The future Mayflower Pilgrims (led by John Robinson, William Brewster and William Bradford) and the first English Baptists (led by John Smyth and Thomas Helwys) were influenced by their years in Amsterdam's 'melting pot'.

The Pilgrims were Independents, not Puritans as is often stated. Although sharing the Calvinist doctrine of pre-destination, the Pilgrims retained their convictions about congregational self-governance and separation of church and state, closer to the current Congregational tradition.

Fusing Arminian and Anabaptist beliefs with earlier Separatist ones, Smyth and Helwys' created the Baptist tradition which still has millions of adherents worldwide, along with many other

NAMING THE DEAD

Christians who favour the practice of believers' baptism.

Thomas' Helwys book *A Short Declaration of the Mystery of Iniquity* contained the first plea for religious liberty in the English language, made on behalf of those of all faiths and none. After returning to London to petition King James, Helwys was arrested and subsequently died in Newgate gaol. John Murton then led the Baptist congregation in Spitalfields.

The first Dutch newspaper appeared in Amsterdam in 1616, one of the earliest in Europe. Before that date, the largely literate urban population relied on pamphlets for their news. The Vortius affair divided opinion across the Republic, pitting Arminian "Remonstrants" advocating free-will (general salvation) against Calvinist "Counter-Remonstrants" retaining pre-destination (particular salvation).

Sir Robert Cecil and ambassador Sir Ralph Winwood saw this as an opportunity to further England's interests abroad. Preferring Maurice of Nassau-Orange to Holland's Stadtholder Johan van Oldenbarnevelt, they translated and circulated material bolstering the Calvinist side, including King James' numerous letters and speeches on the subject.

This played a significant role in Oldenbarnevelt's subsequent demise and execution in 1619, which can be seen as an early example of the effectiveness of 'soft power' or unacceptable interference in the internal affairs of another country.

In addition to thanking my family and those who read earlier drafts, I am particularly grateful to Nadine Akkerman and Pete Langman for their 'manual' *Spycraft*, and the late Jeremy Dupertus Bangs, former Director of the Leiden American Pilgrim Museum, for *Strangers and Pilgrims Travellers and Sojourners*.

Alongside a list of the names of the believers, which he extracted from civil marriage and other records in Amsterdam, Leiden, and Plymouth, Bangs quotes William Bradford:

Many worthy and able men there were ... who lived and died in obscurity in respect of the world ... yet were precious in the eyes of the Lord, and also in the eyes of such who knew them

237

Finally, thank you to everyone who has read this far. Please connect with Karen Haden by visiting the following:

Blog: https://karenhaden.blogspot.com (includes character lists and maps)

X/Twitter: @kjhaden17

Linkedin: Karen Haden

There is more information about Christian beliefs at www.christianity.org.uk

Printed in Dunstable, United Kingdom

64014756R00139